Savannah Writes

A Collection By the Savannah Writers Group

Carol North, Editor
Betty Darby, Line Editor
Robert Crisp, Content Editor

ISBN: 978-0-6152-0154-2

First Edition

Savannah Writes: A Collection By the Savannah Writers Group

Published in the United States of America by SWG Press, 310 Tibet Avenue, 53 Brockington Square, Savannah, Georgia 31406. Phone: 912-228-1611.

Cover and Book Design and Art: Carol North

PREFACE

The Savannah Writers Group (SWG) had a humble beginning in 2004 when the two founding members, Trevor Noble and Carol North, met monthly at a Savannah bookstore. The membership consisted of two. To beef up the count, Trevor forced his two teenage children, Elizabeth and Jonathon, to attend. In case we needed to more greatly impress passersby we stationed Trevor's wife, Nancy, on call in the coffee shop and gave her a Nora Roberts novel to read.

During the second meeting, we had a formal election procedure whereby Carol nominated Trevor to be the leader of the group. In an effort to properly fill the ballot box, Carol bribed Nancy with more Nora Roberts novels and the kids with sugary delights from the coffee shop swaying the vote four to one for Trevor. Thus, he was named the leader. The only descenting vote was Trevor's own.

Originally the little group met one night a month. The meeting would consist of either a critique of works in progress or a presentation by a local or visiting author. Little by little, the membership grew until the need for a separate critiquing meeting became apparent. We then began meeting twice a month. The first monthly meeting was devoted to critiquing works in progress and to a brief presentation by a member (usually Carol or Trevor) on a writing technique. The second monthly meeting consisted of presentations by authors, publishers, and other people in the bookselling industry.

We grew and grew and grew until our core group of members numbered 15 to 20 and our author presentations often drew 40 to 50 book buyers. As a result, we outgrew the accommodations of the first bookstore. In October 2007, we moved to our new, larger home in Savannah's premier bookstore, Books-A-Million.

Along with our growth in numbers came an increase in our efforts toward helping our members develop their writing techniques. During this time, Melissa Sanso joined the steering committee of the SWG. Her contributions, including presentations on technique, have proved invaluable to the group as a whole.

As a result of the collaborative efforts of the SWG, three members previously unpublished are published and others are on their way.

This anthology is the result of contributions by a core group of members, some with us early on and others who joined more recently. Their writing experience ranges from new and aspiring to professional-level.

The steering committee thanks the following individuals for their efforts in preparing this anthology for publication:

- Status Management: Ian Robb
- Cover Committee: Ian Robb, John Sonnier, Marli Sieburger
- Editing: Betty Darby, Line Editor; Robert Crisp, Content Editor

On behalf of the entire membership, the SWG steering committee thanks our host bookstore, Books-A-Million in Savannah, for the meeting space and support.

Trevor Noble
Carol North
Melissa Sanso

CONTENTS

PAT ANDRES

This published poet, author, and civil rights freak, morphed from wife, mother, and hairdresser into magna cum laude college graduate at age forty. Her book, *Maggie: A Savannah Dog,* raises money for animal welfare. She is seventy and still a saboteur.

You can contact Andres at Pattyflea@2003@yahoo.com.

An Afternoon Tea

On a typically raw and cloudy Massachusetts afternoon, as I heated water for tea, I watched an unfamiliar old car hesitate as it pulled slowly into the driveway. A bird-like young woman, shivering, drew her black and white coat collar more tightly around her neck as she stepped out of the car. Her face pale, her mousy hair almost tucked under a red wool hat, she reminded me of a small woodpecker I'd seen in the yard. She looked toward the front door that displayed the house number but came to the side door instead.

She knocked lightly.

I opened the door and said, "Hello."

She shifted a large, heavy-looking black purse from one shoulder to the other but remained silent, staring at me.

"Are you looking for someone?" I asked.

"Are you Amy O'Malley?" she finally choked out tearfully.

"No, I'm not," I replied.

By this time both of us were shivering. I invited her into my warm yellow kitchen. She climbed the three cement steps and paused slightly before entering the bungalow. Without a word, she sat down at the table clutching her purse in her lap.

"I was just pouring tea." I said. "A cup would take the chill off this dreary day." She nodded. Still eyeing me closely as I filled the cups, she wiped her eyes and asked, "Do you know where Amy O'Malley lives?"

Sensing that she seemed angry, I replied, "No, I'm sorry, I don't. We're renting this house from her."

"You have to send your rent check somewhere," she quavered.

"Well, yes. It goes to a post office box."

I set the steaming cups on the table and sat down. We sipped in silence.

"What's your name?" I asked.

"Susie. Susie Downs," she answered, as tears slid down her thin cheeks. She opened her purse, pulled out a tissue and a gun and laid them on the table. We both stared at the silver automatic.

"I tracked them all the way across the state from Boston," said Susie. She stole my husband. If I find them together, I'm going to kill him, too. I don't care if I end up in jail."

Yes, Susie was definitely angry. In slow motion, I picked up my cup, sipped and asked, "Do you have children, Susie?"

"Three boys," she sniffed, dabbing her face with the tissue.

I thought of something my ex-husband had said about how I seemed to be the candle to every "mad moth" in the universe. He was right. I attract troubled souls who tell me more than I want to know. People who should say no more than hello often tell me in detail what's bothering them, who's to blame and what they plan to do about it. I must give out empathy vibes or something.

For the next half hour we traded stories about our kids as Susie blew her nose on tissues she pulled from the big purse. I stole glances at the clock above her head, aware that it was almost time for my kids to come home from school.

"Have you thought about what will happen to the boys if you go to jail?" I asked.

Susie was quiet for a few long minutes. She reached for the gun and dropped it back into the purse. "I guess this wasn't such a good idea," she said, halfway smiling. "Thank you for listening." She grabbed my hand and stood. "Thank you."

I had to ask. "Why didn't you shoot me when I opened the door?"

Susie grinned. "I happen to know Amy O'Malley has flaming red hair. My husband is a sucker for redheads."

I watched her back out of the driveway, not realizing I was sweating as I sat down.

A few minutes later I froze as the door flew open.

"It's me." My neighbor and best friend, Jean came in bringing a cold wind with her. "Who was just here? I didn't recognize the car."

As the cold air rushed over me, my heart re-started.

"Amy? What the hell happened?" Jean asked. "You're two shades paler than the platinum blonde we bleached your hair yesterday. Amy?"

Behind My Desk

I have a sign at work. It says, "I wasn't born behind my desk." I hope it causes people to think of how a person proceeds from nothing to something, from nowhere to somewhere.

I wasn't born behind my desk. My Dad was a beat cop in our small New Jersey town and knew all the business owners on Main Street. In the 1950s one of them had a son who was a military doctor on his way to the war in Korea. They needed help with a new baby, I was told. Three times a week I went from my seventh grade classes and walked to their house to wash dishes, dust and clean bathrooms. The new baby's mother left used sanitary napkins rolled up on the floor behind the toilet for me to pick up. I gave him the money I earned but never told my Dad that I wasn't allowed near the baby.

My Mom worked evenings at a sewing factory. From five to ten pm I was in charge of my one-year old baby brother. I'd feed him supper, do my homework and get ready for the next day. On Tuesdays she left ironing for me.

I wasn't born behind my desk. High school years brought several opportunities for part-time work. Dad's friend Nick hired me to work in his deli where the milkman, instead of delivering the milk straight into the refrigerated counter out front, squeezed behind me pressing hard with his body. I left to work in Howard Johnson's on the New Jersey Turnpike as a cashier, standing for whole shifts and collecting money every weekend. I had my pick of boyfriends, though, tough guys from Newark who slicked their hair back with one spit curl on their foreheads like Sal Mineo, alcoholic short-order cooks and married gas station attendants who insisted that I was pretty.

I wasn't born behind my desk. My parents urged me to quit school when I turned sixteen for full time work because they needed the money, but I liked school, made good grades and secretly hoped to go to college. Several friends were planning careers in teaching and nursing, but encouragement didn't exist for blue-collar kids. My senior advisor, in front of the class, told me never to work with people because I had a "face that would antagonize them."

Months before I graduated, my Dad found me an office job in a chemical fertilizer plant to which I went afternoons to process invoices. My family was very proud that I was working and studying. I had an inside job at a desk, learned time-keeping and found a husband. Their job was done.

I wasn't born behind my desk. In 1957 custom dictated that married couples didn't work together. My new sister-in-law found me a clerical job at her office. I hated it and I once again watched thousands of cars racing down the NJ Turnpike and dreamed of hitting the road myself.

Abandoning the idea of college as too expensive and taking too long, I entered beauty culture school. It cost $1,000 for a six-month 1,000 hour course. I got a license and worked in shops until my children were born. Then I worked at home or traveled with kids in tow to people who needed cuts, color and perms. Everyone remembers what he or she was doing when President Kennedy was killed. I was cutting hair and listening to the radio.

I wasn't born behind my desk. Besides fixing hair, I've been a school cafeteria worker and a typist for a friend who was writing a play. I cleaned house for a neighbor who minded children before day care was invented. I cleaned the office at a cemetery where the owner pressed his 75 year old hard-on against me whenever I bent over. He was so proud of that erection. I sold Amway and worked as a library aide. I taught children to read. I never had a job I liked or one with benefits.

I wasn't born behind my desk. In the 1970s, fate, in the guise of a job transfer for my husband, took us to a small town in New England. Far from my blue-collar roots and the people who said I should continue to work at odd jobs to help my husband support the family, I had freedom to dare to dream. Every day I walked my dog and dreamed of doing something with my life other than mothering.

I soon discovered, a few miles away, a state college on a hill. Going against the voices in my head, I sweated through the SAT and took one course to see if I could do the work. I was thirty-six years old. To my delight, I loved the literature course, made an A and decided to go to college. How was I going to pay for it? No idea. How to arrange sitters for my grade school kids? Not a clue. And the answer to my frightened husband's declaration that I would be forty at graduation? It was: How old will I be if I don't go?

I wasn't born behind my desk. Three times a week I trudged up an icy, slippery hill to attend classes with eighteen year-olds just out of high school. I felt as if I were from another planet. My classmates, though, helped me through math and science during lunch and I longed to take them up on invitations to go for pizza and beer at night. But I had to go home to my other life to keep the family from being inconvenienced by my student status.

I graduated magna cum laude with a degree in Psychology without a word from my Dad. Another transfer for my husband brought us to Savannah in 1976.

I wasn't born behind my desk. The country was in recession, the state wasn't hiring and, with my brand new degree and no experience in welfare work, I could not find a job. I volunteered at Georgia Regional Hospital for close to a year when I heard that a new program was starting at Comprehensive Mental Health. It took several months but I was hired to work in an Aging Services program. I finally had a job I loved going to every day and was soon named coordinator.

I wasn't born behind my desk. I got in my own way many times when I believed people who told me that education wasn't meant for me, when I denied wanting to be a professional, when I sought the fastest, cheapest way to have a career, when I tried not to inconvenience anyone. The angel on my shoulder, however, must have been whispering to me all the while even when I wasn't listening.

I re-cycled myself, taking the long way around, but I've been told that the skills I brought to my jobs couldn't have been gotten any other way. I wasn't born behind my desk.

Going to Hell

From Lorenzago di Cadore in Italy came the news that Pope Benedict XVI has reasserted the primacy of the Roman Catholic Church. He said "other Christian communities are either defective or not true churches." Reading this in my morning newspaper painfully threw me back to my childhood in the 1940s when half of my family was Catholic.

When she married a Roman Catholic in 1935, my mother had no idea that she was complicating our lives. She was the third daughter of Hungarian peasants who had come to America in 1906. I've been told that my grandfather, furious that his third child wasn't a boy, left his family and moved to Florida for more than six months.

Their unpretentious Magyar Reformed Church was Protestant in a small New Jersey town that was predominately Catholic, divided along ethnic lines into large Polish, Italian and Hungarian congregations. Interfaith marriages were rare. Offspring were usually baptized into the mother's faith. When the holy water of the Magyar church was poured over my head, I joined a minority that was often taunted and scorned.

For me the gibes started early in my own family. I was jealous of my Catholic cousins. At their first holy communion at age seven, they looked like brides in white dresses with veils, and I was devoured with envy at the fuss that was made over them. They told me I'd never have a white dress because I wasn't Catholic.

When we discussed their catechism, they frightened me by saying, "No matter how good you are, you're going to hell because you aren't a Catholic."

Classmates hauled me to St. Joseph's, St. Elizabeth's and Sacred Heart at every opportunity. Having been warned by my mother that conversion was every Catholic's sworn mission, I kept the visits to myself. Awed by the spectacle of richly draped purple altars and statues of the radiant Virgin Mary, I eagerly learned the Hail Mary prayer. It couldn't hurt.

The crosses with hanging Jesus disturbed me so much I avoided looking at them and the smell of incense unsettled my stomach. Masses sung by the priests in Latin deepened the mystery, and convent nuns swathed in black with only their faces showing were formidable creatures who taught in the schools that were supported by the churches. Their toughness was legendary and they were feared by one and all. You had to pay to go to those schools.

On my eighth birthday on Christmas Eve, my Dad surprised us all by marching down our church aisle and converting to Protestantism. My Mom couldn't stop crying at his public display of love for us. His brothers and sisters never forgave him. A schism formed between us. Years later, as I planned my wedding, my cousins refused to be bridesmaids or ushers because "it would be a sin" to stand up for a non-Catholic.

In contrast to the ornate Catholic churches, the Magyar Reformed Church was a simple square brick building with a double stone staircase. Plain wooden doors opened on a tiny narthex where the steeple bell was rung by pulling two ropes. To the right of the altar stood a pipe organ that was traditionally played by the minister's wife. A staircase on the left led to a carved wooden canopied pulpit from which the black-cloaked minister delivered his scolding Old Testament sermons. Yes, I was going to hell, for sure. The dollar a week we put in the plate couldn't possibly save all of us.

Families filled the wooden pews in Puritan tradition; the men on one side to the minister's right, and the women and children on the other. Everyone wore their best outfits and married women were expected to wear hats. Bulky gold-tinted radiators hissed and clanged in unison with the hymns on winter mornings. The lights, hung on long chains from the slightly vaulted roof, cast a dim yellow light.

The low-ceilinged basement was used for meetings and Saturday school where we learned to read and write in Hungarian, as well as studying a smattering of history of the old country. My favorite part was recess where we played games on the brick courtyard that led to the manse where the minister and his family lived.

The Board of Elders, twelve men who actually governed the church, met there. My Dad served as treasurer and stayed in the office for years, I think, mostly for the hot card games that followed late into the night. Of great interest was his treasury report that appeared in the monthly newsletter that printed the exact amounts each parishioner gave each Sunday.

The place of women was clearly defined. They cooked for banquets, raised money for building improvements by selling Hungarian sausage and baked goods, laundered the communion linens and carried the hymns on Sundays. To my child's ear, it seemed we sang the same ones every week: "Have Thine Own Way, Lord," "Rock of Ages" and "Beautiful Savior." Six Sundays a year, the adults lined the aisle to receive communion, squares of homemade bread and wine sipped from a common cup. The recipe for the bread died with my grandmother in 1956.

Every Sunday my grandparents, my mother, my two aunts and I walked the mile and a half to church. Afterwards, I was sent to get the newspapers from the newsstand while my aunts crossed the street to the bakery from which the aroma of bread, hard rolls, layer cakes and cookies hung over the whole block. I pinched off pieces of bread all the way home.

Although I absorbed the lessons and sermons about the Ten Commandments, I was puzzled by the church members I heard gossiping and denigrating their brethren with such relish the other six days of the week. Weren't they listening to the minister?

What about the mayor who had a mistress and never failed to lead his large family to the front row of St. Joseph's every Sunday? If you happened to be in the bank on Monday morning, you'd meet the priest with his personal collection box under one arm and the church box under the other, unaware that he also bet on horses. What about the politicians who bought up tracts of land right before developments appeared on them? My own grandfather and his cronies played cards for money in our back yard and sent me to the corner bar for pitchers of beer to chase their shots of whiskey.

On hot nights we sat on the dark porch in tall wicker rockers that squeaked rhythmically. I listened intently to stories of adultery, wife beating, bookmaking, crooked elections and illegitimate babies. I would pretend to be asleep so that I wouldn't miss anything. If commandments existed to be broken and sinners were pillars of the church, were we all hell bound? Could my Catholic cousins be right?

If religion was a good thing, why did it divide families? I heard my mother and my father's sister, a devout Catholic with many children, arguing one day. I didn't know the reason, but I know my mother never forgave my Aunt Anna for calling her a "Protestant Jew bastard" in the heat of the quarrel.

Family traditions divided us, as well. Lent was strictly observed by my cousins. I tried to join them in giving something up but never could maintain not eating sweets or listening to the radio for six weeks. Catholics ate fish on Friday, wore saint medals around their necks, fingered rosary beads and recited a different Lord's Prayer. Sorrowful holy pictures hung in their living rooms.

No matter how bad the marriage, they never divorced. My Aunt Anna took back my Uncle Jim after he lived with a girlfriend for two years. Priests and nuns were celibate while ministers had families like mine. In tightly closed booths my cousins went to "confession." I said if I had to confess, I'd probably never sin at all.

In my small town, Jews were even a smaller minority with a tiny synagogue at either edge of town. Judaism was another religion alien to me, with services on Saturdays, strict dietary laws, and different holidays. Intermarriage was strictly forbidden. The sister of my Dad's best friend made the decision to marry a poor Jew from New York instead of the man her family had chosen for her. She was declared dead and they sat Shiva for a week. We never saw her again.

Although different, Protestants and Jews were on the same side in the Masonic Lodge, as opposed to the Catholics who joined the Knights of Columbus.

One Baptist Negro church existed in the Bottoms, a place so distinct from the rest of the town that it might have been on the far side of the moon. The people kept to themselves and mostly worked at laboring jobs like my immigrant grandparents. One of the old men was famously known to speak fluent Hungarian and was often seen talking with one of our neighbors on his porch.

The invisible line between our house and the ramshackle homes a few blocks away in the Bottoms was clear, and although we all walked home from school together, we divided at a certain corner every day , home to cultures separated by more than color.

As a town policeman, my Dad patrolled the Bottoms and knew everyone who lived there. When he worked the school crossing *all* of us would run to him and show our papers and report cards. He'd then stop traffic and walk us across the street in different directions.

In the 1940s, a class went from kindergarten to 8th grade together. In addition to my half-Catholic family, all but three of my classmates were all-knowing Catholics and we often argued about religion, parroting our different teachings.

The sometimes vehement discussions usually ended when we got tired of the subject. Eventually one kid would nod sagely and intone, "But there's only one God," and we'd jump up and play ball– argument over.

Religion has led me in many directions. In 1967 I belonged to a Presbyterian church in Memphis. When the minister told me blacks would, "despite desegregation, never be admitted to our church," I decided that wasn't what God had in mind for all of us and quit.

Later, another minister in Savannah refused to baptize my grand-son because we weren't members; this after my husband had sung in the choir for fourteen years. I became a Congregationalist in New England, attracted by its independent tenets but, after leaving there, for many years was an agnostic who did not attend church at all.

My Catholic cousins have also gone in many directions. One di-vorced and married a Jew, bringing on excommunication. When she was sick and no one from her church visited, another cousin simply quit being a Catholic. "The Fundamentalists from the corner church were the ones who brought me soup," she told me.

Her brother gave up being Catholic when he tired of confessing his love for the bottle. Cousin Irene is the only devout one left. She has a large Italian family with six children, about twenty-five grand children and a few mixed race ones adopted from her days as a foster mother.

After reading and studying widely, sampling many denomina-tions and thinking about religion a lot, I've come to a conclusion. My cousins and Pope Benedict XVI can kiss my ass. I'm not going to hell.

I think we're all already there.

Grandma's Two Worlds

Growing up in a family that still had one foot in the "old country" gave me a split personality, I think. I never knew which world was the real one. Life was led one way inside and another way outside the house. Language, food, values, name it–everything was different.

In the early 1900s my grandparents left their families in Europe to come to America where they settled in a small industrial town in New Jersey and, although they worked very hard, never had the means to go home for a visit. Two World Wars and the Russian Communist takeover of Hungary also kept them on this side of the ocean.

To save money, whole families lived in one house–ours was a two-story reddish brick stucco that stood on a 50 x 100 foot lot. Each story had a big front porch with four wicker rockers. A two car garage took up half the back yard next to the garden. Grandparents, parents, aunts, uncles–all living together and pooling their resources, yet not really getting along. Mostly it was the women who quarreled but the men sometimes chimed in with their voices of discontent. I didn't know it then but our house was devoid of warmth, of kisses and hugs.

We spoke two languages (three if you factor in Ukrainian on my Dad's side) but pretty much it was English outside and Hungarian at home. Although Granma struggled to learn and ordered me to speak to her in English, when she was angry, the curses she laid on you were definitely foreign.

Before I was old enough to go to school, I sat underneath the kitchen table on the carved round piece of wood that joined the supports of the table legs and took it all in. I felt invisible as I watched Granma stage manage the whole universe, barking the orders that we all obeyed. Although she was barely five feet tall, fair and round, her voice could rattle the dishes on the shelves when she was making a point. She rarely smiled and had no sense of humor.

She grew onions, carrots, string beans, kohlrabi and parsley in her garden in the yard. She kept a compost pile long before it became a trend. In the late summer she put up ripe cucumbers and tomatoes in jars that would soon line the shelves in the cellar and last the family all through winter.

Indian summer was a sweltering time to be cooking and bottling and everyone was pressed into washing dozens of jars which were set to dry and be filled on towels covering the table. The vegetables were sliced and cooked in huge pots on the coal stove. The aroma of spices and vinegar clung to the house for days.

Granma cooked every meal from scratch. Breakfast was hot oatmeal or farina and pastry from the day before. Once, I asked for corn flakes because I wanted a secret de-coder ring I'd heard about on the radio. She bought me a box and then served the cereal with hot milk. Lunch was usually a sandwich and fruit.

Twice a week Granma bought meat from the butcher. She served pork with mashed potatoes and sauerkraut. Beef went into soup and stew and on the rare occasion we had steak, she fried it so well done it could have been cobbled to the soles of our shoes.

Granma had a meat grinder that she screwed to a wooden bench. She would straddle the other end and feed the meat for sausages into the opening of the grinder. It was my job to hold the slippery casing tight to the opening where the ground up meat squeezed out. She cooked pig's feet in clear jelly and cooled the bowlfuls on shelves in the pantry. (I didn't want my friends to know about that).

Many nights we simply had noodles with pot cheese or cooked cabbage. At Thanksgiving Granma baked a capon chicken with cabbage rolls on the side and for Easter we had a ham with potato salad and hard boiled eggs.

On a specially made, thick wooden board that covered most of the kitchen table, Granma prepared the dough for noodles and bread. With a homemade rolling pin she'd roll the dough into a big round circle so thin you could see through it. She'd roll the sheet into long flat strips two inches wide and then slice it into various shapes, some long and thin, others wide and squared, depending on what she planned to use them for.

Granma rolled bread dough, shaped and put it into a bowl to rise on the back of the stove. She punched it down and put the shaped dough into greased pans, left them to rise again and then baked them in time for supper. Talk about a heavenly aroma. Granma let me roll and cut and roll and knead to my heart's content on my little corner of the floured board. A cup of sugar was added to the dough if we were using it for jam or fruit filled pastry.

On Thursdays Granma and I climbed aboard the smelly #62 bus to travel six miles to the next town to the farmer's market. We'd get off at the end of the line where the bus turned around for the trip back. The only thing she'd buy was a live chicken. I hated to see her carrying it home upside down by a string tied to its feet. I knew once we got there, she'd take it out back to a big tree stump and chop off its head with an axe. We had chicken soup every Friday.

Rain or shine, Monday was wash day. We gathered laundry from all over the house first thing in the morning. Granma and I sorted and soaked it in the washtubs in the cellar. Very dirty factory work clothes she boiled in a huge iron pot over an open gas burner that blazed next to the tubs. She stirred them with a broom handle as if she were mixing goulash and used the stick to lift and drop them into the washer filled with hot soapy water and bleach where they rolled and pitched. After about fifteen minutes she lifted it all into the tubs to rinse in clear water before she put the load, piece by piece, through the wringer to squeeze out the water. Then it was into the wicker basket and up the stairs to the back porch where she hung them on a line with the wooden clothespins I handed to her.

The clothesline rolled on two wheels and stretched from the house to a tall pole at the edge of the back yard. On rainy days we threw the laundry over lines in the cellar, the inside wall of which was papered with pictures of famous movie stars that came on the cover of the Parade section of the Sunday newspapers. Clark Gable and Lana Turner smiled at me every time I passed them.

During the Second world War sauerkraut, being German, was unavailable so Grandmother made her own by placing sliced cabbage into a three foot high wooden barrel. She covered it with a round piece of wood weighted by a brick. The cabbage was left in the cellar to ferment in salted water for I don't know how long and was ready to eat when it started to bubble and move the brick. How could something that smelled so bad taste so good on a sausage?

On Tuesday we ironed. The heavy iron was heated on top of the stove. Granma pressed and then draped the dampened sheets and clothes all over the house to dry. She let me iron the dish towels and anything else that wasn't starched. The mop and broom skimmed the floors every other day under her busy hands and dusting was my job. Chairs, tables, lamps and windowsills that were within the reach of my rag were fastidiously checked by Granma before we were through.

Twice a year we took down the long lace curtains from the living room windows, washed and rinsed them in tea water to add color, and dunked them in thick starch. On the front porch we'd assemble the curtain stretchers which looked like long yardsticks on legs lined with pins sticking sharp side out. We'd stretch the curtains over the pins and leave them to dry stiffly in the breeze. I managed to get myself stuck every time.

Coming out of the great Depression, most people had little cash and were forced to be frugal. Nothing was discarded until it was fit only for the rag bag. The Singer sewing machine stood open ready to patch work clothes. Granma also sewed dresses and aprons and hemmed flour sacks for towels.

She taught me to darn socks with fine stitches and no knots so that you'd never know they'd been holey. I joke that we were so poor that a pair of shoes counted as two birthday gifts. Not so funny then. When we sat down to rest Granma reached into her yarn bag with the wooden handles and taught me to knit and crochet as well. Of course, I started with scarves made from many colored wisps of yarn.

Morning glories, peonies and a flower she called "snowballs" grew in all the places in the yard that weren't taken by sidewalks. Granma loved showy colors; her roses flaunted themselves like chorus girls. We swept the dirt between them every day as well as the curbs and gutters out front. Years later, traveling in Romania, I saw the same swept yards Granma had re-created in a land so far from her home, fences and all. I wondered if she'd ever been homesick?

Granma repaired just about everything around the house that fell apart and only called in experts for the big jobs like tarring the flat roof at about three year intervals. Two laborers boiled the tar in a red-hot black vat the size of a Jeep and hoisted it up a rope in buckets to two more men on the roof. I watched the exciting show and waited for the bits of tar to come falling to the ground. When Granma wasn't looking, I chewed it like gum. I still like the clean smell of tar.

Granpa, on the other hand, went to work, came home, ate supper and sat on the front porch until bedtime which was usually at dark. He was a hefty six foot tall man with auburn hair and a moustache that tickled my neck when I sat on his lap. He smoked a pipe with a long curved stem and a bowl with a silver lid. His outdoor activities consisted of playing pinochle with three of his cronies around a card table set up in the shady driveway in the summer.

As the game got hotter, Granpa would slip me a dollar to go to the corner bar for a pitcher of beer. In defiance of Granma's dirty looks from the back porch, the men used the beer as a whiskey chaser for a drink they called a boilermaker.

He kept his whiskey in the cellar and every night after supper he'd find a reason to go down there, perhaps to stoke the furnace or add a shovel of coal, and get quietly drunk. Granma wasn't fooled but she never found his stash, either. Every night Her Hungarian curses tumbled down the steps after him.

Granpa was fifty-eight when he died in 1943. I was eight. He'd been in the hospital for two weeks dying of what no one would call by name. The stomach cancer had shrunken him and when I peered at him in his coffin I didn't recognize my grandfather. It wasn't him. I turned to the family and said, "It isn't him." But when I stood up on the red velvet kneeler to take a better look, I saw the long thin scar on the side of his nose. Many times I had asked him where he got the scar; he'd laugh and say that was where his horse kicked him.

All of the parlor furniture was moved and stacked in a bedroom. Granpa's casket was placed beneath a bank of flowers that I can still smell. The rest of the room was filled with rows of metal folding chairs. Neighborhood women prayed and sang most of the day and evening. When they left the old men stayed all night and drank in silence.

To improve her English, she said, Granma went to the movies every Monday night which also happened to be dish night at the Ritz Theatre. During the great Depression of the 1930s and into the early 1940s, premiums were used to lure people into movie houses all over the country. By taking me, she'd get two dishes and I'd get to learn all the songs from those great old musicals with Fred Astaire and Ginger Rogers.

I loved the movies. Many years later the first dog I bought was a wire-haired terrier like Asta from *The Thin Man* series. Every Monday we saw a feature film, a cartoon and a black and white movie like *Gaslight*. During WWII the *Movietone News* reported on the battles being fought overseas by our servicemen. Often it was the only way people could find out where their boys were fighting and dying. I remember seeing the American flag being planted on Iwo Jima and hearing the audience applauding. When I started school, Granma walked me there and back while my mother worked as a riveter in a defense plant. It was then that I became more and more aware that my family was different from the families of my classmates.

I didn't want anyone to know that I spoke Hungarian and ate pig's feet. I wanted store bought clothes from Lerner's and shoes that didn't lace up to my ankles. I was mortified if my Mother came to school for a program. *She looks like a greenhorn*, I thought, *right off the boat, even if she does speak English.*

As I was struggling to balance two worlds, trying to leave the old world behind and be red, white and blue American, I was blind to Granma's daily attempts to do the same. I imagine she had a much more arduous road to travel. She had not only left her mother and father to join an older sister already in America but left her grandparents and a large extended family on a farm in a small village outside Budapest as well.

All Granma had of them were infrequent letters that told of their suffering during World War II and the forced surrender of family property to the Communists afterward. Eventually letters bearing news of their deaths compelled her to say her final good-byes to Europe.

Granma's first two room house on a dirt road was where she gave birth to her three daughters. To earn money she carried milk to the neighbors until the night the barn burned and her single cow was killed. Only after her daughters found work and two of them married was she able to buy a bigger house with their pooled incomes.

Learning to speak English in order to become citizens must have been very difficult, but all I noticed was that my grandparents had heavy greenhorn accents that embarrassed me.

I didn't realize what a hard job taking care of a big family can be. What I remember was that when I was sick with a cold, Granma was the one who made hot tea with lemon and rye toast with butter and bits of garlic on top. She was the one who smeared the warmed piece of flannel with Vicks and tied it around my neck to ease my breathing. If I insisted, she boiled milk and laced it with yesterday's coffee when my mother wasn't around.

While she cooked and looked "old country," Granma was the first on the block to have indoor plumbing and every few years she'd throw out the old furniture to modernize according to the latest home fashions on display in the window of the furniture store on Main Street.

It seemed she wanted to retain parts of the life she had left in Europe like the food and the religion, but she was smart enough to know that she had to embrace new ways in order to succeed in her new country.

When my baby brother was born in 1947 my parents, with a down payment from Granma, bought a house about a half mile away. A grown-up twelve years old, I soon became busy with my brother, school and friends and I drifted away from Granma.

In quick succession, I graduated from high school, got a job and got engaged to be married. I had little time for Granma. Our family was never one for getting together anyway. When my aunt and uncle built their own home, Granma and my spinster aunt were left in the old house.

Without telling anyone, Granma got a job as a chambermaid in a tiny hotel owned by Hungarians and was still employed when she died suddenly of renal failure at the age of sixty-eight. No one knew she had been ill. Her death came three days before my twentieth birthday and two months before my wedding.

People have said that I'm like her, the American version of Granma, busy and bossy and stage managing the whole universe.

My Aunts

The original odd couple lives in New Jersey. Aunt Mary and Aunt Helen have refined sibling rivalry to a point so sharp that they deftly skewer each other and have done so daily for over seventy-five years. Their day begins when one says, "Good morning," and the other says, "What did you mean by that?"

Their parents came to Ellis Island at the turn of the twentieth century from farms outside Budapest in Hungary. They had left their families on the docks and never saw them again. They had no money, spoke no English and came with the clothes on their backs. The only words they could pronounce were *America, citizen, work* and *God*. Many other European refugees landed at the same time and settled in small New Jersey towns.

My grandparents begat Helen, Mary and my mother, Irene. Brunette, redhead and blonde, the sisters were raised in a small house on a small lot on which a vegetable garden and flowers recreated the look of the dirt yards of the old country's villages.

Aunt Helen learned to speak English in public school but couldn't escape the "greenhorn" label that went with high top black shoes and homemade dresses. She never got past the fourth grade and carried milk to the neighbors every morning no matter what the weather, eking out a few pennies a week. The tiny barn burned one night, killing the cow. Ever afterwards, Grandmother slept with the curtains open.

For Aunt Mary, two years younger, school was a happier place. She wasn't taunted for wearing Hungarian peasant clothes. By this time my grandfather worked as a laborer at the Copper Works and modern clothing was bought at Cheap John's. To help support the family, she went to work full time as a maid when she was fourteen.

My mother Irene, the youngest, was able to complete the 8th grade before finding work in a hat factory where she met my father in 1934.

None of them strayed from their tiny industrial hometown on the Arthur Kill across the river from New York city. The Magyar Reformed Church was the core of religious and social life. Banquets, picnics and autumn wine festivals with Gypsy orchestras playing the *czardas* were attended by young and old. Sharing the food, lively dancing and their native costumes and language bound the Hungarians together in their new country.

During my childhood I was able to carefully observe the sisters since, as was the custom, we all lived in the same house. It seemed to me that they didn't like each other. They disagreed over everything.

Just sitting on the Holly Street porch in rockers on a summer evening brought the likelihood of witnessing a good fight. It usually started when a neighbor strolled by.

"Good evening." "Hello, how are you?" Pause–until the person was past the house.

"She looks pregnant." "Shut up. The kid is here."

"Can I ever say anything without you jumping down my throat?"

"Can you ever say anything that ain't stupid?"

"I'm going in." "Who cares?" "Good night." Slam.

The sisters stayed in the house when my grandparents died and my parents, kid brother, and I moved to our own house. In the mid-1940s, spinsters didn't live on their own even if they could afford it, so when Aunt Mary and Uncle Paul built their house, Aunt Helen had to move in with them. Alzheimer's soon killed him and they were left to co-exist. In our culture few women drove cars so they walked everywhere if no one offered to pick them up.

It's her house, so Aunt Mary is the boss. She shops, cooks and keeps the garden and yard in order. At age seventy-five, she opened her first checking account, but still prefers to walk to the bank and post office to pay bills. She pushes a grocery cart she "borrowed" a mile to the supermarket and refuses to call a taxi even to go to the doctor for her B12 shot each month. She says she hates the driver. It's a small town.

Aunt Helen was cursed with poor co-ordination; she was a seven month preemie who wasn't expected to live. My grandmother said she put her in a shoebox behind the stove to keep her warm. She simply can't perform household chores to suit her sister, but she tries to help by washing dishes and cleaning and sneaks dusting and mopping when Aunt Mary is out. She has a gift for malapropism and her interpretation of the evening news can be hilarious.

"Soldiers are on their way to Pepsi Cola in Florida," she might announce. After her mastectomy she reported having a monogram that cost forty-six dollars. People were selling their houses and moving to condoms.

Without fail, on Saturday morning at 10:30 the phone rings and I get the death report from New Jersey. "Do you remember Mrs. Nagy? Well, she went in the bathroom and never came out." Whether I remember or not, I murmur assent to be spared a long history of the person who died.

Aunt Helen, when she finally wrestles the phone away from her sister, uses her time to repeat, "They thought I was finished years ago, but they went first." I can hear her smiling.

Reluctantly, she returns the phone to Aunt Mary, but their simultaneous conversation continues. "I'm talking to her now. Go away. Do you want to talk again? Here. Then shut up. Let me talk. "To me she complains, "You don't know what I go through here. I had a hard life with your drunken uncle. I thought I'd have peace when I got old, but she's here bitchin' in my ear all the time. She hates what I cook. She hates the neighbors. She says I can't take care of this house and why did I build it? So, how are you? How are the kids?"

Aunt Helen regains control of the phone. "How is your neighbor Marion? She was so nice to me when I was in Savannah. I wonder what she wanted?"

As we talk, I remember growing up with one foot still in the old Hungarian world in which gossip was more feared than a fatal illness, where neighbors spoke over stout fences, where no one ever came to dinner and I was forbidden to have playmates in the yard.

I recall coming inside on cold Saturday afternoons to the blended aroma of chicken soup simmering on the coal stove and the smell of freshly waxed floors covered with newspapers to keep them clean.

Returning from school on Mondays meant sniffing the bluing on washday and the starch on Tuesday as the laundry was pressed by a heavy hot iron that was kept hot on the top of the big black stove.

I remember being surprised when these argumentative women cried at my grandfather's funeral when I was eight years old and again at my grandmother's when I was twenty. They cried when my Mother died young.

Through my whole existence they'd never exchanged a civil word that I could call to mind. Could it be that underneath a lifetime of verbal warfare they really loved each other?

Nah, I don't think so.

BESS T. CHAPPAS

Bess T. Chappas was born in Kalamas, Greece, and immigrated to the United States with her family in 1939. She holds a bachelor's degree from Armstrong Atlantic State University in elementary education, a master's degree in education from Georgia Southern University, and an EdS from the University of Georgia. Since retirement after a twenty-one year career as a teacher and school media specialist, she spends time as a professional storyteller and freelance writer. She is a columnist for *Coastal Senior*, a monthly magazine published by the *Savannah Morning News*.

Her published works include a story CD, *Savannah Ghosts and Other Stories* and *Kiki and the Red Shoes*, a children's book based on her life as child in Athens, Greece. One of the many exciting things that has happened since the book was published is its acceptance at the International Storytelling Center at Jonesborough, TN. A sequel, *Kiki and the Statue of Liberty*, is planned for next year.

Chappas has traveled extensively, visiting twelve foreign countries as well as many places within the United States. She collects folk tales as she travels and plans to publish a book of folk tales from around the world. She is a member of Savannah Storytellers, the Southern Order of Storytellers, the National Storytelling Association, the Society of Children's Book Writers and Illustrators, and Toastmasters International.

She has two daughters, a son, and three grandsons. Two of her grandsons have inherited her love of story and plan to be writers. The third wants to be an architect, but she loves him anyway.

Chappas can be contacted by email to Savteller@aol.com.

Visit her website at www.SavannahStorySpinners.com.

Aphrodite

Savannah, Georgia 1976

Standing on the bluff overlooking River Street, Michael watched the large container barge slowly drift down the Savannah River toward the Atlantic. His thoughts drifted like the barge as he envisioned stowing away and leaving his problems behind. He reached into the pocket of his Armani jacket, took out his little flask of Scotch and took a few sips to calm his nerves. "Pull yourself together, Mickey," he told himself. "There's got to be a way out of this."

Women passing by would be sure to notice the tall, well-built man with the startling blue-green eyes. His full, sensuous mouth pulled down at the corners as he ran his hand over curly black hair that almost met his collar at the back of his neck. His slightly off-center nose kept his face from being too pretty.

He turned and walked the few blocks to the DeSoto Hotel, not even aware of the beauty of the live oak trees laden with Spanish moss, nor the flowers blooming in the historic squares. His thoughts were of the events of the previous day.

He had arrived in Savannah the day before to see Pinkie Masters, his father's oldest friend and Michael's godfather. He had come to borrow money, but he didn't ask right away because he didn't want Pinkie to know how desperate and how frightened he was of what happened in Las Vegas.

Pinkie Masters' Lounge was one of the favorite Savannah watering holes. Since Jimmy Carter, a personal friend of Pinkie's, stopped in whenever he was in Savannah, the bar had become a hangout for the local politicians.

"Welcome to Savannah," said Pinkie out of one side of his mouth, the ever-present cigarette dangling out of the other. "How are Gus and the family?"

"They're doing well," Michael lied. He'd had no contact with his family for several years. "Business is good at the restaurant. My sister and brother are both married and have kids. The Andropoulos family is growing."

"Good, good," replied Pinkie. "What can I get you to drink?"

"Well, it's a little early for me, but I'll have a bit of Scotch, single malt, if you insist," Michael said.

"Take a seat at the bar and I'll introduce you to the regulars."

Throughout the afternoon, Michael met many of Pinkie's customers. Some were downtown workers who stopped in for a break, politicians who wheeled and dealed at the back tables, scruffy street people hoping for a handout, and members of old Savannah families. They all greeted Pinkie by name.

With his good looks and expensive clothes, Michael was a magnet for women. This was nothing new. From the time Michael was sixteen, he could have any woman he wanted. Women old enough to be his mother begged to teach him the fine art of lovemaking. In high school, girls considered it an honor to lose their virginity to him. Tonight, however, Michael kept his head down and his eyes on his drink, to the disappointment of several women customers.

During the evening, Pinkie introduced Michael to Walter C. Beaudreau, a Georgia state senator. Michael was impressed with Beaudreau's classic southern charm, his sophisticated bearing, and the power that emanated from him. "Sit down, boy, and tell me about yourself," encouraged Beaudreau. "Call me Senator. Everybody does."

Michael told him that he had dropped out of college after two years to try his hand at acting in Hollywood. He got a few minor parts and did some modeling, but the jobs stopped coming. Michael blamed this on the fact that Hollywood was a closed shop to outsiders. He didn't tell the older man that his drinking and drug use soon gave him a bad reputation with the casting agencies.

When he couldn't find work in Hollywood, he drifted to Las Vegas where he found work in a casino. Michael's job was to greet the guests and entice the high rollers to spend more money. With his striking looks and charm, he was good at his job. Unfortunately, he liked to gamble.

Michael didn't tell Beaudreau that the casino was owned by the Mafia and he was hiding out in Savannah because he owed $50,000 in gambling debts to his bosses.

Beaudreau listened to Michael, sensing more than Michael wanted him to know. "Well, boy, I better be getting along home. Say, tomorrow is Sunday. If you don't have any plans, why not ride out to the old homestead and have supper with us? I'd like to show you my new boat. You like to sail, don't you?"

"Thank you, sir. I'd like that. I did a little sailing when I was in college. And I don't know anyone in town except Pinkie."

"Good. Pinkie will tell you how to get out to the house." With a wave to Pinkie, Beaudreau left.

"Well, Michael, you made a good friend there," confided Pinkie. "The senator is an important man around Chatham County. He's real Old Savannah. His ancestors probably came over with General Oglethorpe. If you're thinking of staying a while, he can help you get a job. He's got a big place out on Highway 17, right on the water."

When Michael reached the DeSoto, he got into his rental car, and with the directions given by Pinkie, drove the 30 minutes toward the Beaudreau estate. Maybe my luck is about to change, Michael thought. Knowing a rich influential man can't hurt.

He turned into a narrow blacktop, passed a sign that read "Magnolia Bluff," and followed a curved driveway to a three-story colonial mansion painted white with green shutters. Four Grecian Doric columns supported the front portico. Stately magnolia trees grew all around the mansion.

He parked the car and stepped under the portico to ring the bell. A tall woman wearing a maid's uniform opened the door. She looked at Michael with sharp ebony eyes. "Can I help you, suh?"

"My name is Michael Andrews. I believe Senator Beaudreau is expecting me."

"Come this way. The senator is in the study."

Michael followed the woman through a spacious foyer into another room where the senator sat in a leather wingback chair smoking a cigar. Soft glowing lights gave a mysterious air to the polished antique furniture and the cases filled with books that lined the walls.

"Here you are, Michael," boomed Beaudreau as he rose from his chair.

"That will be all, Maggie. You can serve dinner whenever it's ready." Turning to Michael, he shook his hand and indicated a chair close by. "Let me get you a drink. Scotch, isn't it?

Michael stood until Beaudreau handed him the drink and returned to his chair. Before Michael could sit in the other chair, a southern voice, like molasses over whiskey, came from the doorway.

"Sorry I'm late, Daddy."

Michael turned to see a tall, slim woman wearing dark slacks and a white silk blouse glide into the room on four-inch heels. Her long dark hair floated around a face pale as cream. Her eyes, dark and heavy lidded, captured Michael's turquoise ones.

"You're not late," the senator answered. "Our guest just now got here.

Stephanie, this is Michael Andrews, new to Savannah. Michael, this is Stephanie, my daughter."

Stephanie held out a slender hand. Holding the cool, strong hand in his a second too long, Michael looked into her eyes. The pupils were like pin points. Drugs, he thought. Stephanie withdrew her hand and turned to her father. "How 'bout one of those drinks for me." She quietly assessed Michael, his handsome face and his tall well-built body.

"Sure," said the senator, "You can take it into the dining room. I see Maggie hovering at the door. Dinner must be ready."

During dinner, Beaudreau covertly watched the pair, sensing a hum of attraction between them as they made small talk about what to do and where to go in Savannah.

After dinner, Stephanie said she was going down to River Street and asked if Michael wanted to go with her. Before Michael could answer, Beaudreau surprised Michael by saying, "The boy and I have some business to take care of. Maybe he'll see you down there later."

After Stephanie exited the room, Michael looked at Beaudreau expectantly, with a glint of annoyance in his eyes. "What's going on, senator?"

"Now, now, boy, don't get your shorts in a wad. Let's go back to the study." He led the way across the hall and sat behind his desk. Taking a cigar from a carved wooden container, he lit it slowly. "Would you like one?" he asked.

Reaching for his cigarettes, Michael shook his head. "I appreciate the dinner and the hospitality, senator, but I'd like to know what is going on."

"You can cut out the act, boy. Who do you think you are fooling? I have friends in Vegas. I made a call this morning and I know all about you and the trouble you're in." Fear coiled in Michael's gut. When he moved to get up, the senator continued, "Sit, sit, I didn't tell anyone that you're in Savannah. Just listen, boy, I'm trying to help you."

Michael was rattled, but he refused to let it show. He was proud that his hands were steady as he lit his cigarette. "There're some pretty nasty people after me," he confided. "But I plan to pay them back. That's why I'm here."

"If you are planning to get money from Pinkie, you can forget it. To tell you that truth, he doesn't have it right now. A land deal went bad on him few months ago. I know because I was involved myself, but I have the resources to take the hit without getting hurt."

"If what you say is true, I'll just have to move on. I can't stay where the guys from Vegas will find me unless I have some money for them. I have other prospects," Michael lied.

"I don't think you do. I've checked around. You are in big trouble and have nowhere to run. But, I have a proposition for you that will solve your problems–marry my daughter."

Michael was momentarily stunned. The heat of the cigarette on his finger snapped him out of his shock. Putting out the cigarette, he got to his feet. "What? Are you crazy? I just met your daughter. I have enough problems without taking on a wife. I'm not that desperate."

"I don't know. I think you are. Sit back down and let's talk about this calmly." He walked to the bar and poured brandy into two snifters, giving one to Michael. "Would a million dollars make you listen to what I have to say?"

Michael downed the brandy in one gulp. He walked to the bar and poured himself another one. Then he sat down. "Okay, I'm listening."

"Good," said the senator. "Two years ago, when my daughter graduated from college, she was engaged to a man she met there. He was from an old influential New England family. He finished law school and was going into his father's firm. Stephanie was crazy about the guy, but his family thought he could do better than a girl from the backward South. They talked him into asking her to wait, and the next thing she knew he had gone back to an old girlfriend. Stephanie took it extremely hard.

"She had a nervous breakdown. When she came out of the hospital, she was not the same girl. Since then, she drinks too much, fools around with drugs, and hangs out with a sleazy group down on River Street. She doesn't listen to anything I say and it's just a matter of time before she gets into trouble. Stephanie is my only child and I'm concerned about her.

"I know you're in trouble, but from what I found out, you come from a good, stable family. If you're finished sowing your wild oats, this could be a second chance for you as well as Stephanie. She's a beautiful girl. I saw that you noticed. She's smart, too, when she is not drinking."

"I'm not saying I'm interested, but what makes you think Stephanie will go for this?"

"Well, that's up to you. You're a good-looking man. I saw the way she looked at you. We wouldn't tell her about our arrangement, of course. I will take care of your debts with the guys in Vegas, help you find a job here in Savannah, give you a million dollars when you marry, and another million when your first child is born. Will you think about it?"

Back at the hotel, Michael's head was spinning. After changing into jeans and a T-shirt, he walked back to River Street and headed for the closest bar. The streetlights had come on, giving the cobblestones a slick, wet look. The Talmadge Bridge, spanning the river between Savannah and South Carolina, looked like a Tinker Toy structure in the moonlight.

After two double Scotches, Michael was mellow enough to think about the senator's proposition. A million now and a million after the first child. That's a lot of money. He wouldn't have to stay in Savannah forever. With that kind of money, he could go wherever he wanted. Stephanie was a beautiful woman. He'd slept with a lot worse, especially when he was drunk.

Then, there was the senator's property. That had to worth a lot. He'd like to see his father's face when he found out how much he would be worth. He'd like to stick it to the old man. Michael remembered his father, his face red, yelling at him when Michael told him he didn't want any part of the restaurant and was leaving for Hollywood. "You're worthless," his father had shouted. "You'll end up in the gutter."

Finishing his drink, he slipped off the bar stool, went outside and walked to the river. He leaned on the balustrade and looked at the dark, dirty water rushing toward the ocean. He had to make a decision. The mob would find him soon.

Michael was so deep in thought, he didn't notice the trio coming toward him until he heard Stephanie's drawl, "Why, here's the Yankee newcomer to our fair city. Guys, meet Michael Andrews, tall, dark, and dangerous."

Michael turned to see Stephanie flanked by two men. They were an odd pair. One was tall and thin with red hair combed up in spikes. Tattoos filled all available space on his bare arms. He was dressed in tattered jeans and a sleeveless shirt. The other had black dreadlocks trailing down his shoulders. He had on slim dark slacks, a white dress shirt with rolled up sleeves and expensive running shoes.

Stephanie had one arm around the elbow of each man. She smiled crookedly at Michael and seemed unsteady on her feet.

"Oh, hi, Miss Beaudreau," said Michael, thinking fast. "Your father hoped I would run into you. He asked me to give you a ride home."

"Hey," slurred Tattoo, "She's got her wheels."

"Yeah," added Dreadlocks, "We ain't through partying yet."

Stephanie blinked and swayed slightly, her eyes fastened on Michael's intense blue-green ones. "Party's over, guys," said Michael as he slipped his arm around Stephanie's waist and led her toward the restaurant on the corner.

"Shit," said Tattoo. "Who's gonna buy our drinks now?"

Michael entered the restaurant with Stephanie stumbling along. He sat her down at the nearest table and ordered black coffee for both of them.

"Well, aren't you Sir Galahad?" Stephanie smirked. " C'n take care of myself."

"You're not afraid someone will roll you one night for the diamond rings you're wearing?" He indicated to the beautifully cut antique rings on her fingers.

"No one will touch Senator Beaudreau's little girl. They're all afraid of him," she laughed.

"I wouldn't be too sure," answered Michael. "Drugs and hunger do strange things to a person. Where's your car?"

"Not sure. Think it's in the parking lot somewhere around here."

Michael wondered at his reaction. What was he feeling for this girl? Compassion? Attraction? There was tightness in his loins. It was just because he hadn't had a woman in a while, he told himself. He just wanted to get her safely home. "Drink your coffee and let's find your car."

Finding Stephanie's car wasn't difficult. It stood out like a sore thumb, a red Mercedes convertible with a parking ticket on the windshield. "Daddy will take care of it," she scoffed.

The ride to Magnolia Hill was uneventful. Michael kept his thoughts to himself as Stephanie dozed, her head pressed against the passenger door.

Lights were on in the house and on the porch when they drove up. Maggie opened the door as soon as the car stopped. "Why, there's my old Mammy," slurred Stephanie. "Bet she tells Daddy all about this at breakfast." Stephanie stumbled out of the car and into Maggie's arms. Maggie slammed the door in Michael's face and turned off the lights.

Michael sat there a couple of minutes, unsure of what to do. Hell, he thought, I'll just take this baby back with me. He turned in the circular driveway, let the top down and enjoyed the ride in the beautiful spring night. He smiled to himself. "Shit, I could get used to this."

Early the next morning, Michael drove up to the Beaudreau estate in Stephanie's convertible. The senator answered the door. "Come in, come in and get some breakfast," he invited, leading Michael beyond the dining room to a large kitchen. "I want to thank you for bringing Stephanie home last night. She would thank you herself if she weren't still sleeping."

Michael sat at the round table in the large, well-equipped kitchen. Maggie poured him coffee and brought a plate filled with eggs, ham, and grits. A large platter of biscuits was on the table along with butter and jelly. "This looks and smells fantastic, Maggie." He attacked the food with gusto.

"Humpf," replied Maggie.

Beaudreau watched Michael enjoy the food while he had another cup of coffee and looked through the morning paper. Three biscuits and a clean plate later, Michael looked up sheepishly. "I didn't realize I was so hungry."

"Don't apologize," laughed Beaudreau. "Maggie is a wonderful cook. Come into the study. We need to have another talk." The senator walked out of the kitchen, expecting Michael to follow.

Michael sat there for a few minutes, trying to collect his thoughts. He still didn't know what to say to the senator. Maggie whisked the plate from in front of him, giving him a look of disdain. Michael looked up at her, "You don't like me, do you?"

"I don't rightly know you. I jes don't know what you and the senator are cooking up for my baby. I've been taking care of her since her Mama died when she was little. She's already in trouble and she don't need nobody from up north to give her more misery."

Michael didn't have an answer. Folding his napkin, he got up from the table. "Thank you for the breakfast, Maggie." He followed the senator into the study.

Beaudreau was sitting behind his desk smoking one of his imported cigars. Michael took the chair he had vacated last night. It's déjà vu, Michael though. What am I doing here?

The senator let out a long stream of smoke. "Michael, I've been thinking. The carriage house behind the garden is furnished and empty. There's no reason for you to stay at a hotel. I'm sure a strong young man like you can make himself useful around here to earn his keep. Also, I spoke to my friend, the manager at the DeSoto Hilton. Seems like he can use a smart fella in his marketing department. Think you can do that?"

Michael felt trapped, but he needed a job. His hotel bill was mounting and he had no way to pay it. "Senator," he said. "I would like the job and I do need a place to stay, but about the other..." He cleared his throat. "I just don't know. I need more time."

"Unfortunately, Michael, there isn't much time."

Fear clutched at Michael. "What do you mean? The guys at Vegas know I'm here?"

"No, no, that's not what I mean." The senator leaned back heavily in his chair. He took out another cigar, looked at it, rubbed his fingers around it, and then put it back in the humidor. "I didn't want to tell you this, but now I see it's necessary."

Beaudreau swiveled his chair around and gazed through the window behind him to the garden outside. He rubbed his hand across his face and turned back to face Michael. "I'm the one who doesn't have much time."

Michael stared, still unable to comprehend what the older man was saying.

"Got the results of the tests from the doctor last week. I have lung cancer, the big C. The doctor is talking operation even though it's rather advanced. Got to admit I'm pretty scared. But the worst part is, what is going to happen to Stephanie? Left to herself the way she is, no telling what she'll do or who will take advantage of her." Beaudreau's voice was thick with emotion, his eyes shiny with unshed tears. He turned back to the window, unable to meet Michael's eyes.

Michael was shaken and felt a stab of compassion, yet at the same time couldn't help but think that this improved his position. Now who was desperate? He didn't want to appear too anxious, but he could already taste the millions. "I'm very sorry," he mumbled. "Why don't we just try it for a while with me living in the carriage house, getting to know Stephanie and see how it goes?"

Beaudreau cleared his throat. "All right, Maggie will show you the carriage house and then you need to go to the DeSoto and see Dave Pinckney, the manager, about that job." He turned back to the window, waving his hand in dismissal.

Michael went back to the kitchen where Maggie was just finishing cleaning up. "The senator said you would show me the carriage house,"

Maggie's head jerked up, black eyes piercing Michael's. "Lordy, this is getting even worse," she muttered. She took a key from one of the kitchen cabinets and went out the back door into the garden.

The garden was professionally landscaped with flowering azaleas, roses, beds of annuals and small trees. In the middle was a goldfish pond. At the rear of the pond stood the most beautiful statue Michael had ever seen.

"My God, she's gorgeous," he exclaimed. "Aphrodite, isn't it?" He went straight to the statue and put his hands on the marble, expecting it to be cool to the touch. He was surprised to find it warm as he ran his hand up the arm of the statue and down one thigh. The statue was standing with one arm across the torso and the other reaching toward the classically beautiful face, which was turned slightly over the right shoulder.

Michael turned to Maggie, surprised to see a strange look on her face. She was clutching something she wore around her neck. "Is there something wrong?" Michael asked.

"No, just in a hurry. I got work to do, you know." Giving the statue a wide berth, she hurried to the carriage house at the other end of the garden. Michael glanced again at the statue and followed.

The carriage house apartment was up a narrow stairway over a double garage. It consisted of a living room, dining room combination, a small kitchen, bedroom and a bath. Michael thought he would be comfortable there. Maggie handed Michael the key, and went back to the big house without a word.

She really doesn't like me, thought Michael. As Michael went back across the garden, he paused and gazed admiringly at the statue of Aphrodite.

Michael found the senator still in the study. "I left my rental at the hotel when I brought Stephanie's car back. Can someone take me back to town?"

"Stephanie is going to a luncheon. She'll take you," answered Beaudreau. "She's in the kitchen having coffee. Let me know how the job interview comes out."

Stephanie sat at the table having coffee and toast. "Good morning, Stephanie. I hear you're going into town. How about a ride?" She was dressed in a royal blue dress that suited her dark hair and white skin. Her hair was piled high on her head with little wisps hanging down around her ears.

Maggie looked up from the sink where she was washing dishes, and glared at him.

"Sure thing, I owe you a favor after last night." Stephanie finished her coffee, picked up her purse from the counter and walked outside where the convertible was parked. Michael, always the gentleman, opened the door for her.

Taking an exaggerated breath as she passed by him, Michael said, "My, my, you look and smell delicious this morning, Miss Stephanie." He went around and climbed in the passenger side.

When Stephanie drove the car to the main road, she gave a sideway glance at Michael. "Look, about last night. Thank you for bringing me home. I admit was too groggy to drive, but I don't want you to get the idea that I need someone to take care of me. I can take care of myself. I have friends in town I could have stayed with."

"Yeah, I met a couple of your friends last night. I hope they weren't the pick of the litter."

"Oh, Mac and Jocko are okay," she laughed. "They don't mean any harm. What are you up to today?"

"I'm interviewing for a job at the DeSoto Hilton. Looks like I may be around for a while. Will that be a problem for you?"

"Why should a handsome guy be a problem? My girlfriends will be wild to get their hands on you, Michael. You'll have to beat them off with a stick. Will that be a problem for you?"

"I've never run away from a woman in my life, but it depends on whose hands they are," he answered pointedly, looking at her pale slim hands on the steering wheel.

"Speaking of women," he continued, "I always get along with them no matter what their age, but Maggie doesn't seem to like me. Any reason why? Earlier when we were in the garden, she was downright strange."

"Maggie is funny about the garden and the statue. Her grandmother was Gullah and filled her head with all kinds of weird stories of spells and ghosts. She's very superstitious. Don't take it personally."

"My Yiayia was like that. She would tell me about people that died or got sick because someone put a curse on them. She worried that someone was going to put the 'evil eye' on me and pinned one of those little cloth amulets to my undershirt when I was in grade school. The guys saw it when we were in P.E. and laughed at me. I had to beat up a couple of them to regain my status." He didn't tell Stephanie that he still had that little cloth protector filled with incense in his suitcase.

Michael met with the manager of the hotel. After no more than thirty minutes, he had the job, filled out the necessary forms and was told to report tomorrow morning at nine. He packed his bag, checked out of the DeSoto and drove back to Magnolia Bluff.

He parked his rental in the circular drive and carried his suitcase into the garden. A man wearing baggy jeans and a plaid shirt was weeding in a corner of the garden. He stopped his work and stared at Michael. "I'm Michael Andrews, a friend of the family," Michael explained. The gardener nodded and went back to work. As Michael passed the statue of Aphrodite, he whispered, "Hello there, beautiful."

After unpacking his suitcase and changing into casual slacks and polo shirt, Michael received a phone call from the senator inviting him to dinner. When he passed the statue of Aphrodite in the garden, he stopped short. This was odd. He was sure the statue was facing the big house, but now it was facing the carriage house. He shook his head. He must be mistaken.

He went in purposely through the kitchen to talk to Maggie. It rankled that she didn't seem to like him. "Good evening, Maggie. Lucky me. I get another of your fantastic meals tonight. I thought my grandmother was a fantastic cook, but you are even better." Maggie gave him one of her dark piercing stares and went back to her work.

Michael went into the dining room to find the senator the only occupant and the table was set for two. "Stephanie is not eating with us tonight?" he asked.

Beaudreau shook his head. "No, she went out with her girlfriends. They're planning some kind of school reunion, I think. Well, how did it go at the hotel today?"

"Very well. I start in the marketing department in the morning. Say, I want to ask you something about the statue in the garden. When I saw it earlier, it was facing the house. Just now when I went by, it's facing the other way. Am I crazy here?"

Beaudreau laughed, "Now, don't you start. I hear enough from Maggie about the statue being haunted. José, the gardener, mentioned that the base was loose. Must have turned it around when he repaired it."

After dinner, Michael walked back to his apartment. He planned to turn in early and be fresh for his first day of work, but about eleven he felt restless and decided to take a walk around the grounds. He walked down to the dock and back toward the house just as Stephanie's car rolled into the driveway. He put out his cigarette and waited under the portico.

"Good evening," he said as she came to the door. Startled, Stephanie dropped the keys she was holding. Reaching into her bag, she pulled out a container of Mace. "Hold it," cried Michael, "It's only me."

"What the hell are you doing slinking around in the dark? You scared the shit out of me!"

"I'm sorry, I didn't mean to frighten you." He stepped forward and took the Mace out of her hand. Realizing she was trembling, he put his arms around her and rubbed her shoulders to calm her. "I was just taking a walk. Too restless to sleep. Are you okay now?"

Stephanie buried her face in Michael's strong shoulder. She could smell a masculine cologne and something else, a sexy male scent. She put her arms around his waist to steady herself. Still shaky, she felt comfortable in his arms.

Michael moved his lips down to her hair. It was black as ebony, thick and silky. She raised her head and his lips covered hers in a soft kiss. When Stephanie gave an involuntary sigh, he deepened the kiss, evoking an emotional response in her that both surprised and angered her.

As soon as she found her control, she pulled away and looked up at his dangerous turquoise eyes. "Shame on you, big guy, for taking advantage of a girl when she is out of balance."

Reluctantly, Michael released her. "You can't say you didn't enjoy it."

Her eyes were smoldering dark pools. "No, I can't say that."

The portico light came on. Maggie opened the door with a smile for Stephanie and a scowl for Michael. She took her by the hand and pulled Stephanie into the house. "Time for you to be in bed, baby," she crooned. The door slammed shut.

Michael walked into the garden and stopped by the statue. He lit a cigarette and looked at Aphrodite. "You wouldn't give me the brush off, would you, beautiful?" He ran his hand over the statue's waist and hip. "I could have sworn you were facing the other way yesterday."

The next week was busy for Michael. He settled into his job, which was mainly scheduling parties for the hotel. The salary was not what Michael was used to, but he didn't mind. He had a place to live and his eyes on the Beaudreau millions.

Since Stephanie was busy with plans for the Savannah Country Day School reunion, the senator invited Michael to eat with him every night. "I like the company," he explained.

One evening when Stephanie was home, the senator suggested that she take Michael out on the boat. "I promised the boy a ride on my new sailboat. Why not take him out this Saturday? Maggie can pack you a picnic lunch."

"I'd love to go if Stephanie isn't too busy." Michael jumped at the chance to be alone with Stephanie, as things were not moving as fast as he had hoped.

"I think I can arrange to be free on Saturday," answered Stephanie.

Saturday broke clear and sunny. Maggie reluctantly handed Michael a basket of fried chicken, potato salad, biscuits, and chocolate cake. Iced tea and beer completed the picnic meal.

On the boat, Stephanie was surprised that Michael did not make a move on her. With the exception of holding her hand a few times, he didn't touch her. He entertained her with stories of his youth and his job at Las Vegas. Stephanie told him about growing up in Savannah and even about her disastrous love affair. Michael took her hand and kissed it. "He was a fool to let you go." The day was pleasant and Stephanie admitted to herself she had a good time.

When they arrived home, Michael walked her to the door and reached up to touch a wisp of hair that had fallen across her cheek. Stephanie felt her pulse race. He put his arms around her, ran his hands down her back, and leaned down to kiss her forehead. When she closed her eyes and raised her face to his, Michael brushed his lips lightly across hers, turned and went into the garden, leaving her stunned and wanting.

The next evening, Stephanie asked Michael if he would escort her to the reunion dinner. "Gorgeous girl like you doesn't have a date? What's wrong with these Savannah men?"

"Well, I did have a date, but he had to go out of town on business. Besides, all the girls want to meet you."

Michael rented a tux and purchased a little present for Stephanie from Levy Jewelers in preparation for the dance. When he arrived to pick up Stephanie, Maggie let him in with her usual dour look. "Do I pass inspection?" asked Michael, making a complete turn.

Maggie rolled her eyes. "Well, pretty is what pretty does, my Mama used to say," and she walked into the kitchen.

Michael shook his head as a throaty laugh came down from the staircase. He looked up as Stephanie floated down, a vision in deep rose. Her dress was a slim column down to the tips of her high-heeled sandals. The front was draped, leaving her arms bare and the back was almost non-existent. Diamonds sparkled at her neck and dripped from her ears. Her shoes were transparent as glass, showcasing manicured toes that matched the dress.

"Wow, you're the classiest Cinderella I've ever seen. You look sensational." Being married to her wouldn't be too shabby, he thought to himself.

"It really bugs you that Maggie doesn't like you, doesn't it?" she smiled. "Good to know at least one woman is impervious to your charm."

"Does that mean that you find me charming?" He teased, kissing her hand and running his thumb on the inside of her palm.

"Not sure yet. I'm still trying to figure that one out," she shrugged as she picked up a cashmere shawl, a shade deeper than her dress, threw it over her arm and walked out the front door.

At the dance, held at the Oglethorpe Club in the historic district, Stephanie introduced him to her friends. The women all checked out his sexy looks while the men wondered who the hell he was. Stephanie's best and oldest friend, Ginger, whispered to Stephanie, "You must be crazy, girl, I'd have jumped him the first time I saw him. He's gorgeous. A real Greek God."

Dancing began after dinner. While Stephanie danced with another man from their table, Michael asked Ginger to dance. "Listen, sugar," she drawled. "Don't know what's going on between you and Steffie, but if things don't work out, give me a call. I promise you the best time of your life." She rubbed against him to punctuate the invitation.

Ginger was the most blatant, but a couple of the other women made it clear that they were more than interested.

Stephanie was pleased to find that Michael was a good dancer. Their bodies fit well as she was only a couple of inches shorter with her heels. He held her close for the slow dances, kissed her hair and ran his hands down her bare back. She could feel his arousal and couldn't help but wonder if they would fit as well in other, more intimate ways. She shook her head to dislodge that thought.

Michael pulled back, "Is there something wrong? I love holding you like this, but how much longer do we have to stay?"

She looked up into those passionate turquoise eyes and whispered, "Let's go now."

Nothing was said on the ride home. As soon as they got inside the house and shut the door, they turned to each other in a hot, desperate embrace, lips and tongues meeting and exploring. Michael had been thinking all evening that Stephanie was wearing nothing under that spectacular dress and he made his move to find out. He slipped the dress off her shoulder and followed with kisses down to the swell of her breast.

Stephanie's breath was coming in short gasps. "No, not here. Come upstairs. Daddy sleeps like a log and Maggie's room is in another wing."

Michael didn't argue, following her up the stairs into a large bed-room. He had impressions of a beautifully decorated feminine room, but his mind was elsewhere as he led her to the large bed and stripped off her dress in one quick move. He was right; all she wore was a lacy black triangle. She was slim but well proportioned with small well- shaped breasts and long slender legs.

As soon as he took off his jacket, Stephanie began to unbutton his shirt. "Too slow," he said and he ripped off his shirt and pants. Then he remembered the little box in his pocket. He willed himself to slow down and get in control. This was more than a one-night stand for him. He had long-range plans.

Taking the little box out of his pocket, he sat on the bed next to Stephanie and took her in his arms. "Stephanie, I have a little gift for you. It's not much but I want you to know that I've become very fond of you. This is more than just a physical thing for me. I want us to ex-plore the possibility of our relationship becoming something more permanent."

He opened the box and took out a little gold ring, with a Greek Key design. " Let me put this on your finger."

Stephanie, on the verge of surrender, looked up at him and her dark eyes turned cold. "You must be out of your mind. Do you think I don't know what you and Daddy are cooking up? I don't need an-other man to tell me how to run my life. I'll sleep with you because I want to, but if you think there's going to be a 'happy ever after' end-ing, you can go right back to Vegas"

Michael's romantic thoughts instantly vanished and he was furi-ous. "I don't need someone to just have sex with. I can have any woman I want. I thought we had something more going here. I guess I was mistaken. You can go to hell." He hurriedly dressed and ran down the stairs. On the way out, he spotted a bottle of brandy on the sideboard in the dining room. Picking it up, he went out the side door.

In the garden, Michael went straight to the statue of Aphrodite and sat at the base. He knew he would have to leave Savannah and had to decide where to go, where to hide. He opened up the bottle of brandy and took a long deep swallow

He drank again. "Well, Aphrodite, looks like it's just me and you. I bet you wouldn't refuse my ring." Yes, it was still in his pocket. "Let's see if it fits your finger." He slipped the ring onto the marble finger of the statue. "How 'bout that? Fits perfectly."

He continued to drink from the bottle as he tried to formulate a plan. Had Beaudreau already paid his debt in Vegas? He wasn't sure. Could he go back home and face his father? That would be too humiliating. He had some friends in New Orleans. That might be a good place to hide. His eyelids grew heavy and he slept.

My God, what a dream! Michael didn't know where he was but it seemed he was floating on a cloud. Next to him was a beautiful naked woman with long blond hair, eyes the color of the summer sky, and full, sensuous lips. And what a body, pale as Italian marble, with lush breasts, narrow waist and full rounded hips. On her finger was a slim gold ring. Her long legs were wrapped around him, her mouth hot on his. She was insatiable. She wanted him again and again. He didn't have to hold back… It was just a dream.

Michael awoke just before dawn, lying naked at the base of the statue of Aphrodite. He looked at the bottle of brandy and saw it was almost empty. No wonder his head was pounding and his body felt sore. He pulled on his wrinkled clothes and started to leave when he looked up and saw the ring on the statue's finger.

"God, I must have been really been wasted last night," He shook his head to clear it but that made it hurt even more. He reached up to remove the ring from the statue's finger, but it wouldn't come off. He turned it and pulled, but it was stuck. "Let it go, you bitch."

"No, you're mine now."

Did the statue say something? Was he going crazy? I'll never drink that much again, he promised himself. He wrapped one arm around the statue, placed the other hand around the ring and tugged, hard. The last thing he saw was Aphrodite coming toward him and she was smiling.

In the kitchen, Maggie handed Stephanie a cup of coffee. "You're up early this morning. I s'pected you to sleep late after the big dance last night. Didn't hear you come in."

"I want to talk to Daddy before he gets away this morning."

"Look here, baby, I should have told you before. Your Daddy's sick, very sick. You need to stop your foolishness and take care of him."

Stephanie's hand shook as she set down the cup, her face white with shock. "What are you saying? There's nothing wrong with Daddy."

"Well, there is. He's got cancer and he's afraid to tell you. I know you love him even though you don't act like it sometimes. Y'all only have each other."

Before Stephanie could answer, Beaudreau came into the kitchen. "Good morning, sweetheart. How was last night?" He walked behind her chair and gave her a kiss on the cheek.

"It was okay, Daddy. Sit down, I want to talk to you." Beaudreau's eyes met Maggie's and she nodded.

Beaudreau sat across the table from his daughter and sighed. "I guess the cat's out of the bag. I just didn't want to worry you." He reached across and took her hand. "I didn't want to make you sick again."

"Daddy, you are the most important person in my life. If you don't know that, it's my fault. I've been very selfish, wallowing in my misery when you needed me. I want to hear what the doctor has to say. In fact, I want to go with you to your next appointment. Has your doctor said anything about going to Duke? There's so much they can do these days. We Beaudreaus are fighters. We won't give up." Stephanie got up from the table and put he arms around her father.

"Thank you, Jesus," whispered Maggie.

Father and daughter were holding each other, both blinking back tears, when José ran in the back door. "Senator, senator, you have to come out to the garden. Something terrible has happened."

When Beaudreau and Stephanie followed Jose into the garden, they found Michael lying under the statue, his clothes rumpled, blood pooled under his head, and his face contorted in fear. "Maggie, call an ambulance," called Beaudreau, even though he knew Michael was dead.

"I don't understand it. I was sure the statue was secure. I fastened it to the base with a steel rod. It's all my fault." Tears streamed down José's face.

"No, José, it's not your fault. It was just a terrible accident," said Beaudreau, turning to lead shocked and crying Stephanie back into the house. "We have to wait for the authorities."

After she made the emergency call, Maggie watched the grim scene from the kitchen window. She clutched the little "wanga" bag she kept around her neck. "I knew that statue was evil. Look at her face. I swear she's smiling."

SHERON COFFEY

Sheron Coffey was born in Louisville, Ky. A graduate of Indiana State University, she also attended Miami University and Rollins College. After 35 years of teaching, she retired to open a children's bookstore and art studio, where she taught classes in art, puppetry, drama, and creative writing. She has traveled throughout Europe and made several trips to her ancestral home of Ireland.

Being an avid reader, having inspiring English teachers, and enjoying an interest in people and other cultures led to her interest in writing. In addition to being active in her church, she volunteers in a therapeutic horse program and Savannah Children's Theatre. She has written two novels, *The Candy Floss Girls* and *Ragged and Funny*, which are awaiting publication. Her latest children's book is *Hannah Banana*. It is about a little girl who colors outside the lines and knows she will be famous some day. It is set for release in the spring of 2008.

Staying current with the writing community is important to her, so she is a member of several state and national writing organizations, as well as local writing groups. She has a daughter, two dogs, and two cats. She resides in Savannah, Ga.

Coffey can be reached at irishcoffey7@comcast.net.

The Mermaid's Song

Brady stood at the edge of the rocky cliff and gazed at the stark horizon of the Atlantic. He closed his eyes, inhaled the familiar aroma, and tasted salt as crashing waves below sent a spray across his face, settling like small pearls on his graying beard. A gust of wind grabbed his plaid wool cap and tossed it down jutting rocks where it finally rested on top of the water. As he watched the cap drift out to sea, his mind wandered to another place in time.

The streets of Dublin were quiet on this Sunday evening, but down a neighborhood street, past the elegant Georgian townhouses with their painted doors, a muffled sound of music drifted from a pub. O'Donohue's was always open as long as people wanted to gather. Once inside, the spell of solitude was broken by the raucous laughter and clapping from patrons packed side by side like sardines in a can, their faces hidden by a fog of blue-gray smoke. Seated in a circle by the front window, an impromptu group of musicians played a rollicking version of, "Fiddler's Green." In the center was Brady O'Shea, holding court, looking like the High King himself. Brady, a well-known singer in Galway, was also becoming a favorite in Dublin and Belfast.

The crowd started to thin, so Brady scooped his tip money from his guitar case, and replaced his guitar. He took time to shake hands with a few tourists and waved goodbye to Tom O'Donohue.

The damp evening fog made him shiver, and he dreaded the long walk to his friend's apartment to sleep for a few hours before the trip home.

Dawn came too soon. He dressed quickly and ran to the street corner to hitch a ride to Galway Bay where the ferry would take him to the island. His da, Culley O'Shea, would be waiting for him in their family-owned pub. He would begin to grumble when Brady came through the door about wasting time running around singing when food needed to be prepped before the noon crowd. Brady would just give his father a bear hug, pinch his ruddy cheeks and tell him how much he loved him. They lived on Inishmoor, the largest of the Aran

Islands, with a population of several hundred residents, a scattering of shops, and twelve pubs. In Ireland, a local pub isn't just a place for a meal, or to gossip over a pint, it is the heart and soul of a town. Inishmoor, a beautiful fishing village with a few peat and potato farmers, is more widely known for fine woolen sweaters and blankets.

Nuala Grace Carey pushed open the heavy wooden door and paused until her eyes adjusted to the dimly lit room. The morning smell of stale smoke, spilled ale and remnants of greasy food, assaulted her nostrils. Her gaze settled on the handsome man behind the bar topping off a pint of Guinness to perfection. A wicked smile appeared on her face as she admired his tall, muscular build, his dark hair curling around his shirt collar and his crystal blue eyes that gave her a knowing look when she entered the room.

"Ah, the gods have rewarded me eyes with a vision of loveliness," Brady said with his hand over his heart.

"And the little leprechauns blessed you with the gift of blarney," Nuala replied as she leaned across the bar to receive an affectionate kiss.

"What will it be today, my love? The specials are the fried egg hamburger, or lamb stew and biscuits me Ma made only this morning."

"No time to eat, I have to get back to the shop. I just came by to see what time you're picking me up tonight."

"We need to catch the seven o'clock ferry to the mainland. There's a new group playing at Paddy's Place I want to check out."

"*Och*, you and your bands. I hoped to go to the cinema."

"You know, you only speak Gaelic when you're annoyed."

"You're changing the subject. Why tonight?"

"I have to check out the competition. It's like scouting in sports. When I'm a big star you'll be glad you have me," he said with a wink. "Then off we'll go, to live anywhere but on the island."

"I don't know if I want to leave the island and our family and friends. How about our life now? Cinema, please?"

"We'll compromise. We'll go to the cinema, and then pop in for the last set of the band."

Nuala leaned over to give him another kiss and muttered, "You're a sly one, Brady O'Shea. Okay, see you tonight."

His Ma came up behind him and spoke softly. "Be careful, son.

You're going to lose herself if you don't forget these crazy dreams. You need to settle down, buy that little cottage overlooking the sea, and have lots of babies. You know this pub has been in our family for four generations. Your brothers have no interest in it, so it will all be yours. It's a good honest living."

"I know Ma, but maybe I don't want it either. Don't you worry that pretty little head. I could never leave my best girl forever," he said as he kissed the top of her head.

Brady walked to the back kitchen door, pulled his jacket collar tighter and braced himself for a blast of frigid winter air. He pushed the door open and greeted the driver who tossed back the stiff snow-covered tarp and lowered the tailgate of his old rusty blue pickup truck.

"Top o' the morn', Mr. McKenna, and how are things today?"

"If truth be known, I'd rather be on holiday on an exotic tropical island. But I can't complain. Heard it told once, as long as you are on the right side of the turf, it's a good day," McKenna laughed as he rolled out a keg of Guinness and Brady hoisted it to his shoulder and headed for the storeroom. As Brady signed the bill, Mrs. O'Shea called out from the kitchen.

"Jimmy, for heavens sake, come in and warm your bones with a hot cuppa tea. I just took a fresh loaf of soda bread out of the oven and there's a slice with your name on it."

"Only got a few minutes, have a full load in the truck and people waiting for me, but I could stand a cup."

Fiona O'Shea, bustled about the kitchen, a white apron tied around her thick waist. Her dimpled cheeks, smudged with flour, were flushed from the heat of the oven.

"I've been baking since daybreak, expect an early crowd today," she said as she sat the teapot and soda bread on the table. "Always happens when a storm heads in. People gather here to keep warm and pass the time of day with friends."

"Not much work going on during these winter months. Too rough to fish and too wet to plow. Good for my business, though. People have more time to drink," he joked as he finished his tea.

"In the name of St. Brigid, pour the good man a glass of Jameson. Ye can't send him out in this weather with a cuppa tea." Culley scolded his wife as he entered the kitchen.

"Thanks, Culley, but it's still a bit early for me, and I have a long day ahead of me."

"Looks like this storm could be a troublemaker, so we better double our order for Wednesday. The ferry may not run after it hits."

Brady swung the door open and put dishes in the sink. "And that, my dear gentlemen, is why I have a plan to escape this torturous weather."

"I understand you're playing a lot in Galway now. That's grand. You always had a special voice. That's probably why you got a gal as pretty as Nuala Grace," Jimmy said with a wink. "Better get on the road, stay safe."

Later, the storm hit with vengeance, damaging thatched cottages, sinking several small boats, and bringing everyday life to a standstill. Islanders are used to bad winter weather. It's just a way of life. A way of life Brady knew he had to leave.

It was a soft day with just a light mist. The cold weather moved out to sea making way for spring showers, budding trees, and blooming flowers. The rolling hills were forty shades of green, giving the Emerald Isle its rightful name. The golden orange of the furze further enhanced the landscape. An Irish spring is a beautiful sight, and residents wonder why anyone would want to live anywhere else.

It was still early evening, so Brady took time to go to Clery's Department Store to pick up a few things his ma had asked for. Trips to Dublin were more frequent now that he landed a steady spot at O'Donohue's with a new band called The Jolly Tinkers. It felt great to finally be paid for performing and not relying on tips. At last, he was a professional musician.

Nuala Grace quickly wrapped an Aran sweater for an anxious young tourist who was fearful of being left by her tour bus. "Enjoy your purchase, and hope it brings fond memories of Ireland when you wear it." The girl thanked her and ran out the door, practically knocking Brady over.

"I hope it wasn't something you said," he joked and discreetly kissed her ear.

"Mind your manners, sir, I'm not in the habit of making out with customers," she teased, but pulled him behind a rack of coats. "When did you get in? How was the band? Tell me everything." The words tumbled out like rushing water.

"Slow down, beautiful, I can only answer one at a time, and right now I'm not thinking about talking at all," he whispered and lightly brushed her lips with his. "I missed you like crazy, and it's just been three days."

"I wanted to be with you, but with ma being sick and having to work, I just couldn't go. I hope you understand." She looked at him with questioning eyes.

"Next time, maybe. I want you to hear the band. They're really good, and the crowd was grand."

"I don't like being away from you. How long will this last?"

"I signed a contract for two months, but they might extend it."

Nuala frowned and looked away. "I'm happy for you, Brady. If you're happy, then I'm happy. I have a customer, so we'll talk tonight. Meet you at the pub." She blew him a kiss and turned to wait on a young couple looking at blankets.

The rest of the week passed quickly, and it was time to return to Dublin. Again, Nuala could not accompany him, and the separation was difficult for both of them. She would not get in the way of his dream, but felt torn between her duties at home and the man she loved. They had grown up together and were best friends, inseparable. As children, they rode horses bareback down dirt paths, picked berries in the summer and baked pies in Fiona's kitchen, and challenged each other to everything from darts to horseshoes. In their early teens, their friendship took a turn, and they began to look at each other in a different way.

One summer afternoon while walking on the beach, talking about anything and everything, Brady suddenly kissed her on the lips. They quickly jumped apart. Surprised, they glanced away but smiled. For the first time, they felt shy and continued their walk in silence.

Things changed after that innocent kiss. They discovered new feelings and were confused what to do about them. They tried to act like just friends, but their eyes told a different story. They always knew what the other was thinking. Several months passed, and they met at their usual place on the cliff at the end of the island. The day was ending, and the orange sun began to disappear into the sea. They sat on a large rock watching the waves roll onto the beach. He was quiet, and she could tell he needed to tell her something.

Finally, he faced her and looked into her emerald green eyes, gently taking her hands in his. "I love you, Nuala Grace, and I can't stand to be away from you, not even for a minute. So...so will you marry me?"

She was startled for a moment. Not knowing what to say, she giggled. "I'm sorry, Brady," she said, hiding a smile with her hand. "You know I feel the same. Besides my da would kill me. We're only fifteen."

He felt the blood creeping up his neck and imagined his face turning red. "No, not now, silly," he said with a laugh, trying to recover from his awkward display of affection, "when we're older. Just promise me you will never marry anyone but me. Promise."

"I'll always love you, Brady. I promise."

He started to kiss her but stopped. "Do you hear that?" he asked, turning toward the sea.

"I'm not sure. I thought I heard something. Maybe it's just waves splashing. "

"No, it was very clear, I'm sure it was voices. The mermaids were singing. That's a good sign. My sister, Brenna, told me a story about the mermaids. When two lovers pledge their love to one another and the mermaids sing, their love will last through eternity. They are blessed by the sea."

"I know the story too, but I think it was just the wind and not singing mermaids of romantic Celtic lore."

"I heard them. I know we're blessed." As they kissed, a mermaid's song gently floated out to sea. Nothing on earth would ever break the bond between Nuala Grace and Brady.

The first set ended with a nostalgic rendition of "Galway Bay," and Brady made his way to the bar. The bartender pointed to a man at a back table waiting to talk to him. Brady didn't recognize the young, light-haired man, but was curious as to what he wanted. They shook hands, and the man introduced himself. Trace Gallagher was from New York and in Dublin on business. He had family in Kilkenny and always stopped at O'Donohue's before returning to the States.

"My cousins come to the city often and told me I should come to hear you play. They were correct in their description of your singing abilities."

"I'm flattered. Please thank them for their comments. Buy you a drink?"

"No, thanks, I have to get back to the hotel. I have a business proposition for you. Do you have a passport?"

"Uh, yes. I'm afraid I only know how to run a pub and sing, so what kind of business are you're in?"

"I have several businesses. I'm sure you're familiar with the St. Patrick's Day Parade in New York. The parade is sponsored by the Hibernians, of which I'm a member. The city is quite a wild place to be on March 17, as well as Chicago, and Savannah."

"I've read all about celebrations of St. Patrick in America, which are quite different from those in Ireland. But what does the parade have to do with me?"

"I'm part owner of Reilly's Grille, and I'm always looking for new talent. You impressed me, and we need a fresh, new face for that week. We have an outstanding house band, and we spotlight guest singers. I like your style, your voice is exceptional and the women will love you."

"It sounds like a great opportunity, but I have obligations here. Thanks for the offer, but I'm afraid I have to say no. If you'll excuse me, looks like break is over."

"Do me a favor. Sleep on it, and call me in the morning. We can talk over breakfast. It's an all-expenses-paid trip to the States and exposure to a lot of important people. I hate to see you miss this chance. You do want a career in music, am I correct?'

"Well, yes, I do. But I plan to stay in Ireland."

"There's so many Irish in New York, you'll never know you left."

The airplane began its descent and banked toward the runway. Brady looked down in awe at the city below, shining in the sunlight. So many buildings on one tiny island. He tried to locate the Statue of

Liberty, but he wasn't sure where to look. There were white-capped waves along a shoreline of the Atlantic. He was told a person could look across the Atlantic and see all the way to Ireland. He tried to imagine earlier immigrants standing on the shore, filled with sorrow, and gazing toward the country they had to leave behind.

He finally made it through customs and saw a man in a black suit and cap holding a large card with, BRADY O'SHEA, written in bold letters. Brady looked confused but walked toward him. The man rushed forward, took his bag, and held open the back door of a sleek black limo. This certainly beats hitching rides to a ferry, he thought. The driver explained points of interest as he expertly negotiated traffic and pulled up in front of the St. Regis Hotel.

After settling into his room, Brady opened the drapes and exhaled a slow whistle. Before him was a vision of towering buildings and people walking fast as if they were being chased. He couldn't believe he was in New York City, in a country that just elected an Irish Catholic as president. The only thing missing was Nuala. He adjusted his watch, and had just enough time to shower and change and meet Trace Gallagher and the band at Reilly's Grille.

The restaurant was situated in an area called Hell's Kitchen, which sounded rather frightening. The brightly painted storefront had stained glass windows and a heavy wooden door with Reilly's Grille written in gold calligraphy. The front looked small, but was spacious inside. Trace was waiting and gave him a warm welcome, and led him to a group in front of the stage. After introductions, the band assembled on stage and for the next hour they experimented with a wide assortment of drinking songs and ballads. A crowd began to gather and soon everyone was clapping and cheering. He tried to be calm, but was bursting with excitement and knew this was going to be quite an experience.

The week's celebration was more than he imagined. He looked out at the crowd, faces painted green, a collection of gaudy beads around their necks, hoisting mugs of green beer yelling, *Slainte*. The phrase "everyone is Irish on St. Patrick's Day" included a lot of crazy people.

The week finally ended, and Brady was surprised how much he would miss his new American friends and even the frantic pace of the city. He was not looking forward to his final visit to Reilly's to say goodbye. Reluctantly, he pushed open the wooden door and saw Trace sitting with two men. He motioned him over, made introductions, and explained they were agents for Quinn O'Hara, the Irish-American singer, beginning her tour in New York.

"I'll leave you gentlemen to talk," Trace said, "I told them you're leaving for Dublin tomorrow, but they have an exciting offer for you."

The dark-haired man, Maury Rosenbaum, spoke first. "Quinn was here with a group of friends earlier this week and heard you sing. She liked you, and we're looking for an opening act for her tour. I heard you last night, and I agree. Are you interested?"

"I...I don't know what to say. I have a job, family, and a fiancé back in Ireland. I need to go back and discuss this with them."

"I don't think you understand. The tour starts in three weeks, rehearsals start Monday. Decide by tomorrow or we move on."

Brady thanked them, and said he would call as soon as he could. His head was swimming with confusing thoughts. *This is the break I've been waiting for.* However, his family depended on him, and Nuala never wanted him to leave in the first place. Would she wait for him? He walked around the city most of the night, unaware of the people around him. He returned to the hotel and fell on the bed exhausted.

The morning sunlight filled the room, stinging his bleary eyes that hadn't closed all night. Today his life would change, and fear caused sharp pains in his gut. Eventually, he picked up the phone and asked for the international operator.

His ma answered the phone, and he had to shout over the rowdy crowd at the pub. He told her about the offer, and he was going to stay longer. He asked her to send word to Nuala, he would call back in an hour. He sat in an overstuffed chair, looking at the lights of the city, waiting, and hoping she would understand.

"Nuala, my love, I miss you so much. I have some exciting news, but I have to talk fast because this call is costing me a paycheck." He gave her brief details, and emphasized what the exposure would mean to his career. There was silence on the other end. "Nuala, can you hear me? Oh, honey, please don't cry, try to understand. I really need to do this. I'll be home before you know it. Go to the cliff, pretend I'm there with you, and listen for the mermaid's song. Remember, I will love you for eternity."

Brady couldn't believe he was on tour with Quinn O'Hara. He was infatuated with life on the road and would never forget the first night he stepped onto the stage with flashing lights creating a haze of smoke, and the deafening roar of screaming fans. He knew he was where he belonged. The tour was a huge success with every concert sold out. After almost a year on the road, it would all end when the show closed in New York. His original contract was for three months but things were going so well it was extended to eight. Nuala became increasingly unhappy as the tour continued and begged him to come home. She hadn't written for the past month, but he felt everything would be alright when he called to tell her he would be home in a few days.

After their return, he stopped at Reilly's and received a warm welcome from old friends. The beer flowed freely, and conversation loud and lively. Trace came in later, and the two men hugged and slapped each other on the back, and he felt they were truly good friends. After catching up on news, Trace handed him a letter the tour manager forwarded to him. It was from Nuala. Brady tucked it in his jacket pocket to read in private.

Later that evening, he settled into his room, poured a glass of Irish whiskey, and opened Nuala's letter. As he continued to read, his hands shook. He ran his hands over his face, and threw the glass of whiskey across the room, smashing it against the wall, a cry of anguish caught in his throat. Shock, pain, and anger traveled through his body. He had lost everything. Nuala, tired of listening to his empty promises, eloped with his best friend, Shamus Rourke. During his absence, she realized Brady would never be happy on the island. Music and performing was his destiny, but it wasn't hers. She tried to tell him before. All she wanted was a home and children. The letter explained she had found that life and wished him well in his career. It ended with "I'll always love you and will have a special place for you in my heart."

Rain flowed down leaded glass panes distorting the images of people rushing by, heads bowed, clutching their umbrellas. Brady sat in a corner at Reilly's staring out the window but not really seeing. He picked up his guitar and started to sing a slow, sad ballad, and stopped midway to down a glass of whiskey. He poured another glass from a bottle sitting on the table, sat it aside, and began another mournful song.

"If you sing one more song like that, half the bar will jump into the Hudson River," a sultry voice said from the next table. "I'd buy you a drink, but it looks like you have that covered."

"Yeah, it must be the rain, I always get sad when it rains."

"May I join you? We can be sad together," she said as she moved her coat and sat across from him and extended her hand. "Hello, I'm Fallon Kincaid."

"Just call me Mr. Sad Song," Brady said, continuing to strum his guitar.

"This have something to do with a woman? Lost love usually causes a man to drown his sorrow. I'm a good listener if you want to talk."

"No talking, just drinking, and playing sad songs. You know how the Irish love a good tragedy. That's why we write songs, and novels, and plays so well."

"In that case, pour me a glass of whatever you're drinking and sing me a song."

A sliver of sunrays shone through the partially drawn drapes, causing Brady to stir. He attempted to open his eyes but nauseating pain shot through his head. His mouth was dry, and his tongue thick. "Please, God, if I'm not dead, have someone shoot me," he murmured and turned on his side. His heart skipped a beat, and eyes opened wide in alarm when he realized he was not alone. A beautiful raven-haired girl with skin as creamy as porcelain was asleep beside him. "Oh, sweet Mary and Joseph, what have I done?" he whispered.

"Good morning," she said as her eyes fluttered open, and she stretched like a kitten.

"Mornin'," was all he could say as he searched his brain for a name or a clue how she got there.

"Be a dear and order coffee and juice while I jump in the shower. I should have been at work an hour ago. Of course, it helps when you own the company."

He stared at the ceiling, gave up trying to recall the night, and called room service. He lay back down to keep the room from spinning just as she emerged from the bathroom in a cloud of steam, wrapped only in a towel. "Your turn," she said with a perky smile.

He mumbled something incoherent, wrapped a sheet around his waist, and retreated to the bathroom. As the hot water pelted his body, pieces of the previous night came back to him. He remembered Reilly's, rain, singing, a beautiful girl, and then things got fuzzy. He opened the door to ask her a few questions, but the room was empty. A note was propped against the sterling silver coffee pot.

Dear Mr. Sad Song, Thanks for an exceptional evening. The song you wrote for me was amazing. Be happy, not sad. Love, Rain Girl.

Several weeks passed and still no sighting of the mystery woman. None of the guys in the band knew who she was, but they were having a grand time teasing him about his first one night stand. He attributed his behavior and lack of judgment to a bottle of whiskey and a broken heart. Later that week, he dropped by Reilly's and watched a new singer trying out with the band.

"How are things going, buddy?" Trace asked when he walked over.

"I'm surviving. How about you?"

"Doing great. Have you decided what you're gonna do now? You going back to Ireland?"

He shook his head. "I can't go back. I couldn't stand to see them together."

"Listen, you know you'll always have a place here."

"Thanks man, but my performing days are over. My stupid pipe dreams cost me the woman I love, and a life I always thought I would have."

"That's the problem with life, we usually can't control it. Why don't you sit in with the band this weekend, and we'll talk again next week."

"I don't know. I'll think about it."

The next Saturday, the band finished the last set of the evening, and Brady waved to the packed house. Several people yelled, "encore," and then a heavy-set, gray-haired man stepped forward and handed him a note requesting the song, "Danny Boy." Brady hesitated for a moment, and knew it would be emotional for him to sing. The man had his arm around the woman next to him, and he could see it was important to them. Taking a deep breath, he cued the band, and began the endearing Irish song. Gradually everyone stopped talking, bartenders and waitresses stood still, the band stopped playing, but Brady continued a cappella, his crystal clear tenor voice casting a magic spell. The song ended, but the silence remained, each person lost in his or her own memories. Finally, wild cheering erupted, and the bartender rang a bell declaring the next round was on the house. Although many had tried, no one could ever take music away from an Irishman.

Sitting alone in the corner, sipping a glass of wine, Fallon Kincaid was captivated by the tall, dark, handsome man on stage. She fumbled in her purse for her compact, dabbed at her mascara, and with a confident smile declared, "This is the man I'm going to marry."

Brady went to the bar and ordered a club soda. The bartender gave him his drink along with a note left earlier. Brady assumed it was from a fan.

Dear Mr. Sad Song, Meet me on the steps of St. Patrick's at 10:00 tomorrow morning. Love, Rain Girl.

The sun was shining in a cloudless, azure blue sky, giving New Yorkers a well-deserved break from cold and rain. Brady couldn't explain why he was walking down Fifth Avenue toward St. Patrick's Cathedral. He was puzzled by this elusive woman, and even more puzzled about the night they spent together.

"I wasn't sure if you'd come," she said, looking even more beautiful than he remembered.

"I always loved a good mystery. Interesting choice of places to meet. Am I being watched by a priest?"

"I go to mass every morning before I go to work. This is close to my office," she explained, putting on her oversized sunglasses and placed her arm through his. "I have just enough time for coffee, your turn to buy."

They talked about the weather, what brought him to New York, and her cosmetics company. She teased him about his brogue, but told him it was sexy. Just as they were becoming better acquainted, he tried to ask her about that night, but she abruptly said she had to get to work, handed him her card, and disappeared out the door.

The next day, Brady met with Trace and agreed to stay with the band for a little longer. His mind began to wander while Trace rambled on about something or another, and he stared out the window.

"Am I boring you, old friend?"

"What? I'm sorry, just thinking. Have you ever heard of a woman named Fallon Kincaid?"

He looked surprised. "Sure. She's all over the society page of the Times, or in an article in the Wall Street Journal. Why do you ask?"

"Just wondering. We met and had coffee. There's something intriguing about her. She said she owns a cosmetics company."

"Not just any company, but worldwide Bellessence Inc. Daddy is Jack Kincaid, a Wall Street investment banker, mother is a socialite, there's a few brothers scattered around, usually in trouble. Just your typical over-indulged rich family. Not people you want to get involved with."

"It was just coffee, it's not like I'm gonna take her as me bride," he laughed.

"Be careful what you start. Jack Kincaid is ruthless, he likes to ruin people's lives, has lots of enemies. I've had a few dealings with him. He takes over companies in trouble, gets controlling interest, and sells the company out from under them. Fallon Kincaid gets her keen business sense from her father, but her integrity from her grandfather, Patrick Kincaid. He died before he could see what his power hungry son did to the company."

"No plans to start anything. I still need to suffer a little longer with a broken heart. Suffering is good for the soul. Gives you character."

"You're crazy, you know that?" Trace said shaking his head.

"I know, but I'm adorable. All the ladies tell me that."

Fallon leaned over and gave Brady a kiss as she set a plate of ham and eggs in front of him. He folded the morning paper and pulled her onto his lap and kissed her again.

"Gorgeous, and she can cook too. How did I get so lucky?"

"I learned to cook for survival because my wonderful mother kept firing the help. Just because I'm rich doesn't mean I'm lazy and brainless. Are you meeting me at the museum tonight? I have that fundraiser I can't miss."

"You know I hate those things. I don't know what to say to those people. I'd rather go to Finnegan's and throw some darts. By the way, we've been together for over six months now, when do I meet the family?"

"I'm avoiding it, because I'm afraid they'll scare you off and you'll realize insanity runs in the family. Hopefully it will skip a generation when we have kids."

"Are we having kids? Shouldn't we talk about marriage first?"

"That was a hypothetical statement dear. Don't panic. I have to go to work early, please try to make it tonight. I don't want to go alone."

Brady thought about what she said the rest of the day. Did he love Fallon? It wasn't like with Nuala Grace. Now, he felt ready to settle down and have a house and children and a dog, but she comes from a world he never knew existed. How could he support an heiress?

A knock at the door brought no response. The maid called out, "housekeeping." Fallon turned over and grumbled about why "do not disturb" meant nothing in this hotel. Brady turned over and ran his finger down her cheek and smiled.

"Good morning, Mr. O'Shea ," she purred.

"Good morning, Mrs. O'Shea," he said and kissed her passionately. "If the maid will stay out, I'll show you some of your fringe benefits."

Fallon laughed and stared at her new husband with eyes full of love, taking in every detail of his handsome face. "You make me so happy. I hope you never regret marrying me."

"I'll always love you Fallon, no regrets. You are my Rain Girl. By the way, we have to be at the Las Vegas Airport in two hours, and then prepare to tell your family to set another place at the table."

"You did what? Were you drunk or drugged? This will kill your mother. We can get it annulled. Plenty of judges owe me favors. I will not have you married to a lounge singer," Jack bellowed. "He isn't even an American."

"No, but at least he's Irish and a Catholic. Call Mother and tell her we'll be at dinner tonight. And there will be no annulment."

Jack Kincaid was not going to have a son-in-law singing in a pub and insisted he come to work at Kincaid & Associates. Brady protested, not wanting anything to do with the company, but knew it would make Fallon happy. Besides, his heart was no longer into a singing career. They gave him an office with a view of the city, but his job was unimportant, making him feel the same. He didn't fit in and everyone knew it. After a miserable year, he was about to tell Fallon he was going to quit, but instead she told him she was pregnant.

Patrick Cullen O'Shea, entered the world with a loud wail, and it was obvious he would be a driving force. He had wavy black hair and crystal blue eyes like his mother. Brady called home to Ireland, and could hear both joy and pain in his parents' voices. He promised they would visit soon. Jack decided their apartment was too small for a family, so gave them a Park Avenue penthouse as a gift. Nothing was too good for his first grandchild.

While working late one night on a financial report, Brady went to a file cabinet in the outer office, and by accident pulled a different file. He started leafing through it, and what he read made his pulse quicken. This file helped make sense of some of the discrepancies in the project he was working on. It proved corruption throughout Kincaid's company. He replaced the file, turned out the lights, and went home.

Patrick blew out the four candles on his cake and quickly ran to the table stacked with brightly wrapped presents, while delighted family and friends looked on. Fallon and Brady were proud of their little boy and never knew a child would bring them so much love. He was the center of their existence. Fallon recently returned to work and although they hired an excellent au pair, Brady was finding more and more excuses to stay at home to care for him.

"I know you don't understand, but I think I should quit my job and stay home with Patrick. He shouldn't be raised by a stranger," Brady explained.

"That's the craziest thing I've ever heard. What's this really about?"

"I hate it! I hate my job. I hate being around the lying and cheating. I have to quit, Fallon. I'm drowning there."

"I'm sorry you're so unhappy. What will you do about a job? Sing in a pub?"

"Would that be so bad? At least the work is honest. I come from a country that enjoys a simple life. Family, home and food on the table is all anyone needs. Why is it so important to keep making more and more money?"

"You don't seem to mind the sailboat, the company jet, and a house in the Hamptons," she snapped. "How do you think they get paid for?"

"By your Daddy of course, and I'm over it. We came from different worlds, but we fell in love and decided to make our own world. Now, it seems all I do is change to adjust to your world. Let's go live somewhere else. You have companies all over the world. I could teach and write music."

"I'm late for a meeting, we can talk about this later."

It had been three months since Brady quit his job, and he was enjoying the challenge of being at home with his son. He had returned to songwriting and renewed his passion for music. He never completed the song he wrote for Fallon when they first met, but he hoped to finish it in time for their anniversary. The phone interrupted his train of thought, and he answered rather abruptly.

"Hello Brady, this is Maury Rosenbaum. I wonder if Quinn and I could come by and talk to you. Or we could meet somewhere."

"My son goes to pre-school over on Eightieth Avenue. I'll meet you at the coffee shop across the street, say nine o'clock."

"Sounds great. Looking forward to seeing you again."

They were already seated when he arrived, and they all hugged and told each other they looked great. The conversation started about the weather, and family, then Maury got started explaining why they wanted to meet with him.

"Quinn is getting ready to cut a new CD and we all feel you added a lot to the tour, and we heard you were back to songwriting. We'd like to have you collaborate on the CD, and we could possibly record some of your songs."

Brady looked at Quinn and joked, "You thought I was that good, huh?"

She punched him in the arm and laughed. "You haven't changed a bit. Marriage and fatherhood haven't done anything to your ego." She was secretly glad he was still the same. "Do you want the job or not? There's more where you came from," she quipped.

"I think it will fit in my busy schedule. When do we start?"

Fallon was not as thrilled as he was, but she was happy to see excitement in his eyes again. The project renewed his sense of accomplishment, and he was back doing what he loved most, creating music.

"I still don't understand why you can't take off just one weekend," Fallon complained. "Every year the family goes to the lodge in Vermont to ski. You've always loved it before."

"I think 'loved it' is a stretch. I don't ski. But you're missing the reason. I have to work. It's the final cut for the CD. We've been working on this all year. The studio is booked, musicians booked, and I happen to be one of them. I simply can't leave."

Brady helped them load their overabundance of luggage in the black sedan and the driver waited while they said their goodbyes.

"'Bye, Daddy," Patrick said through tears, hugging his dad's neck.

"I'll miss you, sport. Be careful and take care of your mother. I love you."

"Have fun baby, I love you," he said and kissed her."

"I love you more. Knock 'em dead, honey. See you Sunday."

Maury tapped on the glass window of the sound booth and motioned for Brady. From the look on his face, he knew something was wrong. Maury quietly began to explain. The Kincaid family decided to stay longer, but they hired a private plane to bring Fallon and Patrick back to the city. It was snowing, however the plane received clearance to take off. No one knows what happened. The plane lifted off then plunged to the ground in flames. There were no survivors. At that moment, Brady felt the life go out of his body. Shock took over and dulled the pain.

Brady spent the next two weeks in a trance. He couldn't eat or sleep, and kept thinking he saw Fallon or Patrick on the street or heard their voices in the house. The tragedy was more than he could bear. Life no longer had any meaning. He refused to talk to anyone. Several months passed before he realized he had to leave.

He mailed the keys to the penthouse to Jack, picked up his guitar, and took a cab to LaGuardia where he boarded a plane to London. There, he could become anonymous and still be close to Ireland.

The CD was released the following summer. *Rain Girl*, was the hit single and went platinum.

A cold wind greeted him as he emerged from the car. He adjusted his cane, and carried his suitcase to the cottage. Earlier, the caretaker laid a peat fire, and the room was warm. A kettle on the stove was warm so he made a cup of tea and settled in a big armchair. A coughing spell set in, indicating his illness was worsening. He just dozed off when a knock at the door startled him. He opened the door to a beautiful woman with graying auburn hair and emerald green eyes.

"Nuala Grace, you haven't changed a bit, I knew you would come."

"*Och*, and you're as full of blarney as always," she said as he took her coat and seated her by the fire.

"I've missed you, Nuala. Tell me, have you had a good life?"

She hesitated a moment. "Shamus was a good husband. We had five wonderful children, and three grandchildren. That's where my figure went," she laughed. "I was so sorry to hear about your family. Such a tragedy."

"Yes, it was very hard. Life can be very cruel."

"Someone once told me, grief is the price you pay for loving."

"I guess. Eventually I found strength to go on. I lived in Europe most of the time, did a little singing, concerts and such, then retired."

"Perhaps we both found what made us happy after all."

They talked about the past, when they were young and so in love. She sighed and said it was time for her to go. They stood in silence, holding hands, their eyes saying everything.

The next day, Brady went to Nuala's cottage and knocked on the door. A stranger answered. He asked for Nuala. She said she was sorry, but Nuala didn't live there anymore. She had died the previous year after a long illness.

Brady stood at the edge of the rocky cliff and gazed at the stark horizon of the Atlantic. He closed his eyes, inhaled the familiar aroma and tasted salt as crashing waves below sent a spray across his face, settling like small pearls on his graying beard. A gust of wind grabbed his plaid wool cap and tossed it down jutting rocks, where it finally came to rest on top of the water.

He slowly made his way down to the beach, and there he heard Nuala's voice. "I'm here, Brady, I waited for you." Dropping his cane in the sand, he waded into the water and glided toward the melodic song of a mermaid, as his plaid cap drifted out to sea.

SUZANNE LAVOIE-STEBEN

Living in a Cocoon has been incubating for twenty years or so; it was time for it to appear in print.

This is Lavoie-Steben's first published work. She has written two children's books, short stories and many essays. A career in varied office environments in state social service agencies, an attorney general's office, historic preservation agencies and museums, private corporate settings, and newspaper advertising sales gave her a diverse pool of experiences from which she draws her characters and settings. She's also a firm believer in her lifelong habit of journaling.

Lavoie-Steben earned a certificate in journalism from the Newspaper Institute of America in New York. She received an Associate in Science degree with an emphasis in developmental psychology from Manchester Community College. She took many writing courses, and formal studies ranged from dance and improvisation at the Harford Camerata Conservatory to her continuing studies toward her bachelor's degree at Eastern Connecticut State University; and, continuing education classes at Armstrong Atlantic State University.

Lavoie-Steben is a member of the International Society of Photographers, and has had her photos published in *America at the Millennium, A Visual Journal,* and *Imprints of Time.* In addition to her lifelong love of learning, her special interests in children and literacy have lead her to work and volunteer in public and elementary school libraries.

The author lives in Savannah, Georgia, with her little poodle, Coco, and Benji.

Lavoie-Steben can be reached at slavoie-steben@comcast.net.

Reinventing

There comes a time in one's life when introspection leads to the necessity of reinventing oneself. Semi-retirement has done this to me.

Reading and writing has inspired and helped me make sense of our world. Having studied Eastern philosophies, one quote comes to mind from the Brihadaranyaka Upanishad 4:4-5, which states:

"You are what your deep, driving desire is.
As your desire is, so is your will.
As your will is, so is your deed.
As your deed is, so is your destiny."

All self-help books say you have to believe in yourself. That is not enough; someone else has to believe in you also. Your friends will support and encourage you. But that's not enough–an agent, editor or publisher must be willing to take a chance on a new writer. This is one of the one of the most difficult hurdles for new writers. Most writers want to see the byline–something published in their specialty genre, or any genre, for that matter. Another quote comes to mind, this one from Agnes DeMille, who advises: "Find the passion. It takes great passion and great energy to do anything creative. I would go so far as to say you can't do it without that passion."

I would do well to follow Audre Lorde's advice: "Our feelings are our most genuine paths to knowledge. They are chaotic, sometimes painful, sometimes contradictory, but they come from deep within us. And we must key into those feelings... This is how new visions begin."

And last but not least, I have followed and admired Simone De-Beauvoir's writing, especially about her attitudes toward aging and the elderly:

"If old age is not to be a derisive parody of our past experience, there is only one solution: to continue to pursue the goals which give meaning to our lives–devotion to individuals, to collectivities, to causes, to social or political works which is intellectual and creative. Contrary to what the moralists advise, we should wish to retain in our old age, passions which are strong enough to prevent us from withdrawing into ourselves. Life keeps its rewards as long as people give of it to others, through love, friendship, indignation, compassion."

I believe this is an excerpt from her autobiography, *Memoirs of a Dutiful Daughter.*

Living In a Cocoon,
The Early Years

Her happy life in the little white house on the hill ended when Adele was seven years old, the year after the great hurricane and floods of 1955. No longer would she be able to play in the backyard that reminded her of the beach because it was all sand, part of the sandpits in back of the house. This little white house in Maine was not theirs anymore. Her parents couldn't afford the payments. She would not be visiting Grammy next door with her older sister Lisette to get those special treats Grammy always baked especially for them. Grammy, as she was affectionately called, didn't have grandchildren of her own and looked forward to Adele and Lisette's frequent visits. Lisette was the oldest and Adele adored her older sister. She followed her everywhere. She acquired the name "me too". She had a hard time keeping up with Lisette and would often stop to catch her breath: "Not so fast, please wait for me." Ruth and Jules, her parents, began to suspect there was something wrong with Adele.

She and Lisette would not be going back to St. Pierre's Catholic School in September with all their friends. They would not be seeing their parents for more than a year, as they were moving out of state to find work and a new place to live without the five little girls. It was impossible to bring the children along. How could they possibly find a place to live and work if they had to care for five little ones–Lisette was eight years old, Adele seven, Claire five, Diane three, and Cecile only two? They were dropped off at L'Orphelinat St. Joseph, an orphanage, boarding school, and hospice, all in one. It was also known as l'Hospice Marcotte, a home for seniors with terminal illnesses. The girls' whole world was turning upside down; it would never be the same.

Adele hated everything about her new living arrangements. Upon arrival they were served a cold vegetable salad consisting of cut-up beets, peas, carrots and squash smothered with mayonnaise. For a snack later that same day they were given raw rutabaga. She hated the food and having to get up at five o'clock almost every morning to go to Catholic Mass. They were woken up from their dormitory beds, row by row until all seventy-five children were awake. Each child was given a number, which was sewn on all pieces of clothing and placed in the cubbies where they kept their toiletries. They would wash up side by side along elongated sinks with waterspouts. They did all of this in silence, of course.

The younger girls were on a separate floor below. This meant that Claire, Diane and Cecile woke up without seeing Lisette and Adele. It frightened them. They often asked Soeur Solange, "When can we see Lisette and Adele and where are they?" They were told, "Go wash up, get dressed and line up for church." Those caught talking in line did not get to watch television on the weekend.

The orphanage was run by nuns called Sisters of Charity. They were strict and mean and heartless at times; the children could not help feeling neglected and unlovable. It was just a job to the nuns. Soeur Stanislaus, who took care of the older girls, those seven years old and up, was a little nicer than Soeur Solange, who took care of the younger girls. The only time the two groups were combined was outside on the playground.

Lisette and Adele had not been able to visit with their little sisters and the only time they saw them was when they passed them in line on the way to the cafeteria. Lisette would often ask Adele, "I wonder how Claire, Diane and Cecile are doing? Let's ask Sister Stanislaus if we can go down to see them, O.K.?"

The answer to this was always, "You'll see them at recess outside." The girls had to go outside in all types of weather. It wasn't uncommon to have two weeks of temperatures ten degrees below zero. The winters in Maine were horrendous. Snow stayed on the ground from September to April sometimes. When it snowed, the accumulation was in feet, not inches.

Little Adele had asthma and the cold made her lungs hurt. She begged to go inside, but the nuns would say "We'll go in a while, the cold air is good for you." On one particular day, the wind chill factor made it fifteen below zero. Adele's lips turned blue and her breathing became very labored. She went into a full-blown asthma attack and had to be taken to the emergency room. Dr. Nadeau, a family friend and the obstetrician who delivered all five sisters, chastised the nuns for not calling him sooner. Adele stayed in the hospital for two weeks. When she returned to the orphanage, her mother placed a call and asked to speak to Adele immediately. She was told we were outside. Her mother forcefully insisted that Adele be brought to the phone immediately; she would wait no matter how long it took. Adele finally answered the phone and explained the reason for the two-week stay in the hospital.

School was hard. There was Catechism and ancient history in French first thing in the morning, then spelling drills in French and English. In the late afternoon they had math, science, and civics. Lisette and Adele went to school from eight in the morning to four in the afternoon, with a small break for lunch. They had to go back for a study period from seven to eight in the evening. The days were long and they welcomed the nine o'clock bedtime.

Adele would often ask, "Soeur Stanislaus, when will we see our parents? Will we see them at Thanksgiving, or at Christmas?" The nuns would answer, "It would depend on the weather and if your parents can get time off from work." This was not very reassuring. Meanwhile, she'd have to be satisfied with reading their letters and answering them.

Adele enjoyed learning both languages; she was particularly good in spelling. She was entered in a spelling bee with several other schools throughout the city. She won that spelling bee and was entered in a statewide spelling bee. She won that too, but wasn't invited to compete at the higher levels as her parents could not be there, so they sent the first runner-up. Music was another love of hers, and Lisette sang the Mass in French and Latin. On Saturday mornings, when the children who did not go home for the weekends were doing the cleaning, Adele would beg sister Stanislaus, "Can we please listen to the radio while we do the mopping and dusting?" She would sometimes say yes and sometimes no, depending on her mood that day. If the nun said nothing and ignored Adele, she would ask again and be told, "Because you keep asking, the answer is no." This would make her so sad. There were so few things to enjoy in this prison, as they called it.

If the children had been especially good during the week, which meant not getting caught talking in line, they were able to watch television. Soeur Stanislaus didn't understand or speak a word of English. Adele was frequently called on to translate. She couldn't enjoy the movie they were watching if she had to translate, which she hated.

There were many times when the children were forced into silence as they lined up and did as they were told most of the time. They would line up in the morning on the way to the Chapel, on the way to the cafeteria, and on the way to class and study hall in the evening. Adele was often told, "Diane cannot watch television again. She was caught talking more than three times this week." Adele knew this was true as Diane, as cute as she was with her curly blond hair, was a little rebellious and mischievous.

The orphanage did have some books, and Adele, the quiet one, read a lot. The books available were the Nancy Drew mysteries. She read the entire series. She also wrote the letters to her parents as she was the oldest left at the orphanage by this time.

In April of 1958, back in New Hampshire the girls had a little brother, Edwin, but they would not meet him until he was fifteen months old. This was the first boy following five girls. Ruth's first had been a boy but he was stillborn. Needing help with the newborn, their mother and father took Lisette out of the orphanage and moved her in with them.

Soon after, the youngest, Cecile, also left and moved to New Hampshire. She suffered from eczema all over her body. She would scratch the itchy rash and make it worse. The nuns would tell her, "Cecile, you must stop all that scratching." Without any medical treatment, Cecile continued to scratch. The nuns would say, "I'm sick and tired of watching all that scratching, get into that closet." Little Cecile would stay in that dark closet for hours. Adele wrote to her mother and father and let them know what the nuns were doing. Cecile was picked up and brought to live with Lisette and Edwin.

With Lisette and Cecile gone, Adele, Claire and Diane became very close, confiding in each other their hopes, dreams and sorrows. They were all old enough now to sleep in the same dormitory and were able to sneak around and talk to each other. They, too, wanted to leave the orphanage and go live in New Hampshire, but that was not to be until Adele finished eighth grade.

One of the things the girls looked forward to were the infrequent weekend visits with Nana and Pappy–their grandparents on their mother's side of the family. Adele and the girls would go to Mass with Nana and Pappy stayed home to fix breakfast. When they got back, sitting on each of their plates was half a grapefruit with a big bright red cherry in the middle. This looked scrumptious and was something they had never had. Besides the visits, Nana sometimes came to the boarding school to visit and brought them each a huge bag of candy. Oh, how they looked forward to those bi-monthly visits.

On the other hand, the visits to Pepere's some Sundays were not as enjoyable. Memere had passed away and he wanted to see the girls. There was no candy and he did things to them that made them feel uncomfortable. Being starved for attention and affection, they allowed it, not knowing what else to do. Claire with her dark straight shiny hair and pretty face was his favorite. She was younger than Adele, so he could get away with doing more to her. He called her "Blackie." Diane, the feisty one, would run away from him. One Sunday, Adele's godmother and godfather happened to stop by unannounced and found the girls running around in their underwear. The godmother didn't like this at all and reported what she suspected was happening. Soon after that the visits to Pepere stopped.

One morning Adele woke up with an upset stomach and told Soeur Stanislaus, "I don't feel well. My stomach is upset. Can I please lie back down and not go to Mass today?"

Soeur Stanislaus said, "I don't believe you, you just don't want to go to Mass." She had to get up, wash up and get dressed with the others. She was getting worse as the day wore on. Finally, they put her in the infirmary. She did not have a fever, and it did not hurt when they lifted her right leg so it couldn't be appendicitis, the staff reasoned. They decided to give her an enema–this didn't work either.

Soeur Stanislaus said, "Maybe we should call Dr. Nadeau since she is still throwing up and her temperature is up to ninety-nine degrees." He came and examined her and asked, "Why did you not call me sooner? This child is very sick." He carried her out of the infirmary into his waiting car, and off they went to the hospital. Adele asked Dr. Nadeau, "Where are we going?"

When he took her to the hospital, Adele lay there in his arms terrified. At the hospital they discovered her appendix was ruptured. Dr. Nadeau knew he had to operate immediately, but had to get written permission from the nearest relative and that was her grandmother, Nana. Someone had to go to Auburn to get Nana's signature before they could operate. Time was running out.

Finally, permission in hand, Dr. Nadeau operated but it was no easy task. The appendix was lodged in little Adele's back and was hard to find, and what made matters worse was she now had gangrene from the ruptured appendix. She then developed pneumonia and pleurisy and stayed in the hospital over a month. During that time she was in a lot of pain from the pleurisy. The fluid had to be removed from her lungs somehow. This required a long needle being inserted through the ribcage into the lungs. Adele was told, "You must bend forward and stay very still–if you don't when you grow up you will grow leaning to one side." Adele listened even though she had to stay in that position for what seemed to be hours. The nurses liked Adele and told her she was a brave little girl. They nicknamed her "Smiley," as she smiled through all that pain. What they didn't realize was she was enjoying all the attention that she so lacked at the boarding school/orphanage.

Meanwhile, Claire and Diane begged Soeur Stanislaus to let them see their sister, as they feared she was dead. A visit was arranged and they came to cheer her up. They sang songs and told her they were so glad she was alive, hugging her all the while. They were terrified of leaving her and did not want to go back to the orphanage.

Adele was not used to all this attention, and she did not want to go back either.

She wrote to her parents to let them know she was in the hospital, not knowing if anyone had bothered to let them know. She thought Nana might have, though. It would have been so nice to see them walk into her hospital room to tell her everything would be alright, and have hold her and stay a while. Sometimes the ache and loneliness was unbearable. Needing them to hold her, she cried herself to sleep many nights.

Recuperation took a long, long time, and the nuns treated her much better now as they had been scolded by Dr. Nadeau for having waited so long to call him. They knew she almost died when the gangrene had spread so quickly. Now, she didn't have to get up as early to go to Mass, and she wasn't attending school yet either. She had to visit Dr. Nadeau periodically for checkups. Adele had a crush on him and thought he was very handsome. She enjoyed walking downtown, with a chaperone of course, for the office visits. He was worried because she was not gaining any weight. He decided to give her some medication to increase her appetite. She was to regret this all of her life. About this time she started menstruating, and when she got up enough nerve to tell one of the nuns, the response was, "Everyone gets that." She also started developing breasts, which embarrassed her tremendously. The clothes assigned to her were very tight on top. Bras were unheard of, as none of the other children needed them.

The holidays were approaching and weekend chores were more than just dusting and mopping. The wooden floors had to be polished with this awful smelling orange paraffin. After a few hours of drying, the floors were buffed by this large machine that was dragged from right to left and then left to right, until the floor reached a high gloss. Again, the children who did not go home on weekends were the ones who did all the housekeeping chores, including washing windows in springtime.

It was so hard to watch the other students go home every weekend, and especially at the holidays. Adele prayed and prayed that her parents would come for Christmas, if not at Thanksgiving, or maybe in the summertime? Would the weather allow them to make the long journey in the snow? Would they have to work? The questions were always there.

Living in a Cocoon,
The High School Years

After seven long years at the orphanage, Adele graduated from eighth grade. There were no public boarding high schools in Lewiston, and St. Joseph's did not offer education at that level. Adele wondered what was going to happen to her, Claire and Diane. Decisions had to be made.

Reluctantly, her parents decided it was time to bring the entire family together. They wondered how they could make room for three more children as they already had Lisette, Cecile and Edwin with them now. Her mother would plead, "We have to pick them up, we have no choice." Meanwhile, her father thought to himself, "How are we going to cope with three more mouths to feed?"

Adele, Claire and Diane were elated when they learned that that coming June they would be reunited with their parents and other siblings. They finally arrived at the little apartment in New Hampshire; it soon became obvious that the apartment was much too small. Her parents began an exhausting search for a larger place that would hold six children, and for someone who would rent to such a large family. They had to have at least four bedrooms; the children were all in bunk beds, and that was fine with them. Finally, someone took a chance on them. The new landlord did not regret it, as the children were well behaved.

Their new home was the second floor of a very large house on Greene Terrace. There was a dike in the back yard that led to the river a mile away. The children found it heavenly to be outside, except for Adele. She was extremely weak from the frequent asthma attacks. She had to stay inside those first couple of months until her body adjusted to its new environment and temperature. She had several environmental allergies and her body was constantly fighting these allergens. As fall went into winter, she began to feel better. The cold weather killed the germs and bacteria; grasses and trees were now dormant. She thought winters were beautiful, especially after a storm, with the snow and ice covering the trees.

Behind the dike near the river, they would ice skate between the trees. Adele was determined to do everything her sisters did. She would skate until she couldn't breathe, take a break, and then start again.

Winter rolled into spring on Greene Terrace and the beautiful cherry tree blossomed. Diane, still mischievous and rebellious, was always breaking the rules. One day as they were playing outside, she said, "Let's climb up that tree and get those cherries before the birds eat them all." Adele said "That's dangerous, Diane, and besides Mummy will see us and make us go inside." Diane, as usual, did not listen and up the tree she went. Halfway up she lost her footing, came falling down, and she lost conscientious.

Adele said, "Oh no, we are in trouble. What do we do with her so that Mummy doesn't see her lying here on the ground?"

Claire said, "Adele, go get that doll carriage in the garage; we'll put her in that."

So Adele quickly got the carriage before their mother looked out the window. After a while their mother came to check on them and discovered Diane in the carriage. She demanded to know what had happened, so they told her the truth

Behind the dike there was a huge cornfield; and, on another play day outside Diane said to Claire, "Let's go get some of that corn."

Adele said, "Diane, you are going to get us in trouble again, and besides the corn isn't fully ripe yet." Secretly, she wanted some corn too, but the land didn't belong to them; they would be trespassing.

Diane said, "O.K., we'll wait until it's ripe."

Lisette and Cecile wanted a cat and Mummy wouldn't let them have one because Adele was allergic, so they found two little turtles in the swamp behind the dike and brought them home. Little Edwin, the only boy in the family with five older sisters was left out most of the time. He did have his own friends to play with down the street. When he found out about the turtles, he couldn't wait to see them. "I'm going to name them," he said.

Claire wasn't going to give in so easily. After all, she was the one who brought them home.

Edwin said, "It's not fair, all of you girls never ever let me play with you, it's as if I don't exist."

Claire said "O.K. you can name them."

After a few minutes, Edwin popped up with: "Herman and Oliver sound like two good names to me." So the turtles had their names. They would walk around the box and then climb up on the rocks and sun themselves every chance they got.

Lisette still wanted a cat and Adele felt bad that she was to blame. A friend's cat had kittens, adorable little fur balls. Adele said to her friend, "Can I have one to bring home?" Denise's mother knew the kitten would have a good home, so she said yes. Since they didn't live far away, Adele decided to carry it home rather than try to find a box for it.

Her mother took one look and said, "You know what will happen." Adele begged and her mother said, "We'll try." That evening Adele started wheezing and continued until she had a full-blown asthma attack and had to be rushed to the emergency room. No more cats were ever allowed in the house again.

Adele was invited to Denise's beach cottage for the weekend. Her mother said no, but Adele convinced her to agree. They rode down to the seaside with their dog in the car for the hour-and-a-half trip. Adele had neglected to tell her mother they had a dog. She started having a hard time breathing, but said nothing to anyone. Their destination was a musty, mold-infested cottage that had been closed up all winter. The family was famished and ordered pizza. Adele ate very little–she could barely breathe by this time. Everyone made up the beds and called it a night except Denise and Adele.

Denise was able to observe Adele a little more closely and noticed she was turning blue around her mouth. She became frightened and woke her mother up. They located a local doctor who agreed to pay a home visit. His face did not hide his dismay. Adele was given a shot of adrenalin immediately, and she started feeling a little better. It was too dangerous for her to stay, so Denise's mother said, "We'd better get Adele home right away." Adele was extremely embarrassed to have caused them so much trouble. Meanwhile, her mother was not surprised when the car pulled up, as she sensed something was wrong–she had not slept all night.

Adele missed an entire week of school this time. High school was hard enough without having to deal with this asthma. Going from an all-girls French-speaking boarding school to an all-English-speaking public high school was quite a culture shock. The boys were nothing like her brother Edwin. They were strange creatures, she thought.

One black boy in English class, Calvin, would go by her desk, take her pencil and bend it to break the lead. Her friends told her he did this because he liked her. She didn't believe them and didn't know what to make of it. She was extremely shy and had trouble making friends at first. She was studious and excelled in all her subjects. Socially and emotionally she was way behind the other students.

It wasn't until her senior year that she loosened up enough to have a little fun. She was invited to a party and had too much punch. She was naive enough to think her friends would not spike the punch. Of course her mother noticed and she was grounded for a while.

During her senior year she took driver's education since she realized that would give her some independence. Her father took a day off work to take her to the Motor Vehicle Office for the test. Of course, she passed with flying colors. Her father did take her practicing for the test. This was one of the few nice things he ever did for her.

The girls and Edwin tried to stay out of the house as much as possible because they never knew when their father would start yelling for no apparent reason. He was under a lot of stress, trying to raise six children on a limited income. Adele's mother went to work but had to stop. The injury she sustained pulling typewriters off a conveyor belt at the Underwood Typewriter factory would not allow her to continue. She had a pinched nerve in her back that caused her constant pain.

That put even more pressure on her father. By this time he had been diagnosed as having manic depression (today known as bipolar disease). The highs and lows were impossible to predict. The girls coped in different ways. When the yelling started for some minor infraction, Lisette would argue with her father, explaining, "I can't let him beat me down." Adele would say, "Lisette, arguing with him only makes him worse and you will never win an argument with him." She coped by removing herself from the situation and running up to her room in the attic. Many, many nights she cried herself to sleep wondering why life had to be so difficult.

Lisette, being the oldest, would come home from school and cook dinner and watch the other girls. She was also on the receiving end of much of the discipline and unreasonable demands for someone her age. Despite all her efforts, her father constantly criticized her for something–wearing makeup, going out with her friends and her new boyfriend, Joe. Adele, Diane and Claire would hide behind the bushes and watch then kiss and hug. Lisette would catch them and shoo them away.

In her junior year of the high school college preparatory program, her father told her, "Lisette, you have to quit school and go to work to help support the rest of the family." Lisette did not want to, but what choice did she have? She loved school and all of her friends, but being the obedient girl she was, if somewhat feisty at times, she did as she was told. When the teachers found out, they were appalled that this could happen to a student of Lisette's caliber. She was one of the most intelligent students and excelled in all her subjects. How could this happen? Lisette never spoke of her resentment toward her father.

Adele attended the same high school, and as a freshman was told she would have to take the business/secretarial program to prepare for work immediately upon graduation. Before graduation, exams were offered that would qualify her for an entry-level secretarial position with the classified service; without hesitation she took the exam and passed with flying colors. She interviewed and was offered a position with the Chief of Administration at the Board of Education and Services for the Blind, which she accepted. She knew the classified service in state government offered great health insurance, sick leave and vacation, a great retirement pension plan, and life insurance.

Adele's asthma still plagued her at times, and she never outgrew the allergic rhinitis. Because of this, she did not catch colds, she caught infections, as the doctors explained. Colds would automatically turn into infections, sinus or bronchial.

By this time, the Sixties, research had let to injections to help deal with the allergies. These injections helped tremendously and she was allowed to get them before reporting for work once weekly.

Their father went away for treatment at an out-of-state hospital, where he received counseling and medication management. Life was more peaceful during that time.

Meanwhile, Lisette married Joe and they had a wonderful life together. Lisette advanced quickly in her career. When retail sales no longer challenged her, she switched fields and became a department head for Colt Firearms. Later, she joined Konica Minolta Business Solutions U.S.A., Inc. as its manager in charge of travel and accounts payable. She would stay with Konica Minolta for approximately twenty-five years. No one suspected she never finished high school. Her work ethic brought her many well-deserved accolades. In fact, she reported for work the day before her death from bronchial pneumonia at sixty-one. Surely she enjoyed her memorial service in the presence of all her beloved family and friends. In fact, at the service, one of her best friends, Todd Calder remarked, "Lisette was one of a kind and will be sorely missed." He proceeded to pull up a chair near the podium and spoke to her directly as he viewed her framed photo.

Adele matured and flourished despite all her past difficulties. She made friends easily now and had many. She enjoyed spending time with them, even if it meant taking the bus to visit with them. She often spent her weekends in a small ethnic neighborhood in the south end of town. There she met Nella, Rita, Rose and Josephine, all of them hailing from various parts of Italy. It suited her just fine that none of her new friends spoke French. Adele and Nella became inseparable and she considered Nella one of her sisters; Nella was an only child who longed for a sister.

It was through her association with this group that Adele met and fell madly in love with Aldo Valera. Aldo was about ten years older, drove a red Alfa Romeo sports car and played bass in a band. They had much in common–love of music, exotic cars, and common friends. Adele was still naive and inexperienced. These were the things Aldo said he liked about her. The first kiss was unbelievable, and Aldo once said after dating her for a while: "Kiss me the way you did the first time." She willingly obliged, giving him a quick peck on the cheek. Aldo's response, "Oh, no, it was much worse than that."

The trouble with Aldo was that he never called ahead of time for a date. He would just show up at her house, and if she wasn't home, he would take Claire, Diane and Cecile bowling.

Oh, how she longed to see him, but he didn't call as often as she'd like. She obsessed about him and would beg Nella to drive by his house, hoping to get a glimpse of him. She was not old enough to go legally to nightclubs where his band was playing. She obtained a fake I.D. and was admitted into the club. She didn't drink, she just wanted to listen to the music and dance.

When she and Nella came of age they frequented the Zodiac, a club in the city. There she met and dated an Englishman from Surrey. Chris raced sports cars as a hobby. He modified a Lotus Elan and raced it at Limerock in New York, among other places. Adele was quite taken with Chris and they dated for a few years. When they broke up, she cried herself to sleep to the sounds of Karen Carpenter's "I'll Say Goodbye to Love."

Would she ever meet the love of her life and marry?

Author's Note: Cecile, Adele's youngest sister, read the following at their mother's memorial service:

"We gather here to give tribute to our mother, grandmother, aunt and friend. We try to find words enough to express our deep sorrow and gratitude to a woman who lived life with courage, strength, humor and tremendous integrity. It was a privilege to be raised by her and a privilege to have been with her in these last difficult weeks of her life.

"She was a steady, nurturing, fair-minded parent who raised us to work hard, live our own lives, do what needs to be done, care for each other and enjoy life. When chores didn't get done or sibling rivalry broke out, she exacted pretty clear, no-nonsense consequences. Usually something like 'I don't care who started it, go to your room,' or 'go run around the block,' or 'If you're going to fight like, that go outside.' She had a knack for knowing when discipline was necessary and when it was not. She understood when we were going through a "phase" without ever having heard about developmental psychology. For an only child, she had an amazing ability to roll with the chaos of a houseful of children, and rarely said no to any activity or project we wanted to take on except for climbing trees–for some reason she was terrified when we climbed trees. 'You'll fall out and kill yourself,' she'd say (this from a woman who went stunting in an airplane). When we wanted to do something because a friend was doing it, we'd hear, 'If your friend jumps off a bridge, are you going to do it too?' or when faced with a daughter whose attire she did not entirely approve of, she'd say 'It's always best to leave something to the imagination.'"

SUSAN MONTANARI

Susan Montanari was born in Atlanta but moved to Savannah, Georgia, as a teen. She attended St. Vincent's Academy and Armstrong State College. She married and raised three daughters in Savannah.

Montanari recently moved to Lantana, Florida, but no matter where she roams, she considers Savannah home. She has written several articles for local publications and is currently working on a novel.

The author would like to thank Jan Spillane, whose sense of irony is unparalleled, for suggesting the title "Alligator Soul." She dedicates "The Boys of Summer" to husband Dan, a lifetime member of The Red Sox Nation.

Susan Montanari can be reached at Telfairsquare@yahoo.com.

Alligator Soul

Deep in the Louisiana bayou, where the Spanish moss hangs low, a baby alligator was lying near the dark water, enjoying the sun. His name was Zydeco. He was just thinkin' about how hungry he was when he felt a thump vibrate through the mud next to his nose. Zydeco's right eyelid slowly rolled open. He saw a beetle bug flip over from its back. The little alligator smiled. Dinner had arrived.

The bug sat up, rearranged its wings, patted down its belly shell with four of its front legs, and wiped its eyes with the feathery tips of its long antennae.

Zydeco swung his head around, and quick as could be, he had that beetle bug between his needle sharp teeth. Now if Zydeco had been any bigger that bug would have been crushed and swallowed in a snap.

"No! *Mon Ami*, you mustn't eat me." He heard the bug squeal.

Zydeco's other eyelid snapped open. He did not think food was supposed to talk to you. Confused, he mumbled, "Why?"

The fast-thinking bug replied, "I make the music that tells the sun to shine. If I don't play my song, there will be no sun to warm you."

Zydeco grunted in disbelief.

The bug pleaded, "*Chere,* this is for true, I am a musician, the sun shines just for me."

Zydeco liked the warm sun on his back, but this felt like a trick.

"Play your music. If it's no good, I'll eat you."

The beetle bug rolled out of Zydeco's mouth, sat up, adjusted its wings, and wiped its eyes with the feathery tips of its long antennae. Zydeco cleared his throat, and looked at the beetle bug expectantly.

The beetle bug started runnin' the sharp tips of its four front legs against the hard, rigid belly-shell. A rhythm filled the air. Chicka-Chicka-Chicka. Zydeco felt his leg start to twitch. His claws began to tap up and down.

Soon a *faut carut*, a very big grasshopper, hearin' the rhythm landed next to the beetle bug. It started slidin' its back legs together. Zing-Zing-Twang. The sound of strings joined the percussion. Zydeco felt his left shoulder move up and down. His right shoulder started to move up and down too. A *peunez*, a stinkbug, joined in and the sound it produced from out of its snout, Wang-Wang-Wang, sounded like the wind bellowin' through the swamp reeds.

As that Chanky-Chank rhythm filled the air, Zydeco felt it fill his soul. Unable to help himself he swung up on his hind legs, threw his front claws together, and started stompin' and clappin' to the rhythm. His little tail was swingin' around. The bugs kept playin' and hoppin' out of the way.

Those bugs and that little alligator they sure passed themselves a good time that day. They promised they would get together every day and have their very own dance party, a *fais do-do*.

So every morning when the sun began to shine, Zydeco would pull himself out of the swamp. The bugs would gather on a *boscoyo*, the knee of a cypress tree, and begin to play. The music would swell up inside Zydeco, He would rise up on his hind legs and dance. The faster the bugs played, the faster Zydeco danced.

The years passed. Zydeco grew bigger and bigger.

It wasn't long before the animals that lived in the swamp came to know that as soon as they heard the bugs begin to play, it would be safe for them to go to the water. They did not have to worry about becoming Zydeco's next meal. They could hear him stompin', clappin', and dancin'.

That was until two Cajun brothers and their Creole friend came sliding by in their *pirogue*. All three of them stared with their mouths hangin' open. They had never seen a dancin' alligator before.

Jean, the oldest brother, hit Ti Jean on the back of the head, "Do you see what I see?"

Ti Jean hit Clifton on the back as he answered. "I see an alligator, look like he got a whole swarm of black flies on him."

Clifton hit Ti Jean on the leg. "I don't see no black flies though."

Tawk, Jean thumped Clifton on the back of the head, "That gator actin' like he gonna make us a pile of money,"

"*Mon Dieu*! How?" Clifton exclaimed.

"Do you remember that dancin' bear at the travelin' show? We paid good money to see that bear shake a leg. We make twice that and more with a dancin' alligator."

"For sure, *chere*, for sure, you are right," exclaimed Ti Jean, thumping his brother on the back so hard the *pirogue* began to rock back and forth.

"Our fortune is there for the takin'," Clifton grinned. He used the long pole to silently push the boat to the bank and tie it to a *boscoyo*.

Zydeco didn't hear a thing as a ring of rope was lowered around his jaws and pulled tight. He fell to all fours pulling against the rope. Zydeco was big but it was three against one. Soon he was tied up and thrown into the bottom of the *pirogue*. Those boys were laughing, *pome*. Rubbin' their hands together with glee, they glided away.

The bugs stopped playing. The animals stepped into the clearing that had been Zydeco's dance floor. They looked to each other in amazement.

"Ya Hoo!" shouted the hare, "No more alligator botherin' us!"

"We can use that waterin' hole whenever we want," yelled the raccoon.

A small cheer could be heard from some of the other animals.

"Yes," interrupted the fox, "until some other bull alligator moves in here."

"And maybe this new alligator, he don't like to dance," said the beetle bug.

"Better the gator we know, then the gator we don't," added the possum who was lounging across a low-lying pine bough.

"We have to get Zydeco back," the hare said, disbelief in his voice.

"I'll find him," said the crow as it took flight.

Meanwhile the boys had taken Zydeco home with them. They put him in a shady pen beside the barn. They used to keep a pig there, *poo-yee-yi*. It stunk!

The boys brought Zydeco plenty to eat, but he wasn't interested.

The boys filled the watering trough with swamp water, but Zydeco didn't care.

Zydeco did not like it there. He grew sadder and sadder. He wanted to dance, he wanted the sun, and he wanted his bugs.

Jean came out with his fiddle and played Zydeco a song. Zydeco let out a sigh.

Ti Jean came out with his guitar and played a merry tune. Zydeco just closed his heavy eyelids.

Clifton came out with his accordion. Zydeco rolled over onto his back and his tongue flopped out. Every day was the same. The boys brought out every instrument they could think of, but Zydeco just lay there.

Late one afternoon, the crow spotted Zydeco. She circled the pen and quickly flew back to tell the others.

The bugs followed the crow back to the barn and landed on the fence post.

They knew that the only thing that could cheer up Zydeco was the music he loved so much.

They started to play.

One of Zydeco's back legs began to twitch, then the other. His tongue rolled back into his mouth. One eyelid snapped open, then the other. He flipped over onto his stomach. That Chanky-Chank rhythm he loved so much filled his soul. It brought him up on his hind legs. He stomped one foot, then the other. He swung around and his tail crashed through the watering trough, smashing it, spraying swamp water all over the barn.

The boys came running. "*Mon Dieu*, what has happened?" Clifton exclaimed.

"What has brought him around?" Jean asked.

"That sound," said Ti Jean, "Listen, I heard the same sound in the swamp that day."

They all heard the bugs' music now.

"Quick," said Clifton, "we must learn to play it." Jean grabbed his fiddle. Clifton grabbed his accordion.

"What should I play?" asked Ti Jean. He could not think of an instrument to match the sound he heard coming from the beetle bug.

He spotted an old *frottoir*, a wash board, and grabbed it. He started rapping his knuckles up and down on it. As the boys joined in, the music got louder and louder. Zydeco was dancing wilder and wilder.

The music was so loud the neighbors came out on their *galleries* to listen. Smilin' and clappin' to the music, they wandered over. The boys were paying so much attention to their new audience they forgot about Zydeco, until he burst through the fence, danced across the yard and fell, ka–plop, into the bayou.

The boys and the bugs were so surprised the music stopped. It stopped just long enough for Zydeco to get his bearings. With a swish of his tail he was gone. The neighbors shouted for the boys to start up their music again. They had a *fais do-do* right then and there.

The boy's new music became very popular. It seemed everyone

who heard it couldn't stay off the dance floor. The boys were asked to play at every *fais do-do* in the parish and they made their fortune after all.

Soon, their music was being played all over the bayou. That is why, to this very day, when you hear Louisiana music, your feet just can't be still. Before you know it, you're on the dance floor stompin' and clappin' and swingin' your tail around. Then you know, for true, you got a little bit of alligator soul.

Glossary of Cajun and Creole Terms	
Bayou	Slow-moving black water.
Zydeco	The beans have no salt (we are so poor we have no salted meat for the beans). Also a type of music created in Louisiana.
Chere	Dear, an endearment.
Faut carut	A very big grasshopper.
Peunez	A stink bug.
Fais do-do	(fay dough-dough) To go to sleep. It also means a community dance. The dance was called a fais do-do because the dance often lasted all night and small children brought to the dance were often made to go to sleep there.
Boscoyo	The knee of a cypress tree root that sticks out in the swamp.
Cajun	People of Cajun descent were French Canadians, exiled from Canada by the British, who eventually settled in South Louisiana.
Creole	People of African/French/Caribbean descent.
Pirogue	A boat pushed through the swamp by a pole.
Tawk	Sound made by thumping your fingers on something or someone.
Pomee	Laughing so hard it brings tears to your eyes.
Poo-yee-yi	Very stinky.
Galleries	Front porches where people liked to visit.

The Boys of Summer

"You've been helping me all morning. Why don't you take a break? Go for a walk or something," Jack's mother said to him as he brought in another box marked "KITCHEN." They had moved more times than he could remember. The Captain, his father, had said this was their last move for a while, at least until the war in Iraq was over. This time they were stationed at Fort Stewart, Georgia, an army base in the middle of a small town, nowhere. Jack put on his Boston Red Sox hat. The blue cap with the red B had been his most prized possession long before it was cool to be a Red Sox fan.

The hat was a sacred reminder of the day the Captain had taken him to see a game at Fenway Park, home of the Boston Red Sox. He loved the memory of watching a ball fly over the "Green Monster" for a home run. He picked up his mitt and a ball. He pushed open the screen door of the big Victorian style house his parents had bought. They had actually bought a house. The whole twelve years of his life they had lived either on base or in rental houses.

Jack worked the ball into his glove as he walked. It was a first baseman's mitt. His mind wandered back to that last town and that last great game. The older players, the eighth grade guys had all been excited because the high school coach was in the stands scouting middle school talent. They all wanted to show their stuff in the hope of impressing the coach before next year's try-outs. The team was really in the zone and everyone played his best game ever. It seemed to Jack like the ball was on fire as it slammed into his glove time after time. It had been a thrill every time the ump screamed, "You're out," as Jack stopped yet another kid from making it to first base.

They had won the game and the guys were jumping all over each other and slapping each other on the back when the high school coach came over. He spoke to some of the guys and shook their hands. Then he held out his hand to Jack, smiling he said, "Great job out there today, kid, hope to see you at tryouts this year."

Jack shook his hand, "I'm only in seventh grade, sir," he said.

"Then I look forward to seeing you at tryouts next year," the coach smiled.

Jack slammed the ball into his glove. "Guess that'll never happen, Coach," he mumbled to himself. He looked around as he followed the sidewalk down the street. All the houses were old and Victorian. They were set back from the street. The giant oak trees with Spanish moss dripping from their limbs seem to stand guard like silent soldiers. Suddenly the row of houses stopped and Jack came to iron bars.

The wrought iron fence was at least eight feet high. The hedges growing behind it towered above the fence. It was impossible to see what was on the other side. Jack followed the fence for nearly two blocks before coming to the gate at the entrance. There was a kid, about his age, leaning against the gate. He had on a baseball cap with the letter A on the front. Despite his curiosity, Jack kept walking.

"Red Sox suck." He heard the kid say. Jack felt his shoulders stiffen as he turned around to face the kid.

"You want to say that to my face?" Jack sputtered.

"You heard what I said." The kid seemed surprised that Jack was confronting him.

"I just want to see if you have the guts to say that to my face," Jack said through gritted teeth.

"Hey, hey," the kid said, flashing a crooked grin, "I didn't mean anything by it. Don't get all bent outta shape. It's not my fault your team can't win a series."

"I don't know what rock you've been hiding under out here in the boonies, but how could you have missed the fact that the Red Sox swept the series last year. Red Sox are the best team 2004 ever saw and probably the best team this century."

"Hey, hold on, Boston, I didn't mean any harm. Hey, guys, you gotta hear this!"

Suddenly Jack was surrounded by a group of boys who all seemed eager to hear about the Red Sox victory.

"This here is Paulie. We call him the Babe after Babe Ruth, the Big Bambino. Babe moved here from Maine. He's been telling us for years about the curse of the Big Bambino. He has always blamed Boston's bad luck on the Bambino, you know, 'cause they traded him to the Yankees and all." The kid had Paulie by the shoulders and was rocking him back and forth.

"Well, the curse is lifted, Babe," Jack said, "and in a big way. See, it was Red Sox against the Yankees in the championship game."

"No way," The Babe exclaimed.

"The Yankees were up three games."

"No way."

"Sox came back, beat them four games in a row to win the championship."

"Who did they play in the series?"

"Seattle, four up, four down, it was a sweep."

Cheers rang out. Jack found it hard to believe that these kids had not seen the game on TV or even heard about it.

"How come . . . " Jack started to ask again when the first kid interrupted him.

"You carry that mitt around just to look cool, or do you want to play some ball?"

"Yeah, I play," Jack answered.

The kids started moving, Jack stepped through the gate onto a huge sandlot, perfect for a game of baseball.

The guys spread out, automatically taking their places. The first kid said, " You can take The Babe's place, seeing as how you got a first baseman's mitt and all. I'm Joe, by the way, Joe Moorehouse."

"Where'd, 'The Babe,' go?" Jack asked.

"I guess it was time for him to go," Joe answered. "That's Martin O'Hare on second, Michael Robinson on third, Drew Daly is catching, I'm pitching. Up to bat we have Thaddeus Blume, David Jenkins, Hank Daniels, Jason Laforge, and Paul Miller. Don't worry if you don't get all the names right away."

"I'm Jack, Jack Walker,"

"Well, get ready for a treat Boston, 'cause ole Thaddeus Blume is just about the best hitter that ever came outta these parts! That right, guys?"

All the guys in the infield started to back up as Thaddeus stepped up to the plate. The bat was snuggled against his shoulder. He stroked the back of his head with his left hand, and then tugged his left ear. He gripped the bat, took a practice swing and nodded to Joe on the mound. Joe smiled, nodded back, and fed him a fastball. Thaddeus swung. *Crack.* The ball met the bat and went flying high over the second baseman's head. It didn't stop until it hit the hedges against the back fence.

"How'd you like that one, Boston! Thad here just fed one to 'The Green Monster,'" Joe shouted as Thaddeus jogged around the bases. Martin ran after the ball and threw it to Joe as David Jenkins stepped up to the plate.

They played ball all afternoon until the streetlights came on.

"I gotta go," Jack called. It felt good to him when all the guys objected.

"Gotta go have dinner with the folks?" Joe asked.

"Yeah, I'm supposed to be home when the streetlights come on."

"Well get going then, you don't want to make the old man mad."

"You guys want to play tomorrow?"

"Yeah, sure, we'll see you tomorrow."

Jack left and ran home. He dreaded the Captain yelling at him for being late and for leaving Mom to do all the unpacking. They were waiting for him on the front porch when he finally got there.

"Sorry I'm late," he panted as he ran up the stairs, "I met some guys and we got up a game, I lost track of time."

"That's OK, honey, we were just worried about you," his mom said, batting his cap playfully.

"We're glad you met some kids, but try to get home on time from now on. We don't want your mom to worry." His father put his hand on his shoulder.

"No sir, I mean, Yes, sir, I'll be more careful."

"Whew, you sure do stink, where were you playing, in a ditch?"

"It's just sweat, Mom, I'll go take a shower."

"Make it quick," his father said. "Dinner is already late."

That began the pattern for the days to come. Jack helped his mom in the mornings, had lunch and then went to play ball all afternoon. Every night Joe would call out, "Lights on, Boston, you better get home."

One night the lights came on during a critical point in a game. "Lights on...."

"I'd rather stay here," Jack muttered.

"Don't ever say that," Joe said. "You should be thankful you have a family to go home to."

"What do you mean?" Jack asked him. Joe started walking Jack to the gate,

"You could have an old man like mine. He'd just as soon knock you across the room as look you in the eye."

"You need to turn him in, call the police or something."

"I did, once."

"What happened?"

"He had turned on my baby sister. She was only three, grabbed her up by the arm so hard the bone snapped like a twig."

"Oh, man, what did you do?"

"I snatched her away from him and ran. I ran all the way to the hospital, three miles with her shaking and crying in my arms. When I got the emergency room, they took us straight in. They asked me what happened. The same doctor and nurses had patched me up more times than I can count. I just couldn't lie that time. That night holding my little sister against my chest, she was so fragile, like a little bird, and I could feel her heart beating a mile a minute. I knew I couldn't let that monster hurt her ever again. I told the truth."

"What happened?" Jack stared at him in horror.

"Cops went out to the house and arrested him that night. So go home, Boston, and have a nice meal with your nice folks."

"Why don't you come home with me, have dinner with us? My mom would love it."

"Thanks but I can't. I gotta get with my mom."

"You sure?"

"Yeah, get out of here, Boston."

Jack could not get Joe's story out of his head. He watched as his father talked with his mother after dinner and helped clean up. His father was a military man, trained to fight, but he could not imagine him turning on his mother or him in a rage. That night as he was going upstairs to his room he called out, "'Night Mom, 'night Dad."

"Dad," his father repeated. "You haven't called me anything but Captain since you were five years old."

"I know, I've just been thinking, guys all over the base call you Captain. I think I should call you Dad."

His father nodded and turned away, "OK, well, good night, son."

Jack smiled as he walked up the stairs.

The next day Jack approached the gate to the sandlot and was surprised that he didn't hear the usual chatter of the guys. When he turned in he saw two ladies and a man walking up the first base line. One of the ladies was holding a vase with flowers in it. The other one held a handkerchief to her face. Jack thought they must be lost or something.

He decided to come back later. He went down to the corner store, bought a Coke, and looked at the comic books for awhile. When he went back to the lot the adults were gone and the guys were back. Jack asked Thaddeus if he had seen them.

"Yeah, we were here. We just get out of the way when they come around."

"Why do they come here?" Jack asked.

"Depends. It's best just to get out of their way and try not to let them screw up your game. Hey, do you want me to show you what's wrong with your swing?"

"Would you?" Jack asked.

For the next few hours Joe pitched the ball and Thaddeus instructed Jack on how to make solid contact with it. After just getting a piece of the ball time after time, Jack decided to mimic Thaddeus's hair and ear tugging ritual. Joe fed him a fastball. Jack swung hard. He heard a crack and then felt a stinging sensation in his hands. There was a wild cheer among the guys and Jack watched his first homerun ball bounce off the "Green Monster." He smiled as he loped around the bases while all the guys cheered him on.

The next morning Jack's mom reminded him that there was only a week left before school started. "Are any of your new friends in your grade?" she asked. "It would be nice to start a new school and already know some people."

Jack agreed with her and decided to ask the guys about the local middle school that afternoon.

"No, I guess you could say we've all graduated from middle school," Joe told him when he asked.

"Shoot," Jack replied, "some of the guys just look too young to be in high school."

"Maybe you'll get to school and meet a whole new group of guys and you won't want to play ball with us any more." Joe replied.

"And maybe I'll bring that group of guys over here so we can show them how the game is played," Joe answered.

Jack laughed. "Take your base, Boston, let's play ball."

Jack looked around. "Hey, where's Hank and David?"

"Guess they had to go," Joe answered as he threw a curve ball into the catcher's mitt.

Jason Laforge swung and missed.

They seemed to be steadily losing guys. By the Sunday before school was supposed to start only Joe, Thaddeus, and Jack showed up to play one last game before summer was over.

"I guess we'll have to play pickle," Joe said. When the streetlights came on, they called it quits. Joe walked Jack to the gate. Jack pulled his hat off and handed it to Joe.

"What's this, Boston?" Joe asked.

"I want you to have it. It's just my way of saying thanks, thanks for a great summer."

"We should be thanking you. If you hadn't come around how would we have found out about the Red Sox winning the World Series?" Joe smiled his crooked smile, "But I'll take your hat, Boston, thanks, and hey, good luck in school tomorrow."

Jack stated walking home, he turned back to wave at Joe, but he was already gone.

The next day Jack started another new school year in another new school. The lunchroom in the new school was no different from any lunchroom in any school he had ever attended.

"Hey, new kid," someone called. Jack looked around.

"Come on over here and sit with us," the kid called.

Jack recognized some of the kids sitting at the table from the classes he had had that morning. The guys sat at one end of the table and the girls sat at the other. He noticed that the red-headed girl who had smiled at him in English was there. He put his lunch tray down on the guy's side of the table and sat down.

"I'm Kyle, that's Jake, and Mikey."

"I'm Jack."

"So, where are you from Jack?"

"Everywhere," he answered.

"Another army brat, just like most of us, except Mickey, here. He's a Georgia boy, born and raised, right, Mikey?" Mikey nodded. They sat around talking and eventually the talk turned to baseball and the upcoming series.

"Nothing's going to beat last year's series," Kyle exclaimed with a dreamy expression on his face.

"Coach has the baseball equipment out on the field for PE, guess he wants to take a look at everyone's game before tryouts in the spring. We're a big baseball school." Jake explained to Jack, "In high school it's all about football but in middle school, baseball is king."

"I played baseball all summer with some guys over on Clayton Street," Jack told them.

"Really, who?" Kyle asked him. "Maybe we could get up a game."

"Sure, they'd like that. Their names are Joe Moorehouse, Thaddeus Blume, man can that guy hit...." Jack noticed everyone had stopped talking and was staring at him.

"What?" he asked.

"That's not cool," Kyle said with disgust in his voice. The other guys pushed their chairs away from the table and walked away.

"What did I say?" Jack asked out loud to no one in particular as he watched them walk away.

He had math and then it was time for PE. He noticed that the kids who had been so nice at lunch were giving him cold stares now. It was his turn to get up to bat. He snuggled the bat into his shoulder then slicked the hair on the back of his head down with his left hand. He tugged his ear and then gripped the bat. The coach pitched the ball and the ball went flying out into left field just as Jack felt something hit him from behind. He fell to his knees.

"Who do you think you are, you son of....."

"Hold it right there, Kyle," the coach yelled and pulled Kyle off of Jack.

"What's going on here?"

"I don't know, Coach," Jack said.

"Jack, go in and shower. I'm going to talk to Kyle."

Jack shook his head as he got up and started walking back towards the school.

The redheaded girl caught up with him.

"What are you trying to do?" she asked him

"I'm not trying to do anything but play some baseball." He answered her.

"Why are you trying to hurt people?"

"What did I do to hurt anyone?"

"Talking about Joe, and about Thaddeus."

"You know them?" he asked. She looked at him strangely.

"Thaddeus was Mikey's brother. You come here talking about him, hitting like him. Of course people are going to get upset."

"Because he taught me how to hit?"

"Because he's dead. He died in a car crash last year, drunk driver.

His mom almost died too."

"That's not possible. I spent a whole summer playing baseball with him. It must be another Thaddeus Blume."

"You think there are two guys in this town named Thaddeus Blume?"

"There has to be some explanation."

"And Joe Moorehouse."

Jack looked at her with dread.

"I'm Ginny Moorehouse. Joe Moorehouse was my brother. He died nine years ago, along with my mom and dad. Our house burned down. I would have died too, but I was in the hospital with a broken arm. Why would you want to hurt me? I don't even know you, so if you think this is some kind of harmless prank, well, you're wrong. It's not harmless at all."

She started to walk away from him. Jack could tell she was about to cry. He took hold of her arm.

"Please, I don't know what's going on. Maybe someone's playing some kind of joke on me, you know, playing a joke on the new guy in town. Come with me to the sandlot. You can meet these guys. Please say you'll meet me after school."

She nodded her head in agreement and walked into the school.

Ginny must have told the other kids what he had said because they were all waiting for him after school. They all walked with him to the sandlot. Jack turned into the gate. Instead of an empty sandlot, there were tombstones everywhere. Not the kind like they have up north that lie flat so the groundskeepers can mow over them. These were big tombstones with statues of angels on some of them. There were dirt paths in the shape of a diamond between the markers.

"Here we go again," Kyle started to say. Then Jack noticed something red, the letter B. He walked across the cemetery to get his hat. It was sitting on top of a tombstone near where third base used to be. Written on the stone was a name: Joseph Moorehouse, born 1982, died 1994.

Jack stared in stunned disbelief.

"Tell them some kids played a prank on you, Boston," Joe said. He and Thaddeus were standing behind the tombstone. "They'll get over it."

"They might get over it, but will I? Who was I playing with out here? Was I running around the cemetery talking to myself all summer?"

The two dead boys shrugged.

"Don't worry about it, Boston, everyone knows you have to be a little bit crazy to be a Red Sox fan," Joe said with a straight face. "I can't tell you how surprised I was, that first day, when I said, 'The Red Sox suck.' I couldn't believe you heard me. You scared the fool outta me."

"Tell them you got the ear tug thing from Jose Mendez. He's a Braves player, that's were I copied it from. They'll believe that. Anyway, at least you learned how to hit the ball." Thaddeus said. " Hey, I know, will you teach Mikey to hit for me? I had always planned to do that."

"Sure, if he'll let me," Jack answered, still stunned. He looked at Mikey and turned back to look at Thaddeus, but Thaddeus had disappeared.

"You came here so we could hear about the Red Sox, and have one last summer playing ball. Everyone's gone but me. I'm waiting for my mom. I'm not leaving, not 'til I find her," Joe told him. "My dad made bail that night. He came back to the house. He was so angry. Mom and I tried to get away. He stopped us. Then he burnt the house down. I ended up here. I don't know where my mom ended up. At least Ginny wasn't there. She was safe, at the hospital. That's what really matters. She was such a sweet little kid. I wish I could see her one last time."

"That's her," Jack nodded towards the group. "The redhead."

Joe looked over in disbelief. He walked towards Ginny. "I can't believe it, this is little Ginny. She's so beautiful, and so grown up." Joe had tears in his eyes. Suddenly a slender woman approached from out of the hedges.

"Mom!" She and Joe hugged. They both had tears in their eyes. With clasped hands, they walked up to Ginny. They each put a hand up, touched her hair, and smiled.

Ginny shivered, and hugged herself.

"Look after her for me, Boston," Joe shouted as he and his mother faded away before Jack's eyes.

"Well, where's your big explanation?" Kyle snarled at Jack.

"This is my hat, guys," he said, shaking his head. "I guess someone played me. Can you forgive a new guy for being stupid?"

They all looked at him. After a moment Kyle said, "Yeah, I guess so. It's hard to be the new kid. One time when my Dad was stationed at Fort Benning..."

"Hey," Mikey interrupted, "do you think you could give me some pointers on hitting? Man, you knocked the snot outta that ball."

Jack put his hat on.

"Sure," he said, thinking about his promise to Thaddeus. "No problem."

He looked at Ginny. She smiled at him, a very familiar crooked smile.

TREVOR NOBLE

"A writer's imagination is like a bird's soaring flight put to words." Those inspirational words began Trevor Noble's writing journey, and were said to him by acclaimed author Ernest K. Gann, Noble's friend and neighbor for several years.

Originally from Anacortes, Washington, Noble was stationed at Hunter Army Air Field (HAAF), Savannah, in the early 1990s. He returned to Savannah with his family in 2003. Prior to that, he spent 10 years in the Seattle area where he journeyed more deeply into the craft of writing.

Noble works for *Savannah Morning News* and has had newspaper articles published. He is currently working on his first novel and several short stories.

A founding member of the Savannah Writers Group, Noble lives in Richmond Hill, Georgia, with his wife, Nancy, and two of his three children, Jonathon and Elizabeth. His elder son, Robert, is currently attending Skagit Valley Community College, Mount Vernon, Washington.

You can contact Noble at trevor.noble@savannahnow.com.

Farley's Crypt

Written by Trevor Noble with his son, Robert Noble

It was October 31, All Hallows Eve, and I was attending a party at one of my friend's parents' homes. The adults outnumbered us by many. As the night grew longer, my friends and I became rather bored just sitting on the front porch laughing and teasing the trick-or-treaters as they came by.

Mike broke several minutes of silence with what most of the group said was a perfect idea. "Who is up for a trip to the cemetery?"

My friends rose and were laughing it up as they headed down the front path. I still sat there pondering the idea. "Hey guys," I called after them. "You sure you want to go there tonight?"

"Oh come on, Robert. It's better than staying around this party," Daniel said.

"What are you afraid of?" said Stacy.

"Ah, let's see...it's Halloween, it's night, and you want to go play in a graveyard."

My friends were shaking their heads in agreement while I just sat there. I watched two of them backtrack to the house for flashlights. The thought of going to a graveyard on a night like this just didn't appeal to me. Then Julie grabbed me by the arm and pulled, saying, "Come on. I need someone to protect me."

Looking up at her, I felt bewildered and my heart was pounding almost out of my chest. I reluctantly got up and headed out with the group. Daniel gave me a look of disgust at the fact Julie was next to me. He hadn't been bit by the girl bug and still considered Julie more like one of the guys than anything else.

The cemetery wasn't far from the house, only a few blocks and across the park. As we entered the park things began to change. The full moon faded behind a cloud and cast an eerie darkness. Fog covered the ground and obscured the path beneath us. The wind blew and ruffled the trees over our heads. If there was a stereotyped picture of a Halloween night, this was it.

Following the hedge line at the end of the park a wrought-iron fence came into view marking the end of the park and the cemetery. Turning, we followed the fence looking for a way in. With no moonlight and the fog getting thicker by the minute, this was not an easy task. Daniel stopped when he reached for what was a possible opening in the fence, but startled a black cat that leaped out of the bushes, crossed in front of our group, and headed off into the night. The harrowing screams that rose from those in our little group would have made a horror film director proud. While the rest of the group jumped, Julie grabbed my arm so tight that I thought she would break it in half.

After recovering from our hysterical state, we continued to follow the fence 'til it and the park ended at the wood line. Turning, we continued to follow the fence and skirted our way through he woods until we came upon a huge, ornamental gate. The gate was much larger than the surrounding fence and the large letters frequent to horror movies proclaimed the area within to be the "Atwood Cemetery." Our group paused. We all shivered in the chill of the night, and all gazes were fastened on the fog thickening and rising to our chests. Daniel lifted the latch allowing the gate to swing open on its own, letting out a creaking sound that filled the night.

Passing through the gate seemed to change the group. Faces that earlier displayed fun and laughter now reflected anxiety. That was all except for Daniel, who was turning on his flash light for the first time. The beam from Daniel's light cut the fog back and we began to explore the cemetery.

The cemetery seemed a lot larger than I expected, or did it just seem larger because we all were stumbling aimlessly about in the fog. The conversation between the six of us was nonexistent, almost as if we were trying to pass through undetected. While contemplating this, I ran right smack dab into a granite wall.

I rubbed my head as Julie helped me up. The others started moving around the structure turning on their flashlights as they went. The large crypt was made of solid granite. The foliage and vines that covered it looked like they had been undisturbed for hundreds of years. The top sloped up like a Roman cathedral. From the other side of the structure I heard someone yell, "Hey Guys. Over Here."

We all moved around the structure until we were standing at what seemed to be the front of the crypt. I recall thinking this structure was defiantly out of place. The other graves near it were just headstones. The crypt towered above them. Reaching up, I moved the vines and moss that covered a large iron door, shining my light on the engraved inscription:

HERE LIES JACOB FARLEY

CONVICTED AND HUNG UNTIL DEAD IN THE YEAR 1885

The front of Farley's crypt had gargoyle-topped pillars and was Gothic-looking, in contrast to the Roman-like slope of the roof. The giant, iron door overpowered the structure and added to its ominous nature. Daniel, showing his fearless stupidity, banged on the door and yelled, "Hey, anyone home."

On the third bang, the door moved and opened as if some force was pulling it from the inside. I cautiously looked through the open door and saw a set of stairs that descended deep into the crypt. The stairway had lit torches on the walls and a large wooden door at the bottom.

"Hey, I dare one of you guys to come in here with me," Daniel said, moving through the door. Julie gave a quick sign of the cross to the building and backed off, showing that she wouldn't go in. The others just looked down at their feet, and muttered excuses as to why they wouldn't go in either.

"How about you, Robert?" Daniel said, moving close to me, "This might be a good opportunity to impress a certain somebody..."

If there is one thing that will get you to do something really stupid, really fast, it'll normally be a girl, so I foolishly moved through the door with Daniel following. Descending the stairs, a musty odor filled my nostrils. The torches gave the stairs a foreboding glow.

Reaching the door at the bottom of the stairs, I pushed on it. The heavy oak door felt cold to the touch but moved with unsteadying ease, allowing the two of us to enter. The inside of the crypt was larger than I expected. Ornate tapestries in somber colors hung on the walls. Black iron torches with murky glass globes were hung in the spaces between the tapestries. The glow from the torches gave the interior a warm feeling, more like a castle room than a crypt. At the far end of the room was an extraordinary, sculptured stone coffin. The designs inlaid into the sides and top made it stand out more as a work of art than a coffin. The only thing that looked out of place on it was the name "Jacob Farley" chiseled into the side in script lettering.

Moving toward the coffin sent shivers up my spine. Daniel followed so close behind that he was almost on top of me. At the coffin I reached out and touched the top. The torches in the room faded and a shadow cast itself over us. Turning around I expected to see our friends but the sight that was before us terrified me to my core. I was too frightened to scream. Daniel stood silently beside me.

A figure stood before us. Shrouded in nothing but a black cloak. Where his face should be there was nothing but shadows, and where his hand should be was covered by the cloak.

The figure partially blocked our exit. Raising its hand and pointing at us, it spoke with a craggy voice, "Who disturbs my slumber?"

Not answering or waiting for another question, Daniel and I ran for the door. Bounding up the stairs two at a time and tripping over ourselves as we went, we exited the crypt at a full run.

Our friends they were nowhere in sight. Stopping for just a moment we heard the door to the crypt behind us close with a load bang. Turning around, I saw the crypt was engulfed by fog so thick that it was completely obscured from view. A scratchy voice screamed, "Go."

Daniel and I turned and took off at a dead run, not stopping until we finally met up with our friends on the other side of the park.

The next day, Daniel and I returned to the cemetery in the daylight. We wanted to find that crypt and see for ourselves what it really was. We made our way through the cemetery to the spot where the crypt should be. Nothing was there. I noticed some of the grave markers that I had seen the night before, but the crypt was nowhere to be found.

Looking down, I moved some leaves with my foot and found a small marker half buried in the ground. Tapping on Daniel's shoulder, I pointed out the gravestone that read:

Jacob Farley

1850-1885

As we turned and made our way out of the cemetery, we agreed that this was one Halloween we would never forget.

Lightwave,
Prologue

From the San Juan Islands, a group is testing a light amplified weapon that is wreaking havoc on air traffic, both civilian and military. From Washington, Steven Clark, a young man with a military background takes up his new post as special investigator for FIST. He is given the assignment that will either prove him the right man for the job or end his career abruptly.

"Lightwave" is a novel in progress with high suspense, plenty of action, and a few twists that will catch you off guard.

It was a warm evening on the tarmac at Macord Air Force Base as Captain Mark Cummins checked his aircraft. The full moon was shining down and giving him enough light so he didn't need a flashlight. Mark preferred to fly at night. The less he had to deal with the brass around the hangar, the better. Several years ago, when just a lieutenant out of flight school, he requested all the night flights and his squadron commander gave him the call sign "Night Owl."

As he finished his inspection of the F-22, Mark headed back into the hanger to complete the rest of his paperwork before he took off. It was only he and his crew chief, Airman John Adams, as he sat down behind the desk to check over the mission brief and the flight plan. John had been his crew chief for two years. They became good friends over coffee and late night chats before and after flights.

"So, sir, where are you headed tonight?"

"Not far this time. Just a little training flight over the San Juan Islands, maybe a few touch-and-go landings at Whidbey. Nothing special. I should only be gone for a few hours."

"I thought you where banned from landing at Whidbey unless it was deemed an emergency by the tower commander? That incident you pulled by buzzing the tower still gets laughs around here."

"I am, but he's on vacation and the new guy doesn't know who I am. It will just add a little excitement to the evening."

After Mark finished his paperwork. he and John headed back out to the aircraft. Mark climbed up into the cockpit and strapped in.

John handed him a helmet. "You be careful tonight, have a good flight, and don't buzz the tower. I don't feel like listening to you getting yelled at again by the commander."

"Thanks for your concern, John. I'll be fine. And I promise–no buzzing towers tonight."

John climbed down and Mark made his final system checks before starting the engines. He had knew the checklist well, but still referred to it. As he taxied out, he recalled the last time he flew the north training mission and the scolding he received from both his commander and the tower commander. To this day, he wasn't sure if Commander Johnson was madder about the incident or about the fact that he dumped an entire pot of hot coffee down the front of a new uniform. Either way, it was a good memory.

Mark continued his taxi and called the tower for clearance. While waiting for them to respond, he thought about what he needed to accomplish while on this mission. Each training flight had a specific number of tasks that needed to be completed or you didn't receive credit for the flight. This flight was fairly easy. He had to do three touch-and-goes; practice bombing an oil refinery, he decided to use the one in Anacortes for that part of the mission; and fly low over the water while avoiding radar. All of the tasks were easy in and of themselves but adding the night flight to the mission increased the difficulty and the level of alertness needed.

After what seemed like an eternity the tower gave clearance. Mark moved onto the runway, easing the throttles forward, he began moving down the runway. Pulling back on the stick with his right hand, he lifted the F-22 into the air as he'd done so many times before.

The night was warm and clear. Visibility was twenty miles in all directions and everything seemed to be going fine. Mark climbed to 20000 feet as instructed by the tower and headed north to the training area. It took him only a few minutes to reach the area. The lights below always amazed him and made him stare in awe. When he flew, Mark felt he was bigger than everything else and the world was full of ants with lights. It was one of the things that he loved about flying.

As he flew over the naval air station on Whidbey Island he contacted the tower to let them know that he was in their air space. "Whidbey Control, this is Air Force 1356 at 20000 feet entering your airspace on training flight. Request vector and clearance for touch-and-go landing."

"Air Force 1356, we have you on radar at 20000. Please descend to flight-level 5, hold in the pattern at twenty miles west, and await authorization."

"Roger, Tower. Descending to flight-level 5 and proceeding to twenty miles west." As Mark made the adjustments and started his decent, he began to feel odd. It was unusual for a training flight to be held in a pattern for touch-and-goes, especially this far out. Something didn't seem right, but he couldn't put his finger on it.

He'd been flying in the pattern for about fifteen minutes, making a ten-mile loop, and getting tired of seeing nothing but ocean below him. Finally, the radio cracked and the controller called, "Air Force 1356, clearance to land granted per the following guidelines..."

Per the following guidelines? Mark thought. He had never been given guidelines for a landing before.

"You are cleared to land on runway 47 east. Winds are out of the southwest at ten. Upon clearing the ground, you are to turn north climbing back to flight-level 5 and upon reaching ten miles, contact control for further instructions. Under no circumstances are you to overfly the base or the tower."

Oh, so that was it. They knew who he was and what he had done. *I guess the commander left instructions for just this instance.*

"Roger, Control. Cleared on runway 47 east. Winds southwest at ten. Will contact tower upon reaching flight-level 5 at ten miles."

Mark began his approach to Whidbey NAS as instructed, running over all the required procedures in his head. He knew the landing checks from the flight manual, but always seemed to forget something minor with every landing.

As Mark lined up with the runway, everything was going smoothly. He was at 2500 feet and two and a half miles from the runway. He looked to his right and saw several boats passing under him. That was something he liked about landing at Whidbey. Most of the time the approach was over water and had great views, especially during the day.

Mark was becoming complacent, as this seemed to be another textbook landing. With the computers on the F-22 it could almost land itself, anyway. He felt a shutter in the aircraft as he passed 2000 feet. Then the aircraft shuttered hard and dropped fast. Mark's eyes quickly moved over the instruments looking for a cause, but he already knew–wind sheer.

Mark mentally ran over everything he knew about handling wind sheer, then took action. In a matter of seconds, he gave the aircraft full power and pulled up on the nose. The aircraft began to level out but he was still dropping at an alarming rate. His eyes darted to the altimeter. He was passing 1000 feet. If he didn't do something fast, he was going to lose the aircraft and, worse, go down with it.

Inside the tower, Commander Alder was watching Mark through binoculars to make sure that he did as he was told. His chief had told him about the incident with the other commander and Alder had decided that it wasn't going to happen to him. He lowered the binoculars and looked at his chief. "What's his altitude?"

"Just passing 2000 feet, sir."

"Good. Right on the glide path."

Commander Alder looked back at the F-22. Suddenly, the aircraft dropped. *What is this fool doing?* he wondered, then realized what was happening. "Chief, it's wind sheer. Clear all aircraft and get the rescue trucks moving in case he can't recover it. Contact him and tell him…no, he has enough to think about. Close the runway to all flights."

"Yes, sir."

Mark was running over everything in his head. He was checking everything else at the same time. He lowered the flaps. The aircraft leveled out and started climbing. His heart was pumping so hard he could feel it in his toes. He finally took a breath, realizing that he had been holding it since the incident started. Expecting that they saw the drop on the radar, he called the tower. "Whidbey Tower, this is Air Force 1356. Encountered wind sheer at two miles and 2000 feet. Have recovered and aircraft seems to be in good order."

"Roger, 1356. You had us jumping down here. Glad you're okay. Be advised that the runway has been closed so turn right to a heading of 270 and proceed to flight-level 5. Call when reaching ten miles. Good job."

"Roger, Tower. Turning right to heading 270 and will call upon reaching 5000 at ten miles. Thanks." Mark finally took a deep breath. That was as close to a crash as he had ever been and closer than he ever wanted to be. He relaxed as he headed out over the San Juan Islands. He was going to ignore the mission for a little while and just fly until he recovered.

He called the tower and requested clearance to fly a large circle until he caught his breath. His request was granted. That was an experience a lot of pilots don't make it out of, and he was sure that someone was watching out for him tonight. Mark began his leisurely holding pattern and was beginning to calm down. He was thinking that when he got back he would request a few days without flying and relax. He looked out the cockpit window. He was flying at 7500 feet and he was watching all the small boats go by under the aircraft. He always liked the way they looked–like toys with him being a giant. He chuckled at the thought.

Mark wanted to fly ever since he was a kid and his dad took him up. His father was taking flying lessons and his instructor agreed to allow Mark to come on one of his training flights. Mark remembered looking down on all the little people and cars driving around. He liked flying high above them. It was one of the better memories he had of his father.

Mark began to make a turn south so as to not enter Canadian airspace and to continue his loop. He was now flying over the Olympic peninsula and heading southwest over the Pacific. Again as he passed over the water he could see several lights from boats.

Mark turned north and headed toward Whidbey NAS to try another landing. One thing his father always said was, "If you fail the first time, always try again."

"Whidbey Tower, this is Air Force Flight 1356 requesting permission to land."

"Air Force 1356, negative on permission to land. Airfield still closed. Stay in your holding pattern and await further instructions."

"Roger, Tower. Continuing pattern." *Oh, well, so much for that.* Mark checked his fuel. He had half a tank. He could fly around for about three more hours before he had to head back to Macord. He continued north and made an easterly turn over the Strait of Juan de Fuca and headed over the San Juan Islands.

Mark looked out to his left, saw the lights of Victoria, Canada, and thought about going there. *You know, that could be a nice place to relax this weekend and take Natalie.* She was his girlfriend of eight months. Mark met Natalie at the base exchange where she worked and they had been going out ever since.

Mark looked back to the front and knew he was going to have to make another turn soon. Out of the corner of his eye he saw a bright flash of some sort. He turned in time to see another one and realized that it was coming from a small ship moving through the islands. The flash seemed to be coming from the foredeck of the ship. Mark wasn't sure what it was. He decided to make a turn and take another look. If the ship was in trouble he could radio the tower and let them know. As he leveled out and was heading back toward the ship he saw another bright light, this one was steady and a yellowish color. The light was pointed west and didn't seem to be dispersing with distance. It was one long and steady beam.

Mark pushed the call button to hail the Whidbey tower and let them know about the strange light, when the light suddenly swung around and pointed right at him. Mark immediately closed his eyes and turned his aircraft on instinct to get away from the light. Mark opened his eyes after he had turned a little. He looked through several dark spots caused by the blinding light, closed his eyes, and rubbed them quickly. Opening them again he found some of the spots were gone, but the light seemed to still be pointed at his aircraft. He pushed the radio button again. "Whidbey Tower, this is Air Force 1356 declaring an emergency."

Inside the Whidbey Tower, Commander Alder just received his evening cup of coffee and was taking a sip of it when the emergency call came in. He never had to deal with an actual emergency and this would be his second in the same night with the same pilot. As he thought about that he realized that he was dribbling the coffee down the front of his new uniform, but for now he didn't care.

"Roger, 1356. This is Whidbey Tower. Declare your emergency."

"Tower, there is a ship of some sorts pointing a light at my aircraft..."

Both men in the tower looked at each other, obviously wondering why that would be an emergency.

"The light is very bright and blinded me temporarily. The light is still pointed at my aircraft, and the aircraft is beginning to shutter."

Commander Alder looked at the chief with a seriously puzzled look on his face. *How could a light cause an emergency?* He knew that this pilot was sometimes a joker but he knew the rules and knew he could and would lose his license if he declared a false emergency.

"Tower, do you read me?"

"Roger, 1356. What are your intentions?"

Mark began to think. What *were* his intentions? *Land? Fly? Run? Ditch?* He didn't know. He wasn't sure what to do. The light was still pointed at his aircraft and the aircraft was still shaking.

"Tower, intentions unsure, aircraft vibrating and getting worse..."

Just then Mark heard a load bang. He looked out his right side to see the outer half of the wing break free and fall away.

"Mayday. Mayday. Lost outer right wing. Vibrating worse. Am punching out..."

Commander Alder looked at his chief in disbelief. "Mark that position and notify the search and rescue chief."

"Yes, sir. Sir, how are you going to write this up? It almost sounds too weird to be true."

"I know, Chief. Get the tape on this. I'll need it to back up my report, and if this guy pulled one over on me I will have him court-martialed."

"Yes, Sir. But I don't think he was making it up, sir. I've been here for six years, Sir, and that's the most frightened I've ever heard someone over the radio." As the chief finished his sentence, he looked out the tower window behind the commander. "Sir, look."

Commander Alder turned around. Over the top of the trees he saw a beam of light shooting off into the night sky.

"You know, Chief, if I didn't see it, I wouldn't believe it."

"Sir, me neither."

Lightwave,
Chapter 6

Neal opened the door to the office allowing Steven to enter. The office was situated in the corner of the building. *It's nicely furnished,* thought Steven, *with a seating area on one side and a large oak desk by the windows.* The walls were covered with a light birch paneling but what Steven noticed right off were the wolf prints and photos on all the walls of the office. Steven immediately gravitated toward the photo over the couch, which was the largest in the room. It depicted two wolves jumping over a fallen tree in winter. Steven moved around the room studying each photo and print in the room, before finally falling into his chair behind his desk. Turning in his chair, Steven momentarily marveled at the view. The immense grounds with the Potomac River as a backdrop were picturesque.

"Does the king approve of his castle?" Neal inquired dropping into a seat on the other side of the desk.

"Very funny." Steven replied. "I bet it was you who informed them I have a thing for wolves."

"Actually, no. When Dan was doing a background check on you he spoke to your mother, and she told him. She was also the one who sent some of the photos including the big one over the couch. I'll have to admit, she has good taste in photos."

"Only because I mentioned that photo to her about five hundred times. I think she got it because she was tired of me complaining I couldn't afford it."

"Give your mom some credit. I think it was nice of her to send it. Consider it a 'welcome to your new job' gift."

"True, she was pleased when I got this job. But I think she bought the photo because I nagged her so many times about it."

"You're hopeless."

"Why, thank you."

They both started to chuckle as Neal got up and looked at his watch. I'm going to get some paper work done in my office before my inbox is as stacked up as yours."

"Go ahead. I'm going to call Trent. Then go over everything we have and see if we missed anything."

"Okay, if you need me, I'll be across the hall."

Neal headed for the door, but stopped just before opening it. "By the way, do you want me to tell everyone there'll be a meeting later?"

"No. I'll let them know. I told Dan we were going to have one but I am not so sure we need one today. I might wait 'til tomorrow."

When Neal left, it was the first time all day Steven had a chance to relax. Turning toward the window, Steven enjoyed the picturesque view and considered the events of the day. Going from college student to government agent was overwhelming.

Checking the time, Steven turned back to his desk and calculated the change from East Coast time to West Coast time. Picking up the phone, he dialed the number for Trent's Seattle studio.

"Crypto," said a nice, but somewhat authoritative, female voice.

"All Steven can think to say was "Uh...hello."

"Can I help you?" she asked with more than a little agitation in her voice.

"Yes I was trying to make an outside call."

Cutting him off, she said curtly, "Dial nine, then the number."

Steven thanked her and heard her complain about newbies as she hung up the phone. That thought brought a smile to Stevens face remembering all the newbies he had to train while in the army. Steven dialed nine and Trent's number.

Three thousand miles away, Trent was settling into a lunch of ham and cheese on rye with a side of potato salad and a big glass of cola. He just ended a morning session with an upstart band that would do better to find day jobs than to try and make the demo he was recording for them. Trent's Seattle studio was state of the art and had all the bells and whistles of the major studios in LA and Nashville. He received an inherence when his grandmother died and put most of it into starting a music studio, which was his love and passion. Answering the phone on the first ring, he was greeted with, "Trent, put down that sandwich and get back to work."

"Steve, my man, how are the nightlife and the women in the other Washington?" He leaned back in his chair.

"Not bad, I guess. I haven't had much time to explore either. How are things in the land of endless rain?"

"Same old, same old. Same rain, different day. New band, same bad sound. I just don't get why some of these guys think they sound like some big superstar after singing in the shower a few times."

"I know what you mean. Some of the club bands I've heard recently could use a new vocal singer at a minimum. But that's what you're supposed to do–make them sound like million-dollar bands."

"Fixing that solo tape for you was harder than trying to make my cat sing like Elvis."

"Hey I wasn't that bad," Steven retorted

"Let's just say after I played that tape the first time, I had to buy a new plant because the one I had died."

"Very funny," Steven said.

On the other end of the line Steven can hear the distinctive squeaks of Trent's chair as he twisted back and forth. "I know that you didn't call to reminisce about your beautiful singing voice?"

"Your right Trent. I'm calling in a favor"

"Well, here is a first, Steven Clark needing my help," Trent said sarcastically. "So what is it that you need? A better singing voice for the president?"

"I wish it was that easy." Steven said with a solemn tone. "I need you to analyze a couple of tapes."

Trent voice sounded serious, "So what is on these tapes?"

"It's the recordings from an F-22 that went down in the San Juans yesterday."

"I didn't hear about any planes going down."

"And you won't either. It is being kept out of the press. I have to tell you this is all highly sensitive material. You can't share it with anyone."

"Steven." Trent sighed before continuing, "You know you can trust me, but I don't understand why you are sending it to me. Isn't that what the military has labs to do?"

"I've listened to the tapes but I know something just doesn't seem right. I can't put my finger on it, but I want a non-conformist's opinion."

"So you want me to check them for abnormalities?" Trent asked.

"To tell you the truth I'm not sure. Just perform your magic and let me know if you find anything odd."

The line was silent for several moments before Trent finally spoke, "Give me a number I can reach you at." Steven gave him several numbers including his home phone before Trent hung up the phone. Trent leaned back in his chair and considered the unusual conversation he just had. This was the first time Steven had asked for his assistance on something other than embellishing his karaoke voice. What really bothered him was the fact that Steven was coming straight to him and not trusting the government labs to do their job. Shaking his head clear of that thought, he leaned forward to finish his lunch.

Steven finished the call with Trent and spent the next five minutes looking for the FIST phone directory. After several more minutes of looking through the directory, he found the number he wanted and dialed it. When the senior mail clerk answered the call, Steven explained about the tapes and where they must go, emphasizing the need for them to be there quickly. The clerk said he understood and it should be no problem. Before hanging up, the clerk told Steven he would send someone to get the package.

Leaning forward on his desk, Steven pondered the stack of papers in his inbox. He grabbed several off the top and began to leaf through them. Most of the folders contained paperwork he needed to fill out for various departments. Deciding the paperwork could wait, he sorted the stack and placed it to the side.

Steven was considering which files to take home when there was a knock at his office door. The door opened. A young man entered the office and proceeded toward the desk. Introducing himself as the mail clerk, he said he was sent to pick up a package. The phone rang before Steven could hand him the package. Steven motioned for the clerk to wait while he answered the phone.

"Steven," he said.

"Is this Steven Clark, Special Team Leader of FIST?"

Steven considered the unusually formal question as he handed the tapes to the clerk and began looking for a piece of paper to write down the address to Trent's studio.

"Yes," he responded.

The person on the other end of the line immediately hung up the phone. Steven was surprised at the man's rudeness. He set his phone back in its cradle and proceeded to write out the address for Trent's studio.

Steven heard glass breaking. He turned and saw where a single bullet penetrated the window. Pain surged through his left shoulder as the bullet tore through his shirt and creased the skin, sending blood down his arm. He grabbed for his shoulder. A motion in front of him caught his attention. Steven looked up at the mail clerk standing at his desk. The clerk's facial expression showed extreme pain, then fear, as he reached for the bloody spot forming on the side of his neck. Steven watched as the mail clerk's eyes rolled back in his head and he slumped to the floor in a growing pool of blood.

CAROL NORTH

Someone once said that writers aren't made, they spring up like weeds between cracks in sidewalks. That aptly describes Carol North's journey as a writer beginning when she was five years old. For years at a time, the little weed was trampled and would hide beneath the concrete sidewalk where the roots survived and grew stronger. Then the little weed would reappear.

For more than 20 years, North has worked throughout the continental United States as a freelance business and technical writer. her works include *Introduction to Programming Robots,* "Software Specifications for Global System Mobile Communication/General Packet Radio Service (GSM/GPRS)," and *Total Quality Management: A Course Development Guide.*

North's short fiction has been published in literary journals and ezines. Two of her romance novels, *Love's Reflection* and *Eternally His,* are being published in 2008-2009 by Awe-Struck E-Books and Earthling Press.

A founding member of the Savannah Writers Group, North lives in Savannah, Georgia with her Shih Tzu, Little Miss. She has four grown children (who all turned out great) and a gaggle of grandchildren.

She'd be delighted to hear from you: carol-north@comcast.net.

Her websites are carolnorth.com and carol-north.com.

Love's Reflection,
Chapter One

Love's Reflection is published by Awe-Struck E-Books in electronic format and by Earthling Press in print.

Love's Reflection is a sci-fi romance about Dr. Cort Hirsch, a love-besotted scientist who creates his robot, Alpha, in the physical image of the unattainable love of his life, Zoe Parker, film superstar.

"She looks real."

"Of course, she does." Dr. Cort Hirsch looked down on the balding head of his lab assistant, Robert Martin. The professor removed his eyeglasses and wiped the thick lenses with a corner of his lab coat. "I took great pains to make her anatomically correct." He breathed deeply, replaced the glasses, and touched the edge of the table. The steel felt cold, lifeless, like his creation. And it felt hard, like the heart of the woman he loved. He peered through the glass dome covering the table. *Soon I will know if I have given her life...such as it is.*

Cort walked to a computer. His hands trembled slightly as he entered a code and watched the glass dome rise above the table and reveal a feminine figure. *She looks peacefully asleep, so lifelike,* he thought, *so unlike the miles of wire, hundreds of chips, and myriad pieces of steel and plastic I used to create her.*

He almost smiled when he recalled agonizing for an entire evening over the style, size, and price of her clothing. Now she lay before him fashionably attired in a flower-print blouse and crisp, new jeans. To make certain she would look first-rate when activated, he took the jeans to the cleaners and had them press in center creases. Cort suppressed a nervous laugh when he noticed the toes of her white running shoes stuck straight up from the table and were three inches taller than her reclining body.

"She's beautiful." Robert bent over her face. "And 'anatomically correct,' you say. Does that mean she has everything a real woman has? Even ah...ah...you-know-what?"

"Yes, even a sexual organ." Cort nodded briskly causing his pony tail to flap, hit him in the chin, then settle heavily on his right shoulder. He clenched his teeth anticipating the likely next question from Robert and decided his reason for de-sexing the robot was something he would not share with his assistant, or with anyone else.

"Will it work?"

"Of course it will work. It is fully functioning, but she will not use it because sex is programmed out of her. The word, the concept has been deleted from every piece of information in her database."

Robert looked up. "Why'd you do that?"

Cort narrowed his eyes as he stared into Robert's face. "Because I wanted to."

"Okay." Obviously not wanting to push the subject, Robert turned back to the robot. "So she's almost the perfect woman."

"She *is* perfect. Low-maintenance and programmed to do everything I say. She will gratefully cook and clean and be my secretary twenty-four hours a day, seven days a week because she doesn't need sleep or food or expensive clothes and jewelry." Cort raised his chin in the pompous way he did for his university students. Good practice since his sabbatical would be over in only nine weeks and he'd become lax in expressing himself in academic ways. He looked at Robert beneath lowered lids. "I programmed 'grateful' into her." Cort grabbed Robert's skinny shoulder and squeezed.

"Ouch." Robert's eyes were moist with tears. "What's that for?"

"You signed the nondisclosure agreement. I assume you've read it and know if you divulge anything about what you are about to see, you will be driven to the poor house and you will never again work in a scientific field."

"Yes, I understand everything. I had an attorney look it over before I signed it." Robert wiggled his shoulder as if to toss off Cort's grip. "You can let go now."

"Not yet. There is one more consideration." Cort squeezed harder.

"What's that?" Robert's eyes grew wider and drops of sweat appeared at the edge of his receding hairline.

"If you break our agreement, I will have to kill you. First, I will tear your head off your shoulders, then I will grind up your privates and feed them to the dogs." Cort tightened his bicep until the arm of his lab coat looked about to split.

Robert dropped his hand to his crotch. "You're kidding, aren't you? I mean, you don't have dogs, so you're kidding."

"I do not *kid*. I will *buy dogs*, big, vicious dogs." Cort released Robert's shoulder and pulled a transceiver from his pocket. He ran his thumb over the keys taking care not to apply pressure. Tremors of anticipation undulated up and down his backbone, an unwanted reaction for the man who prided himself on the ability to control his emotional responses. Emotion interfered with the optimal use of his intellect and diminished his physical strength. *Calm down. Release the emotion,* he told himself. *Release the emotion.* Cort took a deep breath and slowly let it out.

Robert turned away from the robot and toward the device in Cort's hand. "What's that? It looks like a miniature computer."

"It's a transceiver with which I can activate and control the robot. I send commands and receive her operating information. Inside her is a transceiver so miniaturized that it is no larger than the vitamin pill you take every morning."

"Thanks for reminding me." Robert reached into a pocket on his lab coat, pulled out a pink pill, popped it into his mouth, and swallowed.

Cort waited until Robert's Adam's apple stopped bobbing. "She also has a GPS tracking and data logging system with remote downloading capabilities. I'll know her every move, not that I'll need to because she will never leave this facility. The farthest she will travel is upstairs to the observation deck for a recharge of her solar batteries."

"She runs on sunlight?"

"That is just one of her energy sources. She contains a redundant, fail-safe system and is internally rechargeable." *And,* he couldn't tell Robert this, *duplicates of all her parts and programs are stored in an area to which only I have access, and knowledge of. She is fail-safe.* Cort sighed.

Robert reached out to the robot and stopped, then looked up at Cort. "Can I touch her?"

Touch her? Cort took off his eyeglasses and feigned interest in wiping them slowly with the corner of his lab coat. That was something he hadn't considered–that others might touch Alpha. He fought back a shudder. Even the thought of anyone else touching her felt like a violation of their relationship. Until this very moment no one but he had ever touched her. He had let Robert fetch and carry materials for her creation and do grunt work, but she was covered with a sheet and the dome was down except when Cort was alone with her. She had belonged exclusively to him, but soon her existence, and his creative genius, would need to be announced to the world. He sighed. "Might as well. She has to get used to the dirty world."

Robert looked startled. "But I washed before I came in here."

"I didn't mean you're dirty, I meant 'dirty' as in any place but this 'clean' room and any touch but mine." Cort waved his hand toward the robot. "Go ahead, touch her."

Cort watched as Robert reached forward and pushed on her cheek with the tip of his finger. Cort flinched. *That seemed a bit rough,* he thought, and opened his mouth to protest but by then Robert had removed his finger.

"Cold, but soft." Robert stroked her cheek and turned to Cort. "It feels just like a baby's skin."

"Yes, and it will never grow old. It's taken me twelve years to perfect that artificial skin. I was a graduate student when I began. The skin is in two layers. The lower, dermis layer is constructed to be a type of scaffold for the upper layer, and the skin has a blood supply. Not real blood, of course. It's a synthetic." Cort caressed the robot's forehead. "Developing her skin is one of the crowning achievements of my career." He felt something, an unrecognizable emotion, for his creation. *Interesting.* Instead of pushing away the feeling he allowed it to flow as he arranged the robot's long, flaming red hair around her face and over the small white pillow supporting her neck. *Is this,* he wondered, *how a pet owner feels about his dog or cat?*

Robert bent over the robot. His gaze was directed at her face. "She looks kind of like that movie star —"

"Never mind that. It is time, Robert. It is time to initialize her." Cort waved toward a computer. "I'll program her via my transceiver and you will confirm the displayed commands." Cort could easily see the giant computer monitor screen from any place in the room and needed Robert's confirmation only to free himself so he could focus totally on the robot.

"Yes, Sir." Robert turned toward the monitor.

Cort pressed several keys on the transceiver. "Battery and solar energy levels–Full."

Robert pointed to a dial displayed on the monitor. "Roger."

"Radio frequency transceiver–On."

"Roger."

Cort saw a graph display an undulating wave. He felt encouragement then told himself it was far too early to be optimistic. On the graph, a second wave joined the first. The robot could now receive commands and send responses. He pressed several buttons on the transceiver. "GPS tracking and data logging–On.

"Roger."

Cort looked at the monitor and read a stream of binary math made up of ones and zeros. *So far, so good.* Again he told himself it was too early to feel optimism.

"Three-D and sonar vision system–On."

"Roger."

Cort saw the robot's eyes open, and turned to the monitor. A grid appeared on the screen. It showed a view of the raised glass dome and ceiling above. Cort's heart thumped. *She can see.* He felt transfixed by the vision grid. *My robot and I are seeing identical images. We are in communion.*

Robert turned toward Cort. "Sir, do you have other commands?"

"Yes. Sorry for the delay. I was deciding on a sequence." Cort pressed several buttons. "Object recognition and avoidance technology–On."

"Roger."

"Olfactory and chemical sensory simulation–On." Cort did not have great expectations for the success of this component of his robot. He had lined her nose with sensors designed to identify odor components on the fly, but smell was perhaps the most difficult of the human senses to emulate and was necessary to having a sense of taste. *Thus far,* thought Cort, *artificial olfactory technology has been primitive. If Alpha is able to actually smell, it will be one of my finest accomplishments.*

"Roger."

"Breathing simulator–On." This system would cause her diaphragm to rise and fall with an oxygen intake and output through her nose. It had no purpose except deception. It was there to make Alpha appear human.

"Roger."

"Pump–On." The pump was a copy of a human heart and caused artificial blood to course through artificial veins and arteries. In addition to being deceptive, the pumping system had a practical use. It cleansed her entire system.

"Roger."

Cort pressed his index and middle fingers against Alpha's neck. Yes, there was a pulse. He laid the transceiver on the lab table and with the other hand he pressed his index and middle fingers against his neck. *My God, we're beating in sync. Amazing coincidence.* He began counting the beats in their pulses. *One...two...three –*

"Sir, do you have more commands for me?"

Cort picked up the transceiver. "Sorry, Robert. I was lost in thought. Audio-video modulator–On."

"Roger."

Cort heard what seemed to be an echo, but was actually the robot's audio. She could now hear and coordinate sound with vision. He decreased the volume. "Recorder–On."

"Roger."

I will not know if the next five functions are working correctly until I have observed her in the field, Cort thought, then pressed another button on the transceiver. "Emotional memory response–On."

"Roger."

Cort watched a blinking red light become a steady green light. "Sensory memory response–On."

"Roger."

"Behavioral conditioning–On."

"Roger."

"Internally directed movement–On."

"Roger."

The next function was akin to free will in a human. Her ability to use it was a long shot at best. Cort told himself to reserve judgment. He took a deep breath and said, "Artificial intelligence with deductive reasoning module–On."

"Roger."

Cort hesitated before entering the ultimate command into the transceiver. This was the command that would expose his success or failure. This was the command that would synchronize all the robot's separate systems. This command would reveal the value of devoting himself to twelve years of near-solitary existence, the wisdom of spending a large portion of his inheritance, the viability of his plans to develop and market a race of service robots. He pressed the key. "Robot–On."

"Roger. Looks like all systems are go, Sir." Robert left the computer and stood next to Cort.

The robot's eyelids flickered, closed, and re-opened. Her face animated, softened, smiled. She looked directly at Cort. "Hello, my name is 'Alpha.'"

Cort stared at her face and allowed himself to feel some excitement. *She is perfect. The eyes are polished amber with fossil deposits perfectly emulating the pupils in human eyes. They are worth the years of searching for just the right stones. The ivory skin is soft and luminous. The lips are sensually full with their synthetic nerve endings poised on throbbing. The cheekbones are high-set and perfectly symmetrical. The hair is a fiery, passionate red. I have recreated Zoe Parker, to delight my eyes, to forever serve me.* Thrice Cort had to tell himself to release the emotion before he allowed himself to speak, "Hello Alpha, my name is 'Cort. Cort Hirsch.'"

"Cort Hirsch." The robot paused. "Dr. Cort Hirsch; six feet, four inches; muscular build; one hundred ninety pounds; blond hair, straight, thick, long; ice-blue eyes; broad forehead; jaw-line strong."

Cort noticed Alpha's eyes took on a faraway, almost sweet, look while she was searching her database for his description. He found her innocence kind of sexy and it made her seem deceptively human. "Very good, Alpha." He placed himself directly in her line of sight. "Is there anything more you would like to say about me?"

The robot became still. Her amber eyes rolled upward until the pupils disappeared behind eyelids. *Hmmm. I'll have to fix that. Can't have her eyeballs rolling around.* He held his breath wondering what was going on inside his robot. Her eyes repositioned.

"Hello, Cort. I am grateful to you for creating me."

Whew. Obviously her emotional memory response programming kicked in and simulated thankful appreciation and obedience. *And her voice is perfect.* The audio simulator had recreated Zoe's voice from the recordings in Alpha's database. "Thank you, Z–, Alpha." For a moment he felt as if he was looking into Zoe's eyes. Of all the women who rejected him in high school and college and later, of all the women who preferred jocks to a nerd with thick glasses, she had hurt him the most.

Zoe Parker's rejection was public. They met at a "People in the News" award dinner. He received the "Scientist of the Year" award and Zoe won "Entertainer of the Year." He came to her table to offer congratulations. She looked him up and down and turned away without a word. He would have been less hurt had she said, "Go to hell" or "Get lost, buster." Instead she treated him as not even good enough to merit a response from her famous vocal cords. It was because of her rejection that he decided to create the robot he was building in Zoe's image. But that was all in the past. Now he was the rejecter by denying his creation, Zoe's twin, her sexuality. "Alpha, can you sit up?"

Alpha lifted the upper half of her body, twisted to the side, and dropped her legs off the edge of the table. "Yes, I can sit up."

"Good. That was a very smooth movement. The math is correct, at least that related to sitting." Cort held out his hand. "Extend your left arm and shake my hand with your left hand."

Alpha obeyed Cort's command.

"Good, it moved well. Now let go of my hand, extend your right arm and shake my hand with your right hand." *Not good,* he thought. *The elbow is extending in increments instead of in a smooth motion.*

"Sir, her elbow looks broken," said Robert.

"Yes, I see that the right elbow has a slight jerkiness. I will fix that, and her eyeballs." Cort ran to the computer and entered several commands. Then, using the remote transceiver, he rotated her right elbow and moved her eyes. "Good. No, better than good. She is perfect." He turned to Robert who looked wide-eyed and slack-jawed and was totally silent. *My assistant is impressed, as he should be,* thought Cort. "What do you think?"

"I'm amazed. She is everything you told me she would be, and more. If I didn't know she's a robot, I'd think she was a human being." Robert shook his head.

Alpha's eyes moved. "Robot. Human being."

Cort nodded and looked at Alpha. "Yes, Alpha. Robot. Human being." He turned to Robert. "She can learn by mimicking. She repeated your words; that's a beginning. And there's more, much more. She's programmed to question and use deductive reasoning to make decisions. Her database contains dictionaries, encyclopedias, literature, textbooks, cookbooks, magazines, catalogs, recordings of television programs and films, emotional memories. It would take a human being many lifetimes to absorb all the knowledge she contains. Of course, I have edited the material to make certain she fulfills the purpose for which she was created, to be my service robot and the mother of a race of service robots."

"Sir, thank you for letting me observe this momentous event," said Robert, his gaze never left Alpha's direction and his sweaty, balding head bobbed up and down.

"That it is, a momentous event, and it is being filmed by the overhead surveillance cameras." Cort frowned. "Perhaps, I should be taking some close-ups. My camcorder is upstairs. I will get it." He looked directly at his robot. "Alpha, *don't* move."

"Yes," she replied. "You are going to the second floor of Taurus. The facility is built within a secluded California foothill. Only the observation deck and its solar-system-scanning telescope are above ground level. Access to the below-ground floors is through a hidden elevator and protected by electronic surveillance and recognition devices. Dr. Hirsch controls the codes that permit or deny entry. His living quarters are on the first below-ground floor. The laboratory is on the second floor, storage on the third, and..." The robot stopped in mid-sentence. "And there are only three floors below ground. Presently, we are in the laboratory on the second floor. Is this correct?"

Cort nodded. "Yes, your database contains the correct information. Thank you for the tour, Alpha." He turned toward the door. "I will return shortly."

The door had hardly closed behind Cort when Robert approached Alpha. She observed him circling the steel table where she sat and read his emotional energy waves. He was not a threat. Alpha turned her attention away from Robert. "Don't move," she said and scanned her database. "Move...To change the place or position of." She moved her arm and wiggled her fingers. "Move."

Robert grinned at Alpha. "So you got the 'move' part, but not the 'don't' part. You're more a self-directed female than Cort realizes."

"I am female?" Alpha scanned her database. "Female...The basic term applied to members of the gender that is biologically distinguished from the male gender. Who are you?" she asked.

"I'm Robert, Robert Martin. I help Cort in the laboratory. And it's polite to face someone when you're speaking to them."

"Yes." Alpha turned in the direction of Robert's voice. Her object recognition system recorded his image: five foot, eight inches; One hundred thirty-five pounds; slender build; dark brown hair; receding hairline; hazel eyes; thin face. She added his name to the file. "Are you female?"

"No, I'm male."

"Is my creator female?"

"No, Cort's a male too."

"A male is the basic term applied to members of the gender that is biologically distinguished from the female gender."

"Yeah, you've got it." Robert nodded his head and smiled. "You even sound like Cort."

"No, I do not sound like Cort. Our voice modulation is not the same."

Robert threw his head back and laughed. "You just did it again. You sound like Cort. No, not *sound like*. You *express* yourself just like Cort. Yes, that's it. You express yourself just like..." Robert looked away and mumbled. "What am I doing trying to explain myself to a robot?" He shook his head.

The word "robot" triggered Alpha's database. She received a reminder about a note she had recorded earlier: *Scan for "human being." Scan for "robot."* She scanned. *Human being...Of, belonging to, or typical of mankind, the human race. Robot...Any manlike mechanical being; built to do manual work for human beings.*

Robert turned back to Alpha. "Sorry about that, Alpha. That was impolite of me."

"Yes, you are impolite." She zoomed her vision and studied Robert. She zoomed back and forth at resolutions so high she could count the pores on his nose. She directed her vision at her hand and found she also had pores. Alpha looked up. "Is Robert a human being? Or are you a robot?"

"I'm a human being."

"Is Cort a human being?

"Yes he is."

"Is Alpha a human being?" She watched Robert drop his head and appear to be studying the floor. She analyzed the materials in the floor: white contamination-control, slip-resistant epoxy coating over preformed concrete. A typical installation. She did not know why Robert was staring at the floor. She scanned him. *Scan results: The subject shows confusion and embarrassment.* Alpha recorded Robert's lack of response to her question, and timed him. It took a full half-minute before he answered.

"No, Alpha, you're a robot."

"I am a mechanical being built to perform manual work for humans?"

Robert again looked at the floor. "You should ask Cort questions like that, not me."

Alpha recorded a note to ask Cort questions about herself.

Hiss. Hiss. Cort paused at the entrance to the lab and waited while electronic recognition scanners examined him. The door opened. He walked to the table where Alpha sat, then turned toward Robert. "I have the camcorder. Did anything happen while I was gone?"

Robert's face was expressionless. "Nothing."

Cort turned his attention to the robot. "Alpha, I grant you permission to move as required. Stand, Alpha."

Alpha created the movements related to standing.

"Wow..." Robert let out a long, low whistle. "She's got perfect proportions." He grinned. "Bet you had fun molding her."

Cort scowled. "That's crude, Robert. In the interest of science, and for no other reason, I created a perfect feminine form." His eyesight blurred as he said in a hoarse whisper, "The Turing Test, I want her to pass the Turing Test." This was his goal, no, his passion since the moment Alpha was conceived in his mind. It was his driving force for the past twelve years. All else was transitory. Alpha and the developments in robotics she represented were forever.

"The Turing Test?" There was a hint of disbelief in Robert's tone.

Robert's tone annoyed Cort. Of course, his robot would ultimately pass the Turing Test. That goal, that belief had carried the scientist through twelve years of hardship and he could not let a mere assistant shake his confidence. He clenched his jaw, then responded to Robert's skepticism. "Yes, Robert. The great Alan Turing set forth the condition to prove artificial intelligence. He said, 'If the machine could successfully pretend to be human to a knowledgeable observer, then you certainly should consider it intelligent.' My robot will pass the Turing Test."

"Yes, Sir. If you say so, Sir." Robert still didn't look convinced. "Okay, so she'll pass the Turing Test, but aren't you worried she might run amuck and hurt someone? I mean, it's not like she's got moral values or religion."

"But she does have moral values. I programmed them myself at the same time I added Isaac Asimov's Three Laws of Robotics to her database. She is programmed to never hurt a human being. In fact, she would sacrifice herself to protect a human."

Robert's head bobbed up and down. "I feel better knowing that, Sir. I'm sorry for having doubted your efficiency." He dropped his head in a contrite pose.

"Forget it, Robert. It was a natural concern." Cort waved his hand at Alpha. "Move forward three steps."

Alpha took three steps forward.

Cort slowly circled his robot. "What do you think, Robert, could she pass for human? I mean pass *physically* for a human. Take a look." He stepped out of the way.

Robert walked around Alpha. "Yeah, she looks like a human, but..." He stopped at the front of the robot. "Sir, I don't mean to criticize. Her clothes don't fit right. The blouse is too tight and her breasts are half exposed. Not that I mind looking at them myself, but if an outsider came to the observation tower and saw her recharging her solar batteries they might get the wrong idea... If you know what I mean. How about we take her to DeepDiscount and get her some clothes that fit?"

Cort studied Alpha's chest while considering Robert's comments. Far too much cleavage was showing. "You are correct in your observations. We don't want to arouse any questions, not yet. We need to complete the testing cycle before we announce to the press."

"The jeans are too big. They're ready to fall off," Robert pointed at Alpha's legs. "And it's not cool to have center creases in your jeans. Where did you get them?"

Cort felt his cheeks burn. How was he supposed to know what was "cool"? He hardly ever went out and when he did, it was not with the cool crowd. He socialized with persons like himself–scientists, intellectuals. "I shopped for her clothes on the Internet. I don't know anything about women's sizes so I guessed."

"Internet," said Alpha. "An extensive computer network made up of thousands of other, smaller business, academic, and governmental networks connected through phone lines, cables, or wireless devices. My wireless is off." Alpha's voice volume dropped. "My wireless–On."

Robert does have a valid point about her attire. Cort started to turn toward Robert, and realized he was being rude to Alpha and hadn't paid much attention to what she said. *Oh, I must acknowledge her comment or she will learn that her observations are not important.* "Very good, Alpha. You are scanning well." He turned toward Robert. "You were saying?"

"With all due respect, Sir." Robert dropped his head in that submissive posture Cort hated. It meant he disagreed with his boss. "You don't know much about style either. The blouse is ugly. It's so bright, I feel like putting my sunglasses on. And her shoes are so big, *you* could fit in them. I'm afraid she'll trip when she tries to walk farther than a few steps. Maybe you should take her shopping so she can try on clothes before you buy them. There's a DeepDiscount store nearby and their stuff doesn't cost a lot."

Cort studied Alpha, took a deep breath, and nodded. "Yes, yes, you are correct in your observations. I don't know anything about women's shoes so I bought her men's shoes. Running shoes all look the same. I didn't realize they're sized differently." He removed his eyeglasses and wiped the lenses on his lab coat. "It is too soon to take her shopping. For now she can wear one of my shirts." Cort replaced his eyeglasses, faced the robot, and pointed at her feet. "Alpha, remove the shoes."

She lifted her right leg, pointed her toes to the floor, and the shoe fell off. She repeated the process with the left leg and produced the same result. "They are off," she said.

What a dilemma, thought Cort as he picked up the shoes and slid them under the lab table. *She's not even real, hasn't been turned on for more than an hour, and is already creating a typical female problem. I have heard it all before–she has nothing to wear.*

"I have nothing to wear to the studio." Zoe Parker walked through her bedroom stopping to sniff the vase of red roses on her dresser. One bloom in the center of the bouquet caught her eye. "Lucille," she yelled, and removed the rose from the bunch.

"Yes, Miss Parker."

"Oh," said Zoe, startled by the quick response of her maid. Lucille must have been following behind, but the woman was so short and nondescript it was easy to overlook her. Zoe turned. "Did you bring in the roses?"

"Yes, Miss Parker." Lucille nodded.

"Lucille, what color is my hair?"

A crease appeared in the maid's forehead. "Red, Miss Parker."

Zoe held the rose against her hair. "And what color is this rose?"

Lucille's hand flew to her mouth. Her shoulders slumped. "Oh, it's orange. I'm so sorry, Miss Parker. I don't know how I missed it."

"Lucille, you are—" Zoe stopped herself in mid-sentence. Should she fire Lucille? She'd fired maids for less, but Lucille took good care of her wardrobe. Besides, the black-haired, pale-faced maid coordinated with the color scheme and was attractive enough not to offend Zoe's eyes but not so pretty that she could offer competition. Zoe decided to give Lucille a second chance.

"Yes, Miss Parker." Lucille's eyes and mouth were wide open.

It pleased Zoe to see the fear-stricken look on her maid's face. She smiled and arched an eyebrow. "We'll go through this once more, Lucille. I expect you to remember and make no more mistakes. *Everything* in my house is black or white except the roses are red and *must* match my hair color. Oh, and I allow an occasional accent of silver, solid sterling silver, *never* plate. There is only one item in my entire house that breaks the rules, my gold Oscar."

"Yes, Miss Parker." Lucille nodded. "I promise to remember." She nodded again.

"Those rules apply to my wardrobe too." The reasoning behind the rules was that people should be attracted by her face and body, not by the color of her clothing, but she couldn't tell her maid that. "Everything in my entire wardrobe is either black or white. The only color is the red of my hair." Zoe tossed her head to fluff her red curls and emphasize her statement. "And the silver for my home is replaced by platinum and diamonds on my body." She held out her right hand and moved it so the diamonds caught light and sent out blue-white flashes that reminded her of the Fourth of July sparklers she had as a child.

"Yes, Miss Parker, I do remember that."

"Good. Now go on and finish whatever you were doing, then meet me in the closet in five minutes."

Lucille looked at her watch. "Yes, Miss Parker."

After Lucille left the bedroom, Zoe entered the closet, her "dark womb," the one place where she could truly relax. So far, the morning had been difficult, which was usually the case when Frank negotiated her next film. Her gaze caressed the black cabinets hugging the walls from floor to ceiling and corner to corner. She felt tension flow off her forehead, her neck, her shoulders as she more deeply penetrated the dark womb.

Zoe paced through the closet, stopping now and again to slide open a door, tug a sleeve, and tap her foot in dismissal. Soon she felt Lucille's presence at her back and turned. "Lucille, I have nothing suitable to wear to the studio." Zoe caressed the silk robe clinging to her body. "I certainly can't wear this." She smiled at her little joke and looked at Lucille.

Lucille laughed.

"And I've already worn everything once." Zoe noticed the price tag hanging from a black satin blouse. "Umm...almost everything." Zoe expressed a deep sigh, turned to a floor-to-ceiling shoe cabinet, and pulled a pair of white sandals from a glass drawer. "What was I thinking? These heels are too low." She dropped the shoes and heard two carpet-muffled *thuds* when they hit the floor.

Lucille retrieved the shoes and replaced them in the drawer.

"I must shop." Zoe sucked a strand of hair that had fallen across her face, released the strand, tossed her head, and slid into the nearby chaise lounge. She closed her eyes and stroked the silken white fabric of the chaise. *No one understands how hard it is to maintain my image. I can never relax. I have to always look my best. Sometimes I feel like running away to a place where I can wear jeans and go without makeup.* Zoe sighed.

But if there was no makeup, there probably wouldn't be any plastic surgeons either. What an ugly life that would be. Zoe straightened her shoulders and opened her eyes. She saw Lucille standing at attention at the foot of the chaise. "Tell Frank I want him here–now."

Soon Frank was in the closet and standing dutifully at the foot of Zoe's recliner. "Lucille, said you want to shop?"

"Yes, today. Phone Claudia's and tell her to close the shop." Zoe crossed her legs revealing a bit more thigh. She loved to tease "Old Fatso." Before noon and already his cheeks and nose were red. He was drinking earlier and earlier each day. Why she kept him on as her business manager was a mystery, even to herself.

"What time?" Frank raised his knit shirt and removed the cell phone from his belt, revealing a flabby, white belly dotted with short black hairs. Actually, he had more hair on his belly than he did on his head.

Disgusting, she thought, and felt her stomach lurch, but answered in a composed voice, "Three." There were more benefits than money and fame to being an actress. Obedience by underlings was important too. She smiled at Frank.

"You have a dinner date tonight with that new actor the studio is pushing. That's at nine. Will three to six, six-thirty be enough time?"

"Yes, I just need to find something to wear to the studio for the contract signing. Certainly, it won't take you more than a day or two to convince them to agree to the increase."

"Give me until the end of this week to set it up. You want thirty-percent more. That'll take a lot of convincing." Frank paused. "We know you're worth it, and they know you're worth it. They're just cheap." Frank pressed a speed dial and put the phone to his ear. "Miss Claudia, please. Frank Lanconni for Miss Parker."

Zoe rose from the chaise and walked to the sportswear section of her closet, opened a glass door, and rummaged around. She pretended to be concentrating on selecting something to wear but was listening intently to Frank's conversation.

"Hello, Claudia. Yeah, Frank Lanconni. How are you? That's good. Me too. Hey, I just called to make arrangements for this afternoon. Miss Parker wants to shop. She'll need you to close the store to other clients from two-thirty to seven." There was a lengthy pause in Frank's conversation. "No, she can't come tomorrow. She wants to come today."

Zoe turned to her business manager and put her hands on her hips. "Frank..."

He looked at Zoe, then at his feet. "Claudia, I understand your problem, but you need to reschedule your appointment with Victoria. Hell, she hasn't even been *nominated* for an Oscar, much less *won* one. And need I remind you that Miss Parker spent a half-million in your store last year. How much did Victoria spend with you?" After a short pause, Frank looked at Zoe and nodded.

Zoe smiled. *That bitch, Claudia,* she thought, *was going to turn me down because Victoria had an appointment. I just might take my business elsewhere...but not today.*

"I thought you'd reconsider. Miss Parker will be there around two-thirty." Frank ended the call and hung the cell phone on his belt.

"Tell Thomas I'll be taking the limo, and tell Lucille to come here and help me dress."

"I'm here, Miss Parker." Lucille's head peered out from behind Frank.

Zoe leaned back in the limo seat and smoothed the waistline of her halter top. Lucille was right, today was a good day for wearing white. Black would have been depressing. She stretched out her legs and looked through the limo's tinted window at the shops on Rodeo Drive. "Frank, when did you tell Claudia we'd be there?" She glanced at her watch.

"Two-thirty."

"It's three-five now. Tell Thomas to pull over. I don't want to arrive until at least three-fifteen." She watched Frank speak into the intercom connecting him to her driver. The limo turned onto Santa Monica Boulevard, drove several blocks, and made a couple of turns.

Zoe heard the familiar *thump, thump* of their tires on a cobblestone section of Rodeo Drive and knew they would soon be at Claudia's. She looked at her watch, three-fifteen, covered her head with a silk scarf, and put on sunglasses.

At exactly three-seventeen, Zoe stepped out of her limo and

walked under the canvas awning marking the entrance to Claudia's, the most prestigious shop on the Drive. She struck a pose and waited. Usually she could count on a few paparazzi hanging around hoping for a shot of a star. Thomas was already out of the limo and standing guard behind her. Frank was slowly getting out of the limo and, as he always did, giving her a chance to be seen and recognized.

Zoe noticed a crowd of tourists walking toward them. She shook her head slightly, just enough to cause the silk scarf to slide off her head and reveal her signature red curls.

"Look," screamed a touristy-looking woman, "It's Zoe Parker."

My fans are so loyal. Seeing me will be the biggest event of their vacations, maybe even of their lives, she thought as the crowd rushed forward and encircled her, taking photos with their disposable cameras, and begging her to autograph everything from guide books to the shirts on their backs. Zoe signed autographs and basked in the adoration of her fans.

Thump. Thump.

Thump. Thump. Zoe's awareness was captured by the sound of tires on the cobblestone street. With a collective gasp, the crowd dispersed. Zoe turned. A car was coming straight at her. "Eek." She froze.

Crunch. She felt Thomas's gorilla-strong arms wrap around her and carry her to safety. Her heart was pounding. Her body went limp in Thomas's protective embrace.

Crash. She heard the car hit Claudia's. The side of her face was held firmly against Thomas's chest. Zoe saw shards of glass fly through the air and knew some were hitting Thomas as he shielded her. Thomas carried her to the limo and gently deposited her in the back seat. As soon as Frank was also in the limo, they sped away.

Eternally His,
The Ghost

Eternally His will be released during Winter 2008-2009
by Awe-Struck E-Books in electronic format and by
Earthling Press in print.

Eternally His is a paranormal romance about Erica Petersen, a bridal salon owner who is haunted by a matchmaking ghost wearing a Victorian wedding gown. The ghost has an ulterior motive.

A veil of dust hung in the stagnant air of the locked tower. Dirt coated the wicker rocker and an old leather trunk with tarnished brass fittings. Spider web festoons hung from the domed ceiling. Rays of sunlight struggled to penetrate the grime-clouded window but managed only to cast a yellow glow. The round walls were covered with faded and peeling red rose-strewn paper against which two gowns languished on bent steel hooks.

The once-beautiful gowns were tattered and laden with residues of the passage of time. The black taffeta had paled to rust leaving only traces of its original richness deep in the folds and in the jet beads dangling on loose threads from a ripped collar.

The years had been even less kind to the wedding gown. Its sheen was worn away to a coarse dullness into which dust had burrowed and turned the pale ivory a somber grey. The satin fabric weighed heavily on fine stitching until seams burst and left only the front of the skirt attached to the bodice. Three tiny seed pearls clung defiantly to a limp fringe that was once a delicate lace ruffle, while their comrades lay scattered on the floor below, waiting for time to claim the others.

Suddenly, in the unmoving air, the wedding gown fluttered and shook itself free of the layers of dust. Slowly, ever so slowly, the dress took form. The ripped skirt gathered and joined the rounded waistline. A bosomy shape filled the bodice. Shoulders straightened. Hips swelled. Seed pearls once again adorned the lace ruffle. The gown rose and released itself from the hook, then settled in the center of the room with its train neatly arranged behind.

Dainty feet in satin slippers unfolded from beneath the skirt. The sleeves fluttered and delicate hands appeared. One slender finger wore a diamond-encrusted, gold, love knot. The gown quivered. From the lace collar burst a red pompadour and green eyes set in porcelain-fine skin. A mist of tulle covered her from head to toes. She pinched her cheeks and bit on her lips to add color to her ivory face. Oops, she almost forgot her bridal bouquet of gardenias. Poof...it was in her hands.

The ghost was properly dressed for a haunting.

ALLENE PRALL

Native Californian Allene Prall has traveled extensively and accumulated a wealth of experiences as a military spouse. She earned a bachelor's degree in English from Armstrong Atlantic State University in Savannah. Although she has a full-time job in another field, writing is her first love, and she concentrates on short stories and essays, with the seeds for a novel in the back of her mind. Her contributions to this anthology are her first published works.

Her other interests include genealogy, artistic projects, gardening, and spending time with her daughter, son-in-law, and new granddaughter. She lives in Savannah with her three cats, Othello, Iago, and Cassio.

Prall can be contacted by email to aprall@juno.com.

Transcendental Reflections

Nothing is so peaceful and therapeutic to me as the sense of renewal I receive when I sit on my front porch and survey my garden. Like television, which is a form of entertainment when taken in small doses and a form of boredom when overdone, nature's beauty must also be viewed in small doses to be fully appreciated and not taken for granted–and yet it is difficult for me to follow this philosophy. It is very hard to tear myself away from this tranquil, quiescent observance.

My garden contains a mixture of plants that were favorites of my mother and my grandparents, and I am reminded of these long ago gardens, as well as the people who tended them, as I admire the beauty. I see the yellow canna lilies peeking out through a swirl of unfolding chartreuse and yellow leaves, the small nosegay of multiple pink roses all crowded together on a single stem, the welcoming yellow lantana fanning out over the sidewalk, daring me to cut it back, the deep purple verbena cautiously spreading as if respecting the right of the Plumbago to do the same, the orange daylilies crowing about their height, and the yellow sunflowers, surprise volunteers from a suet cake once hanging in the magnolia tree above the garden.

Still, the abundance of weeds peeking out through the flowers, as well as the overgrown bushes, and the grass which needs mowing, are Mother Nature's reminders that with appreciation goes responsibility. If the beauty of nature is to be enjoyed, it must be cared for–lessons my mother and grandparents knew well–and yet this responsibility does not deter me from my love of this gardening pastime. I now know how spiritually inspired my maternal ancestors–all farmers–must have felt while walking in their fields daily, surveying nature's abundance, or how spiritually bereft my grandfather must have felt when he was no longer physically able to care for his California farm and made the decision to sell it. I wonder if he felt as though he were somehow letting down generations of forebears who danced to the circadian rhythms of crop regeneration and failure, the abundance or lack of natural elements, forces of nature, and acts of God–their occurrences building character through the adversity they bring and the toil that they necessitate.

I like to think that what I am feeling as I study my garden is innate–my sentient genes descending from those of a long line of forebears and nurturers who respected and understood Mother Nature and her powers enough to practice a symbiotic relationship with her. Whether my genetic inheritance has left me with a green thumb, or an oft-suspected brown one, it has instilled in me a desire to know more about my ancestors. There is something God-like about these people who lived a simpler, yet more difficult, life. Their transcendental knowledge of God, through nature, is inspiring. The lives they led, the struggles they had, the children they sacrificed through sicknesses and wars, the abolitionist causes they embraced and the dangers they faced hiding slaves simply because they knew intuitively that it was the right thing to do–all these factors increase my thirst for knowledge about them. Their sturdy brick and frame houses in Ohio and Pennsylvania, centuries old with their historical markers, still stand as testimonies to the extraordinary examples they set for future generations.

Sadly, I have recently learned that the hand of progress, much held in suspicion by Emerson and Thoreau, has slowly encroached upon the California farm once owned by my grandparents. It was the end achievement of a manifest destiny dreamed centuries ago by my great-grandfather, who migrated from Ohio to California in search of a better life for himself and his future family, coalescing rich earth, abundant crops, sturdy timbers, and years of toil into sustenance and shelter, a concrete example of what he hoped to be a far-reaching future for his descendents. The house, with its redwood timbers–impervious to the destructive power of insects–has not been impervious to the destructive power of the machinery which was used to tear away at the heart of its foundation, dissecting chambers which were once the life-blood of a loved and loving family. I am told that a new high school stands on a part of the property now, its newly-built rooms and academia intended as the life-blood of knowledge for future students. A new street cuts into the land, allowing ingress for the industry that has claimed the once-fertile fields that provided food for nourishment, with giant warehouses and distribution centers now nourishing the material desires of the consumer.

Like the uninterrupted flow of farmland that surrounded it, my grandparents' farmhouse, with its red frame exterior and silver roof, was a symbol of continuity during my childhood. As long as it stood there, its spiritual and moral significance was repeated to me by the many examples my relatives set before me, the stories about their childhood on the farm, and by their strong sense of family. Although I had never been inside the house–it was sold when I was an infant–my occasional drives past, and my overnight stays with my grandparents in another house I grew to know intimately, resulted, after much begging on my part to know about the farm, in bedtime stories of community harvests and barn raisings, nighttime chicken thieves scared off by my grandfather's shotgun fired out the window, transients asking to sleep in the barn after riding the rails in front of the house, the one-room schoolhouse my mother and her siblings attended, and funny new spinster schoolteachers who temporarily boarded with my grandparents.

These stories were filled with color and excitement, and helped me connect with the farm and the sense of community it represented. Although it has had several owners throughout the years, the townspeople always referred to it by my family's name to signify ownership; and, in the same breath, many would speak fondly of my relatives and their generosity, as if the house served as a monument to my family. Perhaps my grandfather knew this–that the real immortality of a house lies not in who owns it, but in the record of spiritual and moral accomplishments of its occupants. Perhaps this is what he was trying to teach my family when, upon selling it, he said "It's just a house."

He had to be proud of his own heritage. He had to be proud of the five children he and my grandmother raised, and their achievements. His transcendental communion with nature and its challenges undoubtedly taught him that there is also a time to–as Thoreau put it–"Simplify." This simplification led him and my grandmother to buy a smaller house in the city after their children were on their own. This smaller house is one which I grew to know intimately, having spent many joyful holidays and family celebrations there, and occasionally staying overnight in a bedroom wallpapered in a soothing pink decorated with large cabbage roses, comfortably tucked under my grandmother's thick handmade quilt–symbols of warmth in my occasional reveries of this other marvelous house and its cozy environment.

As I take note of the future challenges of my own house and yard, and my advancing age, perhaps it is time for me to "simplify" and downsize, but I am not yet ready to let go of my surroundings. My garden is a great stress reliever, as well as a source of creativity and spiritual knowledge. Although I am three thousand miles from my roots, gardening helps me feel connected to my forebears. I feel as though they are here watching over me. Perhaps I will "simplify" by starting small, separating the verbena and the plumbago as they eye each other's territory with respectful envy. Graduating to the back yard, my simplification will necessitate clearing a lot of kudzu and weeds. Next will come a spring cleaning inside the house, allowing a therapeutic purging of the material shackles which hinder my enjoyment of this environment I love so much.

All things in good time. Meanwhile, as I work in my garden, the genetic imprint of my ancestors will allow me to continue to learn from nature, and their spirit will be with me always.

Words Unspoken, Things Unsaid

The year 1963 was not only a year in which the Kennedy assassination forced the nation to reckon with its complacency, but a year in which my own eleven-year-old innocence was called into question, the beginning of an atonement of sorts for the halcyon days I had enjoyed until then. It also marked the beginning of a realization that my life would never be the same again.

If atonement was in order for my carefree days as a child, Shanteussy, California, a small, friendly town with approximately 16,000 people, made it easy to live an uncomplicated life. Originally founded by a lucky 20-year-old Frenchman who came west in 1849 and struck gold, the town was unofficially named "Sans Souci" by the Frenchman as a symbol of his new, carefree lifestyle.

Expanding this small encampment by buying surrounding land, and selling it at a discount to anyone who could provide a trade or business, he appointed himself mayor and ruled with an iron hand. By 1880, our 51-year-old mayor had few friends and little money left. Taking to the bottle became a habit. It was during one of the mayor's "binges" that a census taker, stumbling upon the little town with hardly any people left, and no clear identification, happened to see him wandering aimlessly and mumbling to himself. The census taker tried as best he could to understand the mayor's garbled answer when asked the name of the town and wrote down "Shanteussy." The name reminded the townspeople of the many saloon singers of ill-repute who lived in the town. Never missing a chance to get back at their tyrannical mayor, they kept their mouths shut and decided not to correct the census taker.

My great-great grandfather, Zebulon Hollingsworth, became the mayor after the Frenchman's death, inheriting most of the town. A sturdy, hard-working man who never took life too seriously, Zebulon was known to say that with all of the peculiar characters who inhabited the town, not to mention the name itself, one had to have a sense of humor to live there. I suppose that is how he lived to the ripe old age of 100. The inheritance was a fitting reward for his patience with the Frenchman, and provided handsomely for Zebulon, his wife Anna, and their three sons.

Charles Hollingsworth, my great-grandfather, was the only son who stayed in Shanteussy. Great-grandpa Charles, his wife Pearl, and their two sons, Richard and Charles Jr., were well-respected by the population of Shanteussy, which had grown to about seven or eight thousand people. If the original mayor was a tyrant, the Hollingsworths enjoyed a certain status because of their benevolence. It was within this social environment of giving and taking that Margaret Louise Hollingsworth, my mother, was born. My grandparents had almost given up trying to have children, managing, at the worst of times, to have her during the Depression. Although slowed down by these economic circumstances, my grandparents, as well as the rest of the town, fared better than most. They persevered as small farmers do, growing their own vegetables and raising cattle, while the women, thrifty as they were, did their own preserving, with pantries and root cellars full of canned and stored vegetables, and old clothes turned into quilts. Many times my grandfather, while just barely feeding his family, would give food to a family in less fortunate circumstances.

His benevolence was not forgotten by the townspeople, and when the country began to get back on its feet economically, the town spoiled this first child of Charles Jr. and Ellen. She lacked nothing, much to my grandparent's dismay, who kept trying to instill self-reliance, responsibility, and firm discipline. It became a little easier to instill discipline after my grandparents had three more daughters, but the pattern had already been set; my mother usually got her way. I had heard that when Mama quit college at the age of twenty and announced that she was engaged to Jack Williams, a man they had never met, my grandparents, after much consternation, decided to give my father a chance. Soon they were married and settled into a tiny house that was a wedding gift from my grandparents. In time, my grandparents came to love my father and his devotion to my mother.

By this time, the town had doubled in size and was known for its sense of community, where neighbors talked over back fences and the women met for coffee each morning. Mama settled into the business of trying to have children, and in short order, I, Cassandra Anne Williams, came along, followed three years later by my sister Samantha. Daddy took his responsibility as a father seriously–so seriously, in fact, that making a lot of money seemed to be his goal. When translated to the job market, this meant that he never seemed to be satisfied with the job he had. He was always searching for a better job. The grass always seemed to be greener somewhere else.

Several times when his bosses would hear the rumor that he was seeking employment elsewhere, they would hurry the process along by firing him. This made it hard for my father to find another job, which worried my mother, who planned on having more children. Many arguments followed in which their stubbornness made it hard to compromise. But compromise they did, keeping their original intentions hidden beneath a façade of conjugal diplomacy for our sakes, but surfacing again only to be tested in the same manner. Silence would eventually ensue, with compromise soon after, but no real talking between them to solve the problem.

In 1963, by the time I was eleven, this cycle became a normal routine and didn't worry me. I somehow knew that things would always get better, and they usually did. I took it for granted that my parents would be together forever. I did not want to imagine what would happen if they weren't together.

When the leaves of the large, ancient oak trees in the park across the street from our house would shudder violently in reaction to the cold north winds, making it impossible for Samantha and me to go outdoors during our winter vacation from school, we would play indoors, stretching a sheet over the A-framed wooden rack that Mama kept near the wall furnace to dry laundry, and using it as a house. Gathering our dolls, or "children" together, we would pretend that we were widowed sisters who shared a house. Our romantic imaginations did not stretch far enough to acknowledge that two women with children might be living together not by choice, but because of economic necessity. Instead, in our idyllic fantasies the living room rug became our yard as we ventured out of our makeshift house to go swimming in our make-believe pool, or to have outdoor tea parties to which all of our "society friends" were invited.

On quieter days, when bored with pretending, we would get out of the closet a large box containing construction paper, crayons, paints, glue, chalk, and other craft items–a gift from our Aunt Lyda–and explore our creativity.

A schoolteacher who never married, Aunt Lyda's tenacity was

admired by everyone except Mama. Whatever Lyda Hollingsworth pursued in life, her fearless determination usually guaranteed that she would get, which is probably why she did not stop once she obtained her teaching degree and chose to pursue a master's degree. That, I suspect, gave her the idea that she was better than most men, and she chose not to marry. I suppose Aunt Lyda knew that visiting Samantha and I would be as close as she would ever come to having children of her own.

Like Mama, she was rather set in her ways. Nevertheless, she could be very caring in her own way, and would clean out her school-room twice a year, bringing the leftover supplies to Samantha and me. A box decorated with Christmas wrapping paper, originally used to hold the children's Christmas cards, was brought to us during our Christmas vacation filled with these leftover supplies. At the end of the school year, Aunt Lyda would use another box she had saved, this one decorated with lace doilies and hearts, which had been used as a container for the children's valentines. We would look out the window with anticipation when hearing Aunt Lyda's car chugging up the driveway, backfiring as it came gasping to a stop.

"When are you going to get a new car, Lyda?" Daddy would ask, and would receive the same standard answer.

"When it starts to rain money," Aunt Lyda would shoot back, hurriedly getting out of the car. Her next movement was crucial; if she grabbed the back door handle, we knew she had the box in the back seat. If she didn't, and continued toward the house, we knew there would be no box.

If Mama nurtured our emotional and spiritual needs, Aunt Lyda and her boxes nurtured our creative needs. I sensed that this seemed to irritate Mama in some way. "You don't have to bring those boxes all the time, Lyda," Mama would say. It was as if Aunt Lyda were somehow encroaching into Mama's territory.

"I enjoy seeing the smiles on their faces," Aunt Lyda would say. "Please let me enjoy the moment, Maggie."

Mama would frown and disappear while we carefully inventoried the box with Aunt Lyda. "I guess a master's degree isn't enough for her; she has to be a mother, too," Mama would mumble to Daddy.

Spring's warmth created a special bond between Mama and me while we planted flowers in her garden. Mama had started a new job, so our ritual was to water the garden on weeknights after supper, talking about how our day went, and to plant on weekends when Mama didn't have to work and I didn't have school. Like a lot of eleven-year-olds, my pre-adolescent, self-centered mind wanted to be able to choose how I helped Mama. This usually involved anything creative and fun, like planting flowers, and letting Mama do the weeding. If any real work was to be done, indoors or outdoors, I would usually find a way to get out of it. Mama's garden talks that year centered around the topic of responsibility, which seemed strange to me, since I knew about her spoiled childhood.

"We all have to do our share," Mama would say, "not just to earn money, but to help each other. You're getting older now, and must learn the difference between arbitrary help and responsibility." Naturally, I balked at anything that involved giving up my independence.

Mama didn't mind weeding, saying that gardening was therapeutic and relieved the day's stress. I asked her what kind of stress she meant, although I already knew, but Mama didn't seem to want to talk about it. Sadness would appear on her face as she said this. I knew she wasn't just referring to her new job, but was also referring to the arguments she and my father had. Sometimes Daddy would sleep on the living room sofa after one of these arguments, explaining to us the next morning that Mama had one of her "sick headaches" the night before, and that he didn't want to disturb her. He would then take us out for breakfast. After stuffing ourselves with pancakes and listening to my father's corny jokes, we would come home to find Mama in a better mood. Daddy would scoop her up into his broad arms, I suppose for our benefit, giving us a little reassurance by their long embrace that whatever problems they had no longer seemed to divide them.

Samantha and I spent the hot summer days participating in recreational activities that the city provided in the park. Evenings were spent trying to extend the day as long as possible by playing with friends in the park, until forced by Mama's call to come inside. My shyness had always caused my friends to be few, and my relationship with Samantha to be close.

The month of August was both reluctantly and eagerly awaited. Because it was the last month to enjoy ourselves before going back to school, our reluctance meant we did not want to come in at night, as we tried to make the most of our remaining summer vacation. Although the Robbins County Fair was a cap off to the end of the summer, this mid-August event was one that we eagerly looked forward to all summer. Having doubled up on extra chores during the summer for fair money–the only time Mama had no trouble getting us to do chores–budgets and schedules were drawn up around our saved allowances, with every expenditure carefully planned. Candy apples, cotton candy, souvenirs, games, and rides: choices were made after much pondering and written down on a sheet of paper we would tuck into our pockets, along with our money, the day of the fair.

Our family routine was always the same. Back from church, we would hurridly change clothes, empty our piggy banks, grab our budgeted lists of proposed expenditures, and speed to the car, trying to hurry Mama and Daddy as much as possible.

We usually attended the fair on its last day, a Sunday, because of the Lion's Club barbecue. We savored the pit-roasted beef, delicious pinto beans, tossed salad, and coconut cake for dessert. Then, Mama, Samantha, and I would make our way to the horticulture building, where small garden plots would be landscaped according to a theme, and prizes awarded to those participating in the contest. Mama and I really enjoyed this, hoping someday to enter the contest ourselves. After taking our time carefully studying each plot and deciding whether it deserved the prize it won, we would rejoin Daddy and slowly make our way through the fairgrounds until coming to an area near the public stage, where Mama and Daddy would usually spread a blanket on the ground to listen to various local talent, including organ music provided by Stell Moynahan, a permanent fixture at the fair every year.

Walking to the three exhibit buildings was next, with their giant Quonset-hut shapes. We would linger around the agricultural exhibit with its display of irrigation pumps, and marvel at the one feeding water into a huge tank in which a giant catfish was swimming. We always wondered if the catfish was released after the fair ended, or became someone's dinner.

Moving down to the end of the building, representatives of the local lumber company handed out wooden yardsticks. As we walked outside, we would look with anticipation in the direction of the midway with its calliope music and colored lights. Mama would take our yardsticks as she gave us the nod to enjoy ourselves while she walked back to the public stage with Daddy. Budgets and money were pulled out of our pockets and we would head for the midway, walking around once on a reconnaisance mission to see what rides and games were new before settling down into the business of spending our money.

This year we were disappointed to learn that Mama would not be accompanying us to the fair.

"Stomachache," she said, as she urged Daddy to take us anyway, knowing that we had saved our hard-earned money and had been looking forward to attending the fair for a long time.

Daddy was very quiet as we drove to the fairgrounds. I suppose he was worried about leaving Mama alone. It was strange for Mama to let a little thing like a stomachache keep her at home. Mama never got sick. If she was ever in pain, she hid it well. I noticed that she had looked a little pale and had been restless during church services, but I said nothing to Daddy in fear of adding to his worries. He was between jobs again, and had been arguing with Mama before we left for church. I thought that with everyone out of the house, Mama might be able to get some rest.

As we drove into the parking lot at the fairgrounds, the smell of barbecue took my mind off their problems. But this year the barbecue did not seem to have its usual savory taste, although Daddy and Samantha seemed to be enjoying it. I suppose it was all in my mind because I missed Mama. Skipping the horticulture exhibit, which just didn't seem the same without Mama, I followed Daddy and Samantha to the usual spot by the stage. Daddy was determined to make our day as pleasant as possible under the circumstances and helped us plan our upcoming midway visit with enthusiasm, taking us there after our usual visit to the exhibit buildings, and treating us to cotton candy, candy apples and rides on the ferris wheel and whirligigs.

After buying our usual souvenir-a snow globe with the words "Robbins County Fair" inside, and red, white, and blue sparkles instead of snow—we came home earlier than usual to check on Mama. We were definitely in higher spirits than when we left. Approaching the house, we were surprised to see Aunt Sara's car in the driveway, followed by Dr. Blevin's blue Ford. We were met by an eerie silence as we entered the house. Aunt Sara came toward us, and took Samantha and me aside, telling us that Mama was all right, and engaged us in small talk about the fair, while Dr. Blevins took Daddy to the bedroom to see Mama. Daddy looked somber as he re-emerged.

"If I had known she was pregnant, I never would have taken the kids to the fair, especially since she was in pain this afternoon," Daddy was saying.

"She wanted to hold off telling you for as long as possible, with things the way they are..." Aunt Sara's voice trailed off.

"Sometimes these things just aren't meant to be," Dr. Blevins said softly, "But she will be able to have another when the time is right."

Things were very quiet after that. Samantha and I went to our room. Aunt Sara eventually went home, and Daddy stayed by himself while Mama slept. I didn't have to explain a lot to Samantha; she seemed to know or guess what happened. I didn't know how much she was affected by the situation until I looked into her face, which was turning red.

"Does this mean that they will stop fighting?" she asked me tearfully.

"I don't know, Samantha. I hope so," I said.

September and October were months that brought a reprieve to their arguing. Mama was quieter than usual–not quite her old self. She spent weekdays at her job, and helped us with our homework in the evenings. She and Daddy went through the motions of normal, but strained, conversation. If the conversation lacked any deep meaning, it wasn't because of a lack of effort on Daddy's part. Daddy was working once again and in good spirits. Try as he did to get Mama to open up, she seemed to retreat to a place deep within herself, where only silence existed–a place that no words could reach. It was as if she needed that silence in order to get to know herself, and examine her life.

"I know you're still thinking of the baby we lost," Daddy said finally. "It isn't that I didn't want to have another baby, it's just that, financially, the time just wasn't right. That's what I meant when I said things worked out for the best. We would have done a lot of struggling. I'm sorry if I hurt you."

I could see tears in Mama's eyes, but she said nothing, choosing to leave the room.

One November day, our principal, Mrs, Hughes, came into the classroom sobbing. After waiting for Miss Morris, our teacher, to calm her down and receive whatever the bad news was, we learned that President Kennedy had been shot.

At some point we were excused early from school and allowed to go home. Mama had gotten off from her job and picked us up from school. I could tell she was in a state of shock, which wasn't a large jump from where she had been for the past few months. She loved the Kennedys. They were young and represented all the hopes and dreams of a nation prosperous with postwar growth and headed in a direction that included new technological advances and new opportunity. Mama especially liked Mrs. Kennedy and often identified with her. A woman with two children who placed her family above everything, Mrs. Kennedy was seen by Mama as a woman who also may have given of herself a little too much, after the miscarriages she suffered and the death of her third child.

We watched with amazement as events unfolded on television—the casket being loaded onto the plane, the vice president and others accompanying Mrs. Kennedy to the plane to be flown back to Washington, the news that Lee Harvey Oswald was arrested as the killer. I looked at Samantha, who was shaking the snow globe we had bought at the county fair. My head began to feel as if it were spinning. I became very scared. It seemed to me that the world had suddenly gone mad. It was as if we were all living in a snow globe that someone had abruptly turned upside down, releasing the snow, and we had all lost our balance. Trying to regain my composure, I asked Samantha to stop shaking the globe.

"Caroline and John-John don't have a daddy anymore, do they?" asked Samantha.

Mama was very still, as if this were affecting her on another level. "No, they don't," she said quietly.

Mama had been phoning her sisters a lot over the past month. The hushed but insistent tones of her voice did not reveal what she was saying, which made me curious. When she wasn't talking to her sisters, she did a lot of closet cleaning, packing boxes with clothes that Mama, Samantha, and I had supposedly outgrown. Once, when I looked into the box that came from the closet that Samantha and I shared, I noticed that a few of the neatly folded clothes were those that still fit us. Mama said nothing in the way of an explanation, but mumbled something about making boxes to give to Goodwill. The boxes stayed in our closet instead of being put on the front porch for pickup.

On Sunday, while the world was still in shock awaiting the funeral of President Kennedy, Aunt Sara stopped by to pick us up for our usual ride in the country. She had Grandma and Aunt Lyda with her. I liked taking rides in Aunt Sara's big station wagon, but it seemed very small all of a sudden with Grandma, two aunts, and Mama in the seats and Samantha and I in the very back. Our usual country travels were replaced with a city route that took us to the middle of town, with its quaint two-story Victorian houses painted in colorful shades of yellows, greens, and blues, and trimmed in complimentary colors.

One such house stood at the corner of Elm and College streets. A massive two-story house, with a corner entry and basement apartment, it had been built around the turn of the century for a very large family. An elementary school stood directly across the street. Aunt Sara slowed down the car. I turned my head to see the women whispering in a huddle. I couldn't hear what they were saying.

"Look, the basement apartment has a 'for rent' sign," Aunt Sara said, the sound of feigned surprise in her voice.

"I've been looking for another place," Aunt Lyda said, somewhat unconvincingly. "Yes, I'd love to know what it looks like."

I wondered what was going on. Aunt Sara pulled the car over, parking it in front of the apartment. It seemed strange that Aunt Lyda would be looking for another apartment since I knew she rented her current apartment from Grandma and Grandpa at a very modest price.

"Yes, let's all go look," said Mama, with a bit of over-enthusiasm that usually came when she was trying too hard to persuade us to do something we didn't want to do. My stomach began to feel funny. I began to feel that this whole trip was deliberately planned. Everyone got out of the car, including Samantha. I stayed, declining to see the apartment. Mama and the others looked at each other bewilderedly.

"We can't leave you here in the car," Mama said, with desperation in her voice.

"Why not?" I asked. "I can stay by myself."

"Because it's important to Aunt Lyda to know if we like the apartment," she said in a high-pitched voice that indicated she was beginning to panic. I started to feel that I was somehow ruining their plans. I thought back to all the secrecy that had taken place over the past month. It was all beginning to come together–Mama and Daddy's arguments, their eventual silence, the hidden boxes of clothes in our closet, the long phone conversations between Mama and her sisters, and now, the importance of getting me out of the car to see the apartment. I now began to sense that the apartment was for Mama, Samantha, and me, and not for Aunt Lyda.

The image of the shaken snow globe came back to me. Inside the globe, I saw Aunt Sara's station wagon. Opposite the car I saw the house with its apartment. In between, I saw Mama, Samantha, and I being tossed about, among the falling snow, being hurled into the apartment, unable to stop. I knew that a dreadful change was about to happen in my life–something I had little control over. It was as if crossing the threshold of the apartment meant meeting a dark, un-known force and those who entered could not turn back. My fear made me feel completely alone with no one to turn to.

Aunt Sara approached with the owner. "I saw you pull up. Sorry I didn't come out right away, but I've been watching the TV. That poor Mrs. Kennedy is in the Capitol rotunda now with John-John and Caroline, kneeling beside her husband's casket. How sad that their lives have been turned upside down."

"Yes," Mama said. "It is sad. We will be ready to see the apartment as soon as we can persuade my daughter to get out of the car. Come dear, let's not hold the lady up," Mama directed me, trying very had to maintain her composure.

"NO." I demanded, desperately trying to put a stop to something I knew I could not change.

"I think she knows," Aunt Lyda whispered to Mama, who was softly starting to cry.

The owner, oblivious to Mama's crying, went on talking about Mrs. Kennedy. "Yes, it's just so sad that she has to go through all of this."

Grandma, who had been listening, answered her. "Yes, it's really sad that life as she knew it has been taken away. She has no choices; the gunshots decided her life for her. At least we have the ability to choose," Grandma said, looking at no one in particular, "and some of us are afraid to do so. We go through life making easy choices. When the hard ones come along, they frighten us, ultimately making us realize that the easy ones were only a very small part of what we really want. Even then, it is difficult to get back on the right path."

Everything was quiet. I looked at Mama, who seemed to be at her lowest point emotionally. Her sisters were now comforting her, putting their arms around her shoulders. Mama seemed to have heard what Grandma was saying, and had stopped crying. Suddenly, Mama didn't seem so vulnerable. My two aunts had not moved; their arms were still around her shoulders. They all gave the appearance of one massive impenetrable wall of defense. I began to understand their alliance. This sisterhood, even with its occasional squabbles and jealousies, was united in unconditional love. As my mind scanned the past, I remembered that they had always been there for each other to face whatever lay ahead. It seemed that fear was an unknown word to my aunts.

I suddenly wondered where I fit in. Mama needed my support and my fears and stubbornness prevented her from getting it. I thought about what Grandma had said about choices. I thought about all the other times my fears prevented me from taking a difficult path–fear of failing in school, not wanting to help Mama with work, and with friendships. I had always taken the easy road, afraid to grow and take chances. The possibility of a new house, new friends, new school–all were overwhelming challenges to me, but somehow I knew I had to summon up the courage to face them. My hands were trembling as I pushed open the car door. My imaginary snow globe was becoming clearer.

"Mama, I'll go in with you to see the apartment," I said, biting my lip while slowly getting out of the car.

Suddenly, something happened. It was as if a light went on in Mama's head. "What am I doing?" she said abruptly. "What am I doing? I'm running away again, that's what I'm doing."

I didn't exactly understand what Mama meant. Maybe I did, but just didn't want to think that Mama would run away from anything. Running away meant fear, and to recognize fear in Mama would mean that my judgment of her as a strong person was faulty. It scared me to know that Mama was vulnerable. At the same time, I realized that if someone I trusted completely was fallible, the only person I could truly depend on was myself, and the only way that Mama–and I–could be truly happy was to be happy with who we are. Watching Mama, I began to see why she had been trying to make me more responsible. It was both frightening and self-assuring. I tried not to think about it. All I cared about was the reassuring smile that was slowly appearing on her face. It was as if a fog had been lifted from around her and she suddenly was able to decide which direction she wanted to take.

Grandma seemed to know what was happening, as she told the apartment owner that we wouldn't be looking at the apartment after all, and thanked her for her time. My aunts were smiling, too. Mama and Grandma hugged. We got back into the car and drove home as a lifetime full of fear and jealousy poured out of Mama–fear of taking chances, of standing on her own two feet, of blaming Daddy, and hidden jealousy that Aunt Lyda had accomplished so much in life. I really got to know Mama during that ride, and I began to realize that Mama and I were alike in many ways.

My aunts let Mama do most of the talking, offering her emotional support. It was as if she had emerged from a cocoon after a long hibernation, and become a butterfly.

"Mama, if we were living in that apartment, would I be going to the new school across the street?" I asked.

"Yes, dear. Would that have been so bad?" Mama said.

"No," I said a little unsteadily, trying to strengthen the new bond that existed between Mama and me.

Mama looked at me in a different way than she usually did. She smiled. I guessed she knew I was trying.

Daddy was at the table eating some soup. He had a look of surprise on his face when we walked into the house.

"I wasn't sure if . . . when . . . you'd be home," he said to Mama, "so I made something to eat."

His look indicated that he seemed to sense that something had been unfolding for the past month.

"Why wouldn't I be?" Mama said going straight to the kitchen to get out the pots and pans.

"I'll help you," I found myself saying.

After supper that night, Samantha and I played in our room as

Mama and Daddy talked for a long time. Several times during the evening, I crept out to the hallway to eavesdrop.

Once, Mama was telling Daddy what she wanted to accomplish in life, and Daddy was encouraging her. There was a boldness to her voice. Daddy also told her what he wanted for all of us. A couple of times, I heard laughter. They talked into the night.

The next morning, Mama stayed home from work, and Mama, Samantha, and I watched the Kennedy funeral together. Mama commented that Mrs. Kennedy was a strong woman and showed much courage. I thought the same about Mama. That afternoon I helped her with the laundry. In the evening, while helping her wash and dry the dishes, I told her I wanted to learn how to cook. I remembered the closeness Mama and her sisters shared while cooking the traditional turkey with all the trimmings on family holidays at Grandma's house. I now knew that part of the bonding they shared involved a large amount of respect for who a person is and what he or she stands for. The same goes for friendships. I realized that my introvertedness and self-centeredness kept others from getting to know who I was or what I was about. It also kept me from getting to know myself. I resolved to get what Mama and her sisters had.

Now that I have been an adult for some time, I think back on my childhood and that particular time with positive feelings. It was a time in which the nation got a little stronger and a little wiser, learning from the Kennedy assassination that hatred and violence can develop from misdirected feelings and misdirected paths. I, too, became a little stronger and a little wiser, learning about the misdirected paths our lives sometimes take, and the dangers that face us when fear and irrational action replace talking–the kind of action that comes when words are unspoken, things are unsaid.

IAN ROBB

Retired for just over a year and already wondering why he did not do so many years ago, Ian Robb writes for pleasure, which, he explains, really means nobody has bought any of his "stuff" yet.

Robb has completed two novels and is now working on his third. He has also written several short stories. With only one short-story exception, all his works are fictional. Like many authors he draws his characters and situations from his vivid imagination. These are supported by his 35 years of dubious experience in human resources roles in the corporate world, his life in three countries, and his journeys around the world to countries in every continent (except Antarctica).

Primarily, however, Ian attributes the true essence of his stories to the inspiration he has gained from his widespread circle of friends and from his daughters, Stephanie and Alexis. He credits the diversity, intelligence, and curiosity of all these people as being the essential ingredients in enabling him to create good strong mysteries, each with an odd assortment of players.

Robb can be reached at Ian142Robb@aol.com.

Gardening?

"Are you into gardening?" I asked the attractive woman I had just been introduced to at an otherwise dull cocktail party.

"Why do you ask?" she said rather haughtily, while I struggled to remember her name. She hadn't asked me mine but I gave it anyway. Thought she should have it for her little black book.

Andrea. That was it.

I'd read somewhere that the best way to remember someone's name is to say it back to them a few times. So, following this presumably sage advice, I replied. "Oh, because, Andrea, I'm looking for some free advice on how to turn my overgrown weed-patch into a kind of neighborhood botanical garden. Are you up to the challenge?"

Fortunately, Andrea saw some humor in this request and smiled a smile that overcame her apparent haughtiness. "Well, I have been told I have a green thumb."

I set my drink down, took her hands in mine and inspected her thumbs closely. "Which one?" I asked.

Andrea was either very easily amused or polite enough to laugh out loud at my lame joke. I cautioned myself not to overdo the corny humor bit.

The gardening approach was my latest attempt at finding a way of breaking the ice with potential partners.

Partner? Hmm. I'm never really sure what the politically correct term is for a woman likely to be over the delicious age of forty. Nobody under forty, other than my daughters, would want to be seen talking to me in public, let alone go on a date with me, so the term 'girlfriend' sounds unnecessarily patronizing. Partner is an alternative that we are expected to get used to but I still prefer lady-friend. It has a mature ring to it even though some of those to whom I might wish to attach such a handle have difficulty living up to the airs and graces that the term connotes.

Prior to my selection of gardening as an opening gambit, I had used sailing, carpentry, and travel as ruses to elevate conversation from the "Lovely weather we're having, don't you think?" type of cliché to something more stimulating but not necessarily of the "Your place or mine?" ilk.

Sailing often brought about unwanted and lengthy tales of ocean cruises taken, rather than the do-it-yourself stuff that I was into. Carpentry was a big mistake. It either provoked a disdainful look that I read as "What do you take me for? A frigging blue-collar worker?" or an introduction to an ex-husband with whom I was presumed to have much in common.

Travel. Now that was a different story, and one which I still do use from time to time. The problem is that disappointingly few people have really traveled, hence the conversation is usually destined to revolve around the obligatory trips to Florida, Las Vegas, Acapulco, and, for the more enlightened ones, San Francisco. Those who have actually been brave enough to leave the presumed safety and security of our continent and who have "done" thirteen European countries in five days offer some common areas of exploration. But that runs cold after a while. Those who have been outside of the traditional vacation haunts are the ones I zero in on, but there are not too many such women and most of them are very much free spirits. In itself, this is not a bad thing, but at my tender age of..., let's say I won't be seeing fifty again,–but I digress. Free spirits, ah yes; wonderful women but generally difficult to hold onto, rather like the proverbial wet bar of soap. Still, they do present exciting challenges and conversation with them is always invigorating, albeit confusing from time to time.

"Tell me what you and your green thumb are renowned for," I pressed her, hoping that we might discover at least an ounce of common interest.

"Funny you should ask," Andrea said, a look of pride brimming in her eyes. "I recently won an award for my roses at a local flower show."

Applying my extremely limited knowledge of roses, I sought to get her to tell me more. This clearly was an area of great interest and probable passion to Andrea. I am always curious to see how an individual's pastimes, hobbies, or whatever affect their perspectives on life and their passion for life.

Showing off, I asked her, somewhat rhetorically. "These would be hybrid-teas, I presume, and not of the floribunda persuasion?"

"My, my. Such big words from one who professes to be the proud owner of an overgrown weed-patch. And yes, you are correct. But do you really care, or are you just trying to make small talk?"

Shrewd lady.

"To be honest," I said, accepting that it was now time to cut to the chase, "I do not like gardening. It's too dangerous a hobby for me. But I also do not like a messy yard. I am sure that roses would look great surrounding my meager pad, but if this would necessitate more than bi-weekly attention being paid to them, then I'm afraid they would not last long."

"You really don't want to talk about the dangerous hobby of gardening, do you?" Andrea was looking me straight in the eye as she tried to figure out what I was really after. Her smirk suggested that she had already drawn her own lurid conclusions about my motives, but if that was what she was thinking, she was wrong. Honestly.

I hastened to accept the opening to kill any further discussion about gardening. "No, I don't. What do you suggest we talk about?" No harm in putting the ball back in her court.

"We could venture into the dangerous waters of examining how men and women go about assessing one another at parties like this, or we could just ask each other what he or she is looking for either at this party or in a partner in general. You are single, aren't you?"

This question caught me off guard. Not so much because I had presumed that my lack of the usual marital status should have been rather obvious but because it had not occurred to me that Andrea might be anything other than single, meaning divorced, widowed or otherwise unattached. Could it be that she had an aggressive six-foot-four ex-football player partner lurking behind the closest faux plant, ready to leap on my head the instant I made any remark that might be interpreted as a pass at the love of his life?

"I am indeed," I replied with the necessary amount of emphasis but with a carefully disguised lack of pride at my single status. I have never quite become used to being divorced, even after many years of being so. Perhaps this is because I had previously, and secretly, always harbored a degree of scorn toward those who were unable to keep their marriages together. My own divorce had still not completely rid me of that rather old-fashioned perspective and I often wished I had a woman by my side on occasions such as this. One whom I could introduce as my wife. My acceptance of the invitation to this party had, to a certain extent, been prompted by imagining that Ms. Right would accept her invitation also and that the two of us would meet. A lovely daydream, but after many parties Ms. Right has never been included among the guests.

Perhaps sensing my own insecurities about being divorced, Andrea responded, "Divorce sucks, doesn't it?"

Not quite the words I would I have chosen, but the sentiment was the same as mine.

"Years ago," *Here I go, digging into my murky past,* "I believed that divorcees and smokers fell into the same group of socially unacceptable people. But having dabbled at smoking on occasions and being now saddled with the previously inconceivable title of 'divorced guy,' I have modified my view of social categorization to be more accommodating of the world's blend of characters."

"Well, I can't say that I have quite the same thoughts about being divorced. I'm glad I am, even though the process itself is a pain. Marriage for me had deteriorated to a contest to see who could be more critical of the other." Andrea paused before continuing, pondering, I suspect, whether or not to reveal some of her inner self to this man she had just met. It could have been either my incredible charm or her wish to get something off her chest, but she obviously opted to continue. As she opened her mouth to continue, I immediately chose to attribute her decision to my charm. "I wonder if we all feel that even in marriage there are certain sacrosanct personal habits that must not only be protected at all costs but must not even be challenged. That was the way I felt about my Sunday mornings at church and my husband felt the same way about his weekly Sunday golf games. Obviously these two clashed and with children in the picture something had to give. We both clung fiercely to our rights to do what we had always done, he arguing quite irrationally about his commitment to his golfing buddies and me wanting to maintain my church-going habit."

"And who won?" I enquired.

"Well, of course, no one won. No one ever does in arguments of this nature. Neither of us was going to give in. Even compromise was a bitter pill for each of us. Ironically, I've heard that my ex rarely golfs these days and, I have to admit, I rarely go to church."

"So obstinacy and pride got in the way?"

"Are you trying to judge me?" Andrea said quite testily.

"No, I'm sorry. I didn't mean it to sound that way. I was merely paraphrasing what you've just told me. I think we often fail to acknowledge the deeper emotions that enable or prevent us from changing our ways. I know that was my failing. Among many others, as my ex would have said."

"Such as what?" Clearly Andrea wanted to discover my foibles, of which I had many. This could be a long evening.

During this whole conversation, I had caught Andrea casting furtive glances at my devastating bod. I had determined that she no doubt was curious to know the exact size of my bulging biceps and pecs carefully concealed beneath a loose-fitting jacket. In all probability they would have been just as carefully concealed beneath a jacket several sizes smaller. Although not overweight, I do have to work at it to stay that way. My waist was not the type that was apt to fall over my belt. Other valuable accoutrements were to remain well hidden, perhaps for revelation at a later date. As we had both taken a seat shortly after meeting one another, Andrea was yet to be sent into fits of ecstasy at the sight of the remainder of my physical form. I was sure that the anticipation must be killing her.

I, for my part, had been conducting a similar appraisal of this lovely divorcee. Andrea was younger than me. Most people are, I am beginning to realize. She was probably in her mid-forties and could easily pass for someone about a year younger. She was quite slim and most parts seemed to be where they were supposed to be. The effects of gravity and a few years had been overcome by a vigorous exercise program, surgery, or expensive and uncomfortable underwear. I was inclined to think that exercise was the prime contributor to her surprisingly youthful figure. More to the point though was that Andrea was a remarkably attractive woman who did not choose to plaster on make-up to knock several years off her true age.

Casting aside my traditional testosterone-driven inclinations I was becoming interested in Andrea for far better reasons. She liked conversational challenge. She had a lively mind and wasn't into small talk. She appeared to fight the status quo, and, most intriguingly, there was a beguiling air about her that I hadn't encountered in any other woman in years.

Andrea sat quietly. Was she wondering which of my many failings I was going to confess to, and which ones I was going to keep well-hidden? I would have preferred to have kept them all well-hidden but I had kind of brought this predicament on myself.

"Well?" Andrea said before I could formulate a clever and witty answer that would get me out of this jam. "Would it be easier for me just to call up your ex and ask her for the laundry list of your failings, or do you feel that you can at least give me a quick peek at a couple that are not perhaps as incriminating as the others?"

"You drive a hard bargain. How about for starters I elaborate more on my statement that I don't do well relating my deeper feelings to what is going on around me? I don't think that's quite what I said, but it's close enough."

"Go ahead." Andrea had a look of intense curiosity on her face that I suspected was there to disguise her inward pleasure at watching Big-Mouth squirm a little as he tried to come up with a plausible explanation.

After taking a deep breath, I then spent the next five minutes talking about the disconnect I live with. In a nutshell, I spelled out, as best I could, how for reasons unknown to me I am often at a loss to explain why I can't express my real feelings and certainly can't adapt these to the situation at hand. Pure instinct is usually what drives me.

Discussing serious and meaty emotional stuff like this is generally where I come unglued. I expected Andrea to fall on the floor convulsed with laughter at my amateurish efforts to make sense of a topic about which I know absolutely nothing. Why on earth had I opened the door to this ridiculous diatribe?

Andrea's reaction took me by surprise. "For a man who is obviously not at ease talking about such sensitive matters, you put on a pretty good show." Not only was she not in hysterics on the floor but her voice was tinged with what I took to be compassion. This lady could never be described as being only skin deep. There was a depth to her that I was sure she preferred to keep hidden, but I couldn't figure out why.

"Good show or not, I think I'd rather be wrapped up in a gripping conversation about gardening, even though I don't think my BS around that topic would get past you. But before we go any further, I need to see a man about a dog."

As I rose from my chair, Andrea remarked. "Now there's an expression I haven't heard used for a long time."

"You've obviously been missing out on trips to your local veterinarian's clinic." With that said, I walked off to find our host's and hostess's bathroom. Being male, I was not inclined to ask directions as I wandered around upstairs in search of the bathroom. This led to my inadvertently visiting two closets and a garish bedroom before finding what I was looking for.

Apart from a minor call of nature, my need for breathing space was more pressing. I stood in front of the bathroom mirror looking at the bewildered man staring back at me. I couldn't spend long in here analyzing what had been going on downstairs, but I needed to try and figure out why I felt like I did. In the space of about forty-five minutes, Andrea had planted herself firmly and in a most welcome manner under my skin. Maybe I should just head off home now, sleep off whatever I was feeling and then get on with my life. I thought about this and a few ridiculous alternatives and then splashed water on my face to be sure this wasn't a weird dream. I dried my face, combed my hair and returned to the party below.

Andrea was chatting with a short, older woman who had piled her hair on top of her head in such a way that her overall height had increased by about six inches. This left the impression of her being a short woman with a dreadful hairstyle. Not a clever idea, but one to which vertically challenged women with fragile egos and poor fashion sense seem occasionally driven.

I was introduced to the hairdo, who took one look at me as I scowled at her hair and then found some excuse to scurry away.

"Did you tell her that I was that escaped psychopathic moron that the police have been hunting for days? It appeared that she saw something dangerous and looming in me, and I suspect you've been wondering that yourself. Come on now. Own up," I demanded.

"I told her no such thing," Andrea protested. "But I did tell her that you were a frustrated gardener and probably carried a garden hoe up your sleeve."

"She should see what I keep in my pants."

"Now, now," Andrea said through a big, coy grin. "You should not be making such statements in front of one so shy and sheltered as I."

"I told you that gardening was a dangerous topic of discussion. We should change the subject." I hesitated for a moment, not really sure that I wanted to broach the subject of some of the things that had been going through my head while in the bathroom. "Would you like to take a stroll around what looks like a very elaborately laid out back yard and inspect their horticultural technique?"

"I'd like to. Are you planning on offering your services as a gardener?"

"Only if our hostess's real name is Lady Chatterley."

Andrea gave me a big dig in the ribs and then took my hand and led me out through the kitchen onto the patio where the smokers were gathered.

The backyard was much larger than I had realized as it curved around the side of the house and then down a gradual slope toward a rocky beach way below. Once out of earshot of the smokers, I stopped beside a garden seat that had been carefully placed so that anyone seated there would be obliged to gawk in awe at the wonders of the beautifully laid out gardens and the ocean beyond. Giving a gentlemanly tug on Andrea's arm, I suggested we try out the seat.

Sitting there watching the summer sun set and the magic of the wonderful view wrap us in its beauty, we found a multitude of subjects to discuss, some of which we had a shared perspective, and many in which we saw humor. It was dark and several hours later before I plucked up the courage to say something I had been wanting to say for a couple of hours. I had gradually come to recognize that there was something beautiful happening between us. Andrea sensed my need.

"You have some major pronouncement to make, I take it?" Andrea asked looking at me through the wonderful moonlight that made stark shadows on her face.

"No, but I would like to try something on for size."

"Oh, don't tell me." Andrea exclaimed putting her hands to the side of her face in what I hoped was mock horror. "You're one of those men who walks around in women's underwear. I'm completely shocked and would never have guessed, but, if that's your fetish, which do you want to try on first, my bra or my panties?"

Laughing at this amazing woman's brazen sense of humor, I replied. "You have a great way of taking all the steam out of my serious attempts to broach a delicate subject. I think I'd better just drop what I was going to say. That way I won't run the risk of revealing another of my secrets."

"Ignore me. I've this tendency to want to puncture the balloon of someone I see becoming too serious. Life's too short for us not to be able to see the funny side of most situations. Please go on."

"I'll try to put a lighter face on the topic, providing you promise to let me finish before having me arrested for obscene behavior."

"I promise," Andrea said, although the twinkle in her eyes left me doubting that she would keep her word.

"Fair enough." Summoning up the courage to continue, I said, picking my words carefully. "You and I seem to have managed in a short space of time this evening to establish a relationship I only dream of establishing with a woman after weeks of phone calls, expensive dates, expressions of growing affection, sending flowers..."

"You know how much I love flowers," Andrea interjected. "Does all this mean that I won't be receiving flowers?"

"There, I knew you wouldn't be able to keep your promise."

"I won't do it again. I promise, I promise. Cross my heart and hope to die." All this was said as she acted out the role of a child pleading not to be sent to her room, a look of complete and utter innocence on her face.

As I was about to return to my point, Andrea suddenly added, "I just wanted to make sure you were still going to send me flowers."

Now I was completely flustered. I sat back, thinking that I needed to change my approach. Andrea sat beside me, batting her eyelids as a way of saying "You have my full attention." Smiling, I looked at her for a few moments before leaning over and kissing her on her lips. "I think that that says more than my confused words could ever say."

Feeling pleased with myself for wiggling out of my jam, I was surprised to see a change come over Andrea. She now appeared close to tears. What had I done? Slowly she raised her head and looked me straight in the eye.

"I want you to take me home with you tonight," she said almost in a whisper.

"Why?" Seeing this as my turn now to be glib. "'Fraid I might get lost on the way?"

"No, you callous man. What I'm afraid of, though, is that I may never leave your home once I cross your threshold. I don't anticipate your keeping me a captive, although I'd be quite amenable to that. It's just that I feel as if you've been a part of my life for eternity, not just a few hours. I can't pretend to explain why, but nothing in my life has ever felt so right as being here with you."

Andrea was holding my hands and resting her head on my shoulder. Before continuing she suddenly lifted her head and, looking at me through teary eyes, she let out a little laugh and said, "I think I've just blown any chance I might have had at being crowned the least serious person in the world."

"Maybe so. But then we all blow our chances regularly at being perfectly consistent in all that we do and say."

"That's very profound. If I were in the mood I'd find an appropriately pithy response. By the way, what was it you were going to say to me before you lost track of your thoughts?"

"You mean before I was driven off my tracks don't you? I was going to ask you...oh, it doesn't matter anymore. You beat me to the punch. And, by the way, unless your bra is a size forty-two C cup, it wouldn't fit me anyway."

Going Up

He hated being late for work. As he ran into his office building, he was cursing himself for his stupidity. Although the previous night had ended late, that was no excuse for not being able to make it into his office at his usual time of around eight o'clock. He rationalized that he could lay part of the blame on the train for being some fifteen minutes later than it should have been.

An elevator was standing with its doors open, a full crowd already on board. He figured he could squeeze in. He had almost reached the doors when they slid shut.

Fuck it. More delay.

A few moments later, another one arrived and he and six other passengers entered. He moved to the back of the large, grayish green elevator. He smiled at one of the women whom he recognized, and ignored the other passengers. One of the men was wearing too much cologne. The smell of it hung in the air. No one spoke. Within a few moments, the doors closed.

The elevator started on its upward journey.

Or did it...?

At that same instant, tremendous vibrations shook the elevator and the sound of wind rushing down each side gave the impression it was moving up at great speed. The alarming sounds and sensations escalated and lasted for what seemed like about a minute; he was later to agree they probably lasted no more than about fifteen seconds. During this time, there were other reverberations, that of "stuff" falling on the top of the elevator. It sounded like pieces of steel and chunks of concrete or plaster. He was terrified.

Oh Christ. Is this how it all ends? I don't want to die. I really don't want to die.

He and his fellow passengers were crouched on the floor, stunned and terrified by what was happening. Two of the women were in tears, one screaming hysterically.

Dust started to fill the elevator as the violent shaking and the rushing wind diminished, only to be replaced by a ringing bell, an alarm of some sort. An incessant mechanical voice over the intercom informed the passengers that the building management was aware of a problem and would investigate. The man did not find this terribly reassuring.

He looked over at the woman who was most upset.

Poor woman, she must be so scared.

He went over to her and put his hand on her shoulder. The other woman was on the floor beside her, holding her hand.

Water started to drip into the elevator.

Two men tried to open the doors but with no success.

They all stared at one another, unsure of what to say other than to utter the traditional expressions of shock and pose questions such as "What the hell is going on?"

The intercom to the security desk appeared programmed to continue repeating the highly questionable confirmation of building management's efforts to investigate.

God, that's annoying. Why don't they shut it off?

As if hearing his silent plea, the announcement stopped.

What the intercom did not do was allow them to speak to a live person to whom they could explain their dilemma. The line appeared dead.

They banged on the doors loudly. They called out for someone's attention. No response was forthcoming. Eventually the passengers sat back down on the floor and fell into silence. Obviously, someone knew they were trapped and help must be on its way.

Come on, folks. Open the damn doors and get us out.

Time passed. Too much time, with no apparent effort being made to rescue them.

One man, in an attempt to liven the mood of the trapped passengers, asked everyone for their astrological signs. He was holding the morning paper and he told the others he was going to read from it just what was in store for each one that day. No one's horoscope offered any plausible insights into their being stuck in an elevator with the possibility of death awaiting them.

Probably just as well.

Another man ranted about the inefficiency of the building's facility management team. No one paid him much attention.

Why don't you just sit down and shut up, you moron?

Nevertheless, the moron continued to air his views about the building, and then on life in general, oddly linking the problem of a malfunctioning elevator to the administration in the White House.

Receiving no signs of support or interest in his sermon from his fellow passengers, he wisely elected to pipe down.

We all express our anxiety in different ways.

The silence that had descended once again was punctuated by the occasional and disconcerting thump of a new piece of steel or concrete landing on the elevator roof.

The silence held its own threats.

He grew more alarmed by the lack of apparent activity outside the elevator doors.

About twenty minutes had passed when unexpectedly they heard, faintly, the sound of raised voices on the other side of the door. The passengers banged on the doors again and shouted at the tops of their voices. Again, there was no response. The faint voices subsided and disappeared.

Silence returned.

We're going to be in here forever.

One man theorized that they had risen several floors before the elevator had dropped into the basement of the building. Some seemed to subscribe to this in part and most seemed inclined to believe that they were in the basement.

Someone will realize soon that we are trapped and will rescue us. I hope.

Other theories were raised. None held any strong conviction from their proposers and so the subject died. One thought did prevail, eliciting further debate. The steel and concrete falling on the top of the elevator could very well be coming from

the support structure under the huge elevator motor perched many floors above their heads. This discussion restarted the hysterical crying from the most distressed woman. Everyone else became more keen to get out of what was starting to take on the semblance of a potential tomb.

I wonder what will happen to my daughters if I don't get out of here. Oh, don't think that way, you idiot. Of course we'll get out.

Time dragged. No one said very much; each passenger was deep in his and her own thoughts about the possible outcome of their unwelcome situation.

Will someone tell us when it's time to panic? I feel as if I'm almost at that point.

About an hour after being trapped, tapping could be heard coming from the side of the elevator close to where the man was sitting. He tapped back. A faint voice followed enquiring as to where they were. The caller, a man, was in an elevator next to, or behind, the one in which they were trapped. Had we heard from anybody? No, but how come two elevators had failed at the same time? Had a bomb gone off on the floor where the elevator motors were situated? That was the latest theory.

This is surreal. It's as if we are acting out the part in Dumas' book, The Count of Monte Cristo, where Edmund Dantes is communicating with a fellow prisoner in the Chateau d'If. God, I hope I'm not stuck in here as long as he was in the Chateau. I don't look good with a beard.

The passengers and the man in the other elevator agreed that the first ones out would tell their rescuers that others were trapped. The two-way conversation ended.

It seemed then that all at once they realized that their predicament was becoming increasingly dangerous. The perceived, imminent prospect of a multi-ton elevator motor crashing down on top of them became magnified into a terrifying prospect.

Shit, let's get out of here.

They banged on the door again and shouted for help at the top of their voices. He heard the fear in all their voices, his own being as prominent as the others'.

Nothing.

They banged harder; rubble fell onto the floor through the small gap between the top of the elevator doors and the frame around the doors.

I wonder if that stuff was jamming the doors.

He suggested that they try opening the doors again. Two of the men pulled on the doors from opposite directions. The doors opened a crack. More rubble fell. Through the small opening, they could see a sight they had not expected. The elevator had stopped on or had returned to the lobby. Immediately many hands hooked around the edge of the doors and they slowly parted.

Relief flooded over them all.

Let's get the hell out of here.

The lobby appeared almost deserted.

Where is everyone?

A security guard ran up to the passengers. He was immediately assailed with accusations of incompetence at not attempting to rescue the elevator's passengers. The guard hurriedly explained the building had been hit by an airplane that terrorists had flown into the upper floors. "Get out of the building as quickly as you can," was his only instruction.

Running through what resembled a battlefield, the passengers left the building. The gruesome sight of huge windows tinted red with blood, and of multiple bodies and bloodied body parts were to become a memory that would remain with them all for years.

As he left the North Tower of the World Trade Center, the roar of the fire some thousand feet above him assaulted his ears. He looked up.

Oh my God. My office is in the middle of that inferno.

He ran from the building as the sudden roar from the collapsing South Tower deafened him. Dodging the dense, swirling dust and the cascading rubble, he jumped onto the ferryboat as it was backing out into the Hudson River.

It was to be several days before the full impact of the sight of the fire really hit him. Only then did he realize that while he had been in the elevator, many friends, acquaintances, and colleagues were dying on the floors of the building where he should have been.

He cried.

He was to cry again, at the most inconvenient of times, over the next few months as the effects of the shock released their grip on him.

He had never before suffered shock in such a horrific manner. It took him weeks to understand the confusion it created in his mind, and it took almost six months for his own fortunate escape sink in.

The most difficult part of his recovery was learning to handle the mourning process. It occurred to him that one is endowed with an innate ability to mourn the death of one or two close friends and colleagues, however devastating their passing may have been. Mourning the forty-seven friends and business acquaintances he had lost presented a challenge he found especially troubling. The sense of guilt that manifested itself when mourning just one lost friend at a time, to the exclusion of all the others, haunted him for a very long time.

Thoughts such as "why did I survive?" still, to this day, ring in his brain.

Reigning over the legacy of questions and confused emotions, though, one outcome remains paramount; like many others, he will never, never forget.

Sidewalk Cracks

"One, two, three, skip. One, two, three, skip. One, two, three, skip," Miranda, my little sister, called out as we scampered along behind Mom and Dad, trying but failing to keep up with them. We knew we had to be very careful about not treading on the cracks in the sidewalk. This took concentration and we were not able to do that, and keep an eye on the grown-ups' progress at the same time.

We were heading for the park at the top of the hill. High, solid, wooden fences lined both sides of this street. I think the neighbors here must have been afraid of someone trying to see into their yards. I still wonder what was in those yards that was so secret.

It was a gray day, but it wasn't raining. There were no shadows, and no wind. For whatever reason, the birds had decided not to sing for us. I think they prefer to have sun on them to do that.

We called out to Mom and Dad to slow down. They ignored us. They seemed very intent on reaching the park. I think my Mom wanted a cigarette but did not want to be seen in the street with one in her mouth.

We stopped to catch our breath. Watching for cracks was tiring work. I stared at Mom's and Dad's shoes. Every few steps, they would land on a crack and nothing happened. Andy had told us this was the way it worked. Adults were immune from the evil forces that could suck children through the cracks and down into the ground. Andy was our older brother, our stepbrother actually, and he knew a lot of stuff. We had learned many valuable pointers about life from him. He'd even let us in on the secret about why Mom and Dad's bed creaked loudly on occasion through the night, but Miranda and I knew he was just pulling our legs. Dad would never do something like that that would hurt Mom.

Miranda turned to me and said, "We'd better try and catch up."

"OK, but just watch where you put your feet."

She ran on ahead of me, skipping and jumping over the cracks. Suddenly, she stopped and bent down. She pulled from a pocket in her jeans a small doll with the odd name of Auntie. Miranda led the doll by its hand over the sidewalk's cracks, deliberately forcing the doll's feet into each and every crack.

"See, I told you so," she said to the doll. "I knew that you would be safe from the monsters in the cracks. I think Andy was making up that story just to frighten us."

"I'm not so sure about that," I told her.

"I wasn't talking to you," she snapped back.

"I know. I was only trying to be helpful. Andy may have made up some things, but I've heard from other kids that we should be careful of the cracks."

"Oh. OK." Miranda was quiet for a few moments. I saw a frown cross her face. "Have you ever heard about any kids disappearing into the cracks?"

I had to think about that one. I had not actually heard of any specific kid being sucked down into the ground, but I did know it could happen. I needed to sound more confident in my answer to Miranda. She was wild enough that she would try to do something risky, just because it was risky.

"I do know that Anton's younger brother over on the other side of the park has been missing for months and that his folks believe that he stepped on a crack," I told her.

Miranda stared into my face. "Is that really true or are you making that up?"

"Oh, it's true, all right." Well, the part about Anton's brother being missing was.

"Then I'll be very careful." Miranda stood up, shoved Auntie back in her pocket, and continued on, skipping up the road.

I could not see Mom and Dad. They must have reached the park. They were probably now sitting on one of the benches, with Mom fishing around in her pocket for her lighter.

I wished that I were with them. I didn't like all this talk about sidewalk cracks and the evil monsters that lay in waiting beneath them. I also wanted to be running and playing on grass where there were no such dangers lurking.

"I'll race you to the park," I called to Miranda who was about ten feet in front of me.

"You're on," she called back over her shoulder as she set off immediately.

I knew I was much faster than she was, otherwise I would not have thrown out the challenge. Within a matter of seconds, I had passed her.

"This isn't fair," she whined at me. "You're a boy and you're bigger than me and older than me."

All this was quite true, but I kept on going, still keeping a wary eye on where I placed my feet. I could not afford to get swallowed up this close to the park.

The park was only a few feet away, two huge, stone pillars guarding its entrance. Reaching the pillars, I stopped to savor my well-deserved victory.

I turned to see how far behind me Miranda was, knowing it could only be about five feet. She was not there.

Where on earth has she gone?

Had she given up in despair and gone off in a different direction? No, she could not have done that, there was nowhere for her to go. The high fences were impossible to climb over quickly, which is what she would have to have done.

The few trees lining the sides of the road were scrawny things that could not have hidden a flea, let alone my chubby sister.

No cars had passed us in either direction.

I tried not to think about the only remaining alternative.

Oh, God, please. Please do not allow her to be taken by the monsters. If she did step on a crack it was just by mistake, and I know she will never do it again. Send her back up here to me. I will take good care of her.

Miranda did not appear.

God was not listening to me, or maybe, just maybe, he wanted the monsters to hang onto Miranda for a while to teach her a lesson. He knew that she had been mean to me, telling tales on me about the frog I put in Dad's milk, and the worms I had been able to hide in Mom's bedroom slippers. Yes, that was it. That's what was happening. She would come back soon, full of apologies, and promising to be good forever after.

I waited.

Still no sign of Miranda.

Dad's voice pulled me from my fearful thoughts. He was calling to us from the park. He and Mom must be wondering what we were up to.

What was I going to tell him?

Miranda decided to go home. On her own? I don't think so.

Miranda took a short cut. Over the high fences?

Miranda went off in the car of a friend and they've gone to her house to play. Since when did Miranda get into anyone else's car without our parents' permission?

I wondered if I should tell them what really happened.

I think Miranda stepped on one of the cracks in the sidewalk and must have been sucked in by the monsters that live in the ground below.

I doubted they'd believe me. They'd tell me I was making it all up and that I'd have to spend the next ten years locked in my room if I didn't tell the truth.

I walked into the park with my head hung low. I didn't know what I was going to say.

"Where's your sister?" was Dad's first question.

I started to cry.

"What's happened to her?" Mom sounded scared. "Come on, tell us what's been going on."

I looked at the ground and forced the words out of my mouth. "I think Miranda stepped on one of the cracks in the sidewalk and must have been sucked in by the monsters that live in the ground below."

"What are you talking about, boy?"

Using "boy" was Dad's way of letting me know that I was a complete idiot.

"Just like I told you. She's gone." The words poured out of my mouth. "We were racing to get here and she must have not been watching where she put her feet. When I turned round, she wasn't there. It wasn't my fault."

Mom hugged me and said to me, "Come on; we'll go back into the street. Miranda's probably hiding."

"If she's not there," Dad yelled at me, "you're going to have to come up with a better explanation than what you've managed so far."

We reached the stone pillars and looked down the street. It was still gray and quiet.

And empty.

All at once, I realized that there was only one thing I could do to make them believe me. I ran from Mom's arms and stamped my foot down on the first crack in the sidewalk I came to.

Miranda and I have been down here now for almost twenty years. We have both found ourselves spouses and have children of our own. Life is good. We have made lots of friends, including Anton's brother. The sun cannot shine in our new world, but it never rains.

It's dark now. Time to take the children for a walk. They are reaching that age when they must learn not to reach up and try to grab a star from our sky.

You never know what might happen if they succeeded.

MELISSA SANSO

Melissa Sanso was born and raised in Savannah, Georgia. Growing up in Georgia in a family of fine rednecks, she has plenty of fodder for short stories and for novels, including her first completed novel, "Uncle Daddy."

Sanso has been writing since she was a little girl and always wanted to see herself published, but never had the courage to go the distance. Through the Savannah Writers Group, her friends in her mini-critique group, and the encouragement of her husband and son, Sanso has stories on paper and continues to develop new ones.

She also writes as Melissa Lyn Morris.

Contact Sanso at melsanso@bellsouth.net.

Write on!

A Tractor For Bobby

Bobby entered the toy store to buy a present for his grandson's fifth birthday. *Like all grandpas,* he thought, *I have no idea what to buy.* It would certainly be something better than he had at five.

Growing up poor caused him to spoil his only daughter. She went to the best schools, had the best clothes, and, at Christmas and birthdays, got the best gift. He had come a long way from the poor gypsy sharecropper life of the 1940s.

No, those kids running around the toy store certainly didn't know what it was like to become an experienced farmer by their tender ages. Nor did they know what it was like to have to fish for supper and live off the crops they planted and harvested. Those little hands had never seen the blisters from wielding a hoe every day after school.

The man looked around at the children running from this toy to that. A little girl was wide-eyed over a doll that cried. Another one said, "I would look like a princess in this costume." He smiled at the little girl's excitement and continued walking. Video games, skateboards, and building blocks–nothing struck him as the perfect gift. There were too many choices.

He picked up a baseball glove. Drawing it to his nose, he breathed in the aroma of the leather then placed it back on the rack. It was a fine glove, but still not the perfect gift. Turning, he noticed the bicycles–something else he didn't have as a boy–some with trick bars, others with reflectors. Maybe his grandson would like one of those. Then he noticed the riding toys: jeeps, cars, three-wheeled motorcycles. But, it was one toy that caught his eye.

It sat alone. Almost hidden. Waiting for someone to take notice, and notice the man did. A lump formed in his throat and tears welled in his eyes at the sight of the red push-pedal tractor. It was a fine tractor with bright red paint. The white front grill had "Ford" scribed on it in the old authentic script. It had no battery, no bells, no lights that lit up. It was just like the one he wanted when he was a boy.

Memories rushed back in that moment. The hustle and bustle of the kids in the store was drowned out in that moment as he thought about the day he first saw that tractor.

His family moved around often, usually the move came after the area store would give his mother no more credit to buy things with. They finally moved back to the farm where his great-aunt lived. She owned a general store. One day when he went to pick up some potatoes and asked her to put them on their account, she responded with "I suppose they are going to run up a tab with me too, that they can't pay." Bobby didn't understand what his great-aunt meant by the comment so he simply took the potatoes, thanked her, and left.

The hot Georgia sun was unforgiving, and Bobby remembered how he returned from the store to his mother working in the field as his father lay under the oak tree. He remembered how she looked holding her stomach with one hand as she bent over and with the other hand snatched the peanut bush from the ground. The peanuts that dangled beneath the plant like crystals on a chandelier were plucked and thrown into the bushel basket. She would straighten and arch her back to work the knots out, then push the basket down the row with her foot.

When the day was finished, Bobby watched his mother waddle back to the old farmhouse and disappear inside to prepare for supper. He admired her stamina, and he knew she got tired fast, but somehow kept going. He, his brothers, and the other workers continued the harvest until dusk when they would head to the house for supper.

As they approached the house, Bobby looked forward to seeing his mother through the kitchen window with the light around her. Every day her silhouette welcomed him, but today was different. She wasn't in the window. His sensed something was wrong and he ran toward the house.

When he got to the door, he froze at the sight of his mother lying on the kitchen floor. The water was overflowing from the sink making a puddle around her collapsed body. His father came up behind him and when he saw her, jumped past Bobby to her side yelling at him to get his brother.

Bobby wasted no time running out to the shed to get his big brother Len. With breathless speed, he told Len something was wrong with their mother. Len dropped the basket of peanuts and ran to the house, Bobby trailing behind. When they reached the house, Len froze in the door and Bobby ran straight into him.

His father yelled orders to go to Aunt Sue's store and call the doctor. Len wasted no time and ran as fast as he could, not realizing Bobby was still behind him making the two-mile run to the general store at the edge of the highway. They were both panting as they told their great-aunt the story and she dialed the phone.

While she talked with the doctor, Bobby noticed a red push-pedal tractor sitting on the floor near the counter. It looked just like a real tractor; just like the one in the Sears, Roebuck catalog Christmas past. There was even a little trailer to pull behind it.

For that moment he had forgotten why they were there. He was staring at the tractor so hard he didn't hear his brother calling him to go. He felt a twinge of guilt for thinking of the tractor, which was quickly replaced with fear when he remembered his mother.

They rode back to the house with their Uncle Henry. Bobby listened to Uncle Henry's tirade about what could be wrong with her and what had that no-good husband done to her this time. Bobby didn't know what he meant. He knew his father slept a lot, but his mother always said he was sick.

Uncle Henry was still rambling about Bobby's father being a drunk when they reached the house. Bobby ran around his brother to be the first to his mother. She had been moved to the bed. Bobby went in to see her, but was quickly ushered out of the room when the doctor arrived. When the doctor was finished, he asked to speak to Bobby's father alone.

Bobby followed his father and the doctor to the kitchen and listened outside the door. He heard the words "cancer" and "didn't you know?" Apparently, she had been sick a long time and told none of them. She continued to be a mother, wife, and farm hand without complaint or refusal. She endured his father's needs and got pregnant again despite the pain and the warnings from the doctor. Now it was just a matter of time before she wouldn't be able to do any of those things.

Bobby's heart sank as he heard the doctor's words. He didn't know what cancer was, but he knew what the doctor meant by "just a matter of time." He hung his head and walked back into her room. He reached out and touched her hand. The same hand that always stroked his hair and tickled his neck now lay still.

She was in bed several days before the doctor came to take the baby. It died two days later. He remembered the little coffin and the quick service his mother didn't get to see. A few weeks later the doctor called the family together to say "goodbye" to his mother.

Bobby crawled up into the bed, and she put her arm around him. He nestled his head into the crook of her arm and began to tell her about the red push-pedal tractor, detailing the lights that looked real and the gear shift just like the one on the field. When he looked up at her she smiled and told him how grand it sounded. She told him maybe she could buy it for him one day. He knew she would never be able to, but the idea was enough for him.

Now he stood in front of a little tractor. It was just like the one he wanted as a boy. He wished his mother had lived to see his success. Now that he could afford it, he did not hesitate and pulled the tractor off the shelf.

Meeting Auntie Rhonda

A Chapter from Sanso's Completed Novel, "Uncle Daddy":

Tara Howard moved to New York to start a new life where no one knew about her family. For two years she was able to hide them from her fiancé Carter, but an accident and a dying uncle forced her to return home to her little community in Georgia. Against her protests, Carter made the trip with her only to find a bizarre southern family living every cliché he ever heard about southerners and a few new ones. Will their relationship survive her secret?

Saturday morning rolled around. Tara, Carter, and Tara's father, Mack, sat quietly around the living room sucking on coffee and silently staring off in the distance. Carter still felt tense from the day before, was afraid to speak, and stared blankly at the television set. He thought about how his future mother-in-law, who was still asleep, made it clear that she didn't like her daughter marrying someone outside the family.

Now he understood why Tara kept her family from him, and he began to feel sorry for her. He still couldn't get over the fact that she never told him the family members were all married to one another.

Her father broke the silence. "Hey Fancy, how 'bout we go visit ya Auntie Rhonda?"

"I'll get my shoes." Tara threw down the newspaper and, with a smile on her face, bounced off the couch and ran up the stairs.

A few minutes later she emerged from her room wearing a big, blue sweater and riding boots.

"Ready," she announced.

Carter didn't have to change. Tara always said he woke up clean, pressed, dressed, and ready to go. He supposed she was right about that.

"I'll get the Gator," Mack said, raising himself out of his blue vinyl recliner.

Gator? Carter asked himself as he followed the large man out the back door with Tara close behind.

"You'll like this," Tara said, standing by him on the porch.

He watched Tara's father walk across the bare field that was their back yard to the large garage that sat next to an old mobile home. He wondered again, how Tara could have her refined demeanor and exquisite good taste growing up in a rusting trailer.

The loud roar of an engine caused a look of concern on Carter's face. Just when he wondered what kind of vehicle made that kind of noise, he saw Mack come flying around the corner of the mobile home on a four-wheel, ATV-type vehicle. Apparently, this was the "Gator." His assumption was confirmed when he saw "John Deere" and "Gator" written on the green fender. Carter couldn't help but stare in amazement.

"Hop on in now," Mack said.

Tara walked down the stairs. "Babe, why don't you take the seat and I'll get on the back."

"No, I can get in the back." He said looking at what he was supposed to sit on.

"Are you sure?" Tara gave him an uncertain look.

"Yeah, no problem," Carter said, sliding up on the back of the vehicle. He pulled his long legs up and wrapped his arms around them.

Tara shook her head and took the seat next to her father. She looked back at Carter who appeared uncomfortable. "You ready?" she asked.

Carter nodded, an uneasy smile on his face. Mack took off and turned on a dirt path about ten feet from the driveway. The path, overgrown by trees and shrubs, disappeared into the woods behind the house.

"Somebody lives back there?" Carter asked, but nobody answered him. Just then the woods swallowed them up and a large leafy branch barely missed his head.

"Jesus." he exclaimed.

"You okay, Bubba?" Mack asked.

"I think so." He adjusted himself, then tried a bit of humor, "You know, any minute some crazy man is going to come running out of the trees with a chain saw."

"Oh, don't you worry, son. They caught that old man a long time ago," Mack said.

Carter felt his eyes widen. It wasn't until Tara and her father began laughing that he realized they were joking.

"Funny," he responded. "Very funny."

"Oh don't be angry, babe. We're just pickin' at ya." Tara said, then started another laughing fit.

They reached a clearing at the end of the road where sat a light blue mobile home. As they inched closer, they passed an older model Cadillac with a small pine tree growing up the center of it. Next to it sat a Mustang that appeared to be frowning and another car that was so rusted it was void of identity. Cars of all makes and models littered the yard–some on blocks, others appeared to be growing up from the ground.

A huge oak tree stood between the house and a cinder block garage. The tree almost looked out of place. Its majestic limbs looked crippled by the weight of a car engine hanging from a chain and on another limb a tire hanging from a long rope. Around the bottom of the tree a chain was pulled taut by a large dog wildly barking.

A lone patch of cut grass, scattered with brightly colored plastic toys, bicycles, and a go-kart, invited you into the faded blue mobile home. Carter tilted his head to confirm that the home was indeed leaning to one side. The corners and seams were rusted and a broom handle that appeared it was struggling to hold up the air conditioner in the end window of the house.

Carter was astonished by what he saw. So astonished that he didn't realize they had stopped and Tara and her father were already out of the Gator.

"Gonna sit in the Gator all day, boy?" Mack asked in his gruff manner.

Just then a woman threw open the door and leaned against the jamb. On her hip was a fat baby dressed only in a diaper. The cigarette hanging out of the corner of her mouth added charm to this Norman Rockwell-on-acid photo opportunity.

"Oooooo. Eeeeeee. Look what the cat drug to my doorstep," the woman yelled. "My God, I can't believe it's my little sissy. Come give Auntie Rhonda a hug."

Carter stopped and thought, *Didn't Mack say this was Tara's Aunt Rhonda?* He shook his head as if to dismiss the thought. As soon as he started up the stairs, the rickety stairs lurched to one side catching him off guard. Losing his balance, Carter stumbled forward and caught the rails. He held on to both rails as stairs swayed back and forth.

"Watch ya self, Bubba." Rhonda said.

"Auntie Rhonda, this is Carter," Tara introduced them. Carter stopped trying to make it up the swaying stairs long enough to give Aunt Rhonda an appraising look. She was a short, fat woman with long, stringy red hair that looked as if it has seen one too many home colorings or permanents. She had both ears pierced several times and her nose bore a little diamond stud. Her dirty jeans were cut off to make shorts and the t-shirt she was wearing had the sleeves and the bottom shredded to look like fringe. After he made it up the stairs, Carter stuck out his hand to greet the woman.

"What's with the hand, Bubba?" Rhonda said slapping it out of the way. "Give me a hug."

To his surprise, she threw her free arm around his neck and pulled him down to her height. He struggled not to fall over the woman and his cheek barely missed the lit cigarette hanging out of the corner of her mouth. The smell of cigarette smoke, sweat, and perfume, hit him as he struggled not to touch the overly affectionate woman.

"It's so nice to meet you. Y'all come on in now. Bubba'll be back in a bit. He's just gone for some parts." Rhonda said.

Carter grabbed Tara by the arm, "Why is everyone calling me Bubba?"

Tara answered, "They call everybody 'bubba.' It's like saying 'man.'"

"Don't be shy, Bubba," Rhonda said putting the cigarette out with the heel of her bare foot. Then shouted over Carter's shoulder. "You stayin' Uncle Mack?"

When Rhonda turned to go inside, Carter noticed Aunt Rhonda's T-shirt had the words "Wild Bill Rhonda" written on the back in a blue and black airbrush. There was a black rose airbrushed underneath which was just like the tattoo on her ankle. He tried not to stare at the woman, but he had never seen anyone who looked permanently dirty. He thought to himself that even the guys he worked with at the construction sites looked cleaner than she did.

"Nope. I'll be back in awhile to collect 'em," Mack put the Gator in gear and backed out to the dirt path.

Carter watched the dust settle then followed Tara and her aunt inside. Once inside, an awful smell hit him immediately. Before he realized it, he had put his hand over his mouth and nose. He tried to determine the source of the smell, but from the filth it was hard to determine if it was the kitty litter pan in the corner of the room full of nuggets, the various overflowing ashtrays, or the pile of dishes he could see in the kitchen sink. From the looks of the house, filth was the norm for them. He wanted to turn and run but Tara had taken her place on the couch, which was covered with a bedspread and piled high at one end with laundry. He wasn't sure if the laundry was clean or dirty.

There was one path from the door through the mass of toys, clothes, shoes, and other miscellaneous items that had been discarded into the kitchen. Several dog bones were lying around, some rawhide and some from, he hoped, last night's dinner and not from weeks ago. Two plastic milk crates topped with a wood door served as their coffee table. It sat in front of the couch covered with magazines, more overflowing ashtrays, and drinking glasses that had obviously been there a while.

"C'mon in, Bubba. Make ya self to home," Rhonda invited.

Carter sat next to Tara and felt a pain when a spring poked him in the backside causing him to jump. He looked at Tara who gave him a look as if to say, "Don't be rude."

Rhonda had taken her place on the love seat covered with a towel. She had the baby's changing supplies–diapers, wipes, and an opened, oozing tube of diaper rash cream–at one end. After she laid the baby down and changed its diaper, Rhonda put the dirty diaper in the plastic grocery bag hanging from the arm of the love seat. That explained one of the smells.

It was in that moment Carter realized the baby was a boy and not the girl he thought it was when he saw its long blond curly hair. "What's your baby's name?" Carter dared to ask trying to make conversation.

"This is Jake E. Lee. He is named after the late, great, guitarist for Ozzy Osbourne," she replied. "May he rest in peace."

"Oh, yeah, what a guy," was all he could say with a hint of sarcasm.

Tara cleared her throat then tried to continue the conversation, "I didn't know you had another baby."

"Well, if you came home more often, you would know these things." Rhonda answered. "Ya Mama didn't tell you when you called."

"I haven't spoken to mother in a while. I, that is we, have been so busy with our latest project and, well, the engagement."

"Whoa there, Nelly. What engagement?" Rhonda exclaimed.

"Ours." Tara, delighted that the secret was out, waved the engagement ring in Rhonda's face. The ring that, until now, she had kept hidden in her purse.

"My God, girl. That thing would choke a bull." Rhonda grabbed Tara's hand to get a closer look. "What'd ya mama say."

"Well..." Tara sighed.

"I don't think she is very happy with the idea," Carter said, adjusting himself to keep from sinking deeper into the couch.

Rhonda looked at him adjusting the baby on her lap. "You'll learn, Bubba, that my sister ain't happy with much."

"Sister?" he asked.

"Yeah, Mama and Rhonda are sisters," Tara said like he should have known.

He did see some resemblance but Rhonda was twice the size, width-wise, of Tara's mother, Deena, and the hair color. Well, it is obvious red was not her natural color so that couldn't be a determining factor.

"Well, I'm sure you ain't met all the family yet." Rhonda said.

Rhonda's comment fell on deaf ears as Carter looked around the living room at the wild array of mess. Fortunately, his sinuses had almost adjusted to the smell in the house. He studied the large entertainment cabinet that took up one wall. The very small television in the cabinet was barely visible. There were books, junk, and tapes shoved in around it. The top of the cabinet was covered with souvenir beer mugs, shot glasses, and stuffed animals.

Hung on the wall over the cabinet was a mounted deer head. *Why would anyone want to have a deer head on their wall?* Carter thought to himself. He never understood hunting and never considered it a sport. At least, this head served two purposes. It was a gun rack for a rifle–obviously the one that was used to kill the poor creature–and it held the coat hanger antenna for the television.

The next item that caught his eye was the old, brown recliner in the corner. Its arms and the foot rest were taped with grey duct tape. On one arm sat a television remote control taped together with the same duct tape used on the chair, and on the other sat a bright orange ashtray overflowing with cigarette and cigar butts. There was a small table with a pole lamp running through it. The bottom was a magazine rack and it too was overflowing. The little table was covered with glasses and mugs. Some of them had been there so long they had grown fuzzy.

Carter shuddered at the filth. *How could anyone live this way?* he thought to himself. *Mother would have killed me if I left one glass sitting on the coffee table for more than five minutes.* He was so deep in thought he didn't hear their hostess. Tara nudged him.

"Carter, Auntie Rhonda asked if we wanted something to drink.'

"No, not for me," Carter stuttered. "I'm fine."

"You must be thirsty. I'll get ya some tea."

"No, really, Don't trouble yourself," Carter said almost pleading.

"Ain't no trouble. Here girl, take the baby." Rhonda handed Tara the baby and went into the kitchen.

"So how long y'all stayin?" Rhonda yelled from the kitchen.

"If nothing happens, we have to fly back on Sunday." Tara answered.

"Well at least you'll be here for the pickin' tonight." She returned with two big plastic drink cups that said Krystal on the side.

"Thank you" Carter said as he took the cup from her hand. He gave Tara an uneasy smile and looked at the tea as if something was going to come up out of it.

"Pickin'?" Carter asked.

Another question went unanswered as they were interrupted by the sound of hurried footsteps on the stairs out front. The whole house shook as the door was snatched open. It slapped back against the house as two boys and one very, dirty little girl ran into the house. Rhonda jumped up. "Calm it down. What the hell have I told you about coming into the house like that? You're like a bunch of wild Indians," she yelled. "Now you come over here and say 'hello' to your Aunt Tara."

Rhonda's husband, Bubba, came in shortly after the kids. "Good Lord, Bubba, look at the mud you're tracking in here." Rhonda yelled.

"Baby, don't you start with me. Them is the tracks of a working man," Bubba said. "Now, come over here an' give me a kiss."

Carter watched as Rhonda hugged and kissed her husband.

Bubba who, obviously not noticing their company, squeezed her behind. Carter, who was not a man known to be overly affectionate, especially in front of other people, was taken aback by this display. He turned away just in time to notice one of the dirty boys picking his nose.

When am I going to get out of this? Carter thought to himself as he looked down at the floor between his shoes. Just then a large black cockroach crawled out from the edge of the couch. "Ugh," He yelled as he jumped and pulled his feet up on the couch. Everyone turned and looked at him as the cockroach traveled on. Its destination was the microwave dinner plate that was sitting on the floor by the brown recliner.

The kids squealed and jumped up and down. "Get it, Daddy. Get it."

Bubba's big boot descended on the unsuspecting creature. "POP."

"EEEWWW," the kids yelled in unison, followed by laughs and high-fives to each other and their father.

"Who's the man?" Bubba yelled putting his hands out for the kids to slap.

After the celebration was over, Bubba picked up the cockroach with his bare hand and threw it out the front door. The screen door slapped closed behind him. He turned to Tara, "Well looky whose here."

"Hey ya, Bubba," she said hugging the man. "I want you to meet my fiancé, Carter Brooks."

"Hey, man. Pleased to meet ya." Bubba held out the meaty hand that had just thrown the oozing cockroach corpse out the front door.

Carter reluctantly took the hand and gave it a quick shake. He was stunned. This is not what he expected or wanted of an extended family. He was even more stunned that Tara never told him that her family was a bunch of filthy, inbred, rednecks.

What was he going to do?

This is an excerpt from the novel Uncle Daddy by Melissa Sanso.
Look for the completed novel to find the answer to Carter's question.

J.C. SONNIER

J.C. Sonnier was born and raised in the story-rich land of the Cajuns, down in the bayou country of southwestern Louisiana. He holds an architectural bachelor's degree from the University of Louisiana and a master's degree in adult education from Armstrong Atlantic State University in Savannah. He is an active member of the Phi Kappa Phi Honor Society. His artistic and creative interests include boat building, furniture making, glass carving, pen-and-ink drawing, watercolor painting, and woodcarving. He is a member of the Savannah Art Association, a founding board member and instructor of the Armstrong Lifelong Learning Institute, president of the Savannah Woodcarvers' Club, and an active member of the Savannah Writers' Group. Short fiction is presently his passion, but he is planning a science fiction novel. His writing style combines sensory description with the surprising twists and turns that fill our lives. It is just not enough to read his story; he wants you to experience it.

On Monday She Was Gone

Well, if I had to sit out here, at least it was a beautiful Saturday morning. The coolness of autumn had finally arrived and the South Louisiana sky was a brilliant shade of French blue and cloudless. I was very comfortable sitting on a modular bench between the twin dorm towers of Denbo and Bancroft. I chose this bench because the shadow of one of the towers had just flowed over it. On this particular morning, the exclusive girls' dormitory complex was not a bad place to be. Girls of every size, shape, and disposition were swarming the small treeless, multi-layered plaza, littered with bicycles locked into bike racks. Being the only male student in sight, I was kept quite busy returning many a smile, glance and or "Good Morning" as the girls went by. I was just waiting for Suzie. Patience was very necessary when dating a sorority girl. It was so important for girls like Suzie to be dressed and make-upped impeccably before being seen on campus. Being a sorority girl meant there was a role to play. She reasoned the longer she took, the better she looked, and the more I would enjoy her company. It was a point well taken. And besides, I felt as if I were sitting in the middle of a saltwater tank filled with beautifully colored exotic fish. Suzie could take all the time she needed. I could wait.

Resigned to my fate, I eased my sunglasses to the tip of my nose, studying each passer-by with interest. The sounds of chirping birds and the melodic clicking of ten-speed bike derailers were lolling me. Slowly, I became aware of an echoing sound bouncing between the towers. Female voices were coming from a cranked open window, half way up Bancroft Tower. Tilting my head back, I realized two girls were waving clothes or towels and calling out, "Hey, you on the bench..." Looking around, I looked over to the only other bench in the area. It was empty and I was the sole occupant of this particular bench. Could they be calling me? What's more, it sounded as though someone wanted to talk to me. "Laurie will meet you in the lobby."

This all sounded very strange. Suzie may be behind this. Part of the "glue" holding us together was our love to pull pranks on each other. If this was a prank, whom had she coerced into setting me up? I was willing to play along and see where this was going. Heart pounding, I stood up, placed my sunglasses in my left shirt pocket, and headed for the lobby.

This was all happening in the year 1972. On the University of Southern Louisiana campus, no male students were allowed anywhere inside any of the girls' dorms, except the well lit, heavily couched sitting lounge on the main floor. Passing the lounge, I noticed the usual; guys lingering (impatiently waiting for their current "squeeze"), wallflowers studying together for the next big exam, and a smattering of couples lip-locked and groping whenever one of the walk-around monitors wasn't watching.

The elevator door opened and out floated Laurie. Glancing around the lobby, she quickly found me and called out to me. As she extended her hand to me, she introduced herself and an accompanying friend. In the sweetest of voices, she asked, "Would you have a minute or two to talk?"

What would this goddess want with me? This was the cute little blonde who captured my attention whenever she was near me. I had no idea she knew I even existed.

Zombie-like, I followed her into the lounge. I sat on an over-sized easy chair opposite the couch she graced. She honestly lit up the room. Those eyes, those beautiful eyes were looking directly into mine. Her gaze was so tender, so caring. I knew my eyes were betraying me, exposing my every weakness, but I could not look away.

She began telling me she "noticed" me around and about on campus all semester, but never felt comfortable enough to approach me. My head was spinning. We then spent the better part of an hour talking about everything. We shared music interests, our preferences in art, and what goes best on pizza. Emotions flowed over me as we talked. I never felt so compatible, so enamored with someone. I was unable to gaze anywhere but those soft, beautiful eyes. As we spoke, she giggled, saying I was so funny. She kept mentioning it was such a shame that we had not met before today. Why was this of interest? We had our whole lives to make up for the small period of time wasted this semester. She was a freshman and I, a sophomore. We will be in school here for years. We would have so much to talk about, so many plans to make. What would our children be like and what did she want to name them? How big a house would we need? Where would we spend the rest of our lives together? Heart, quiet down, I'm trying to listen to Laurie.

Suddenly, her friend returned, reminding Laurie about her dad arriving soon and that she needed to finish. Finish what? Laurie thanked her and she grimly looked back to me. Sadly, she told me she was leaving school and returning home with her dad that very afternoon. Her experience at our esteemed university had been less than expected. Seeing me this morning in the plaza, she boldly decided to finally meet me before she left. Then she revealed she was to be married soon to her high school sweetheart. I asked her if this was what she really wanted to do. She answered, 'Yes, I've thought about it a lot and feel it would be best." The bi-plane of my heart, bellowing smoke and in flames, began to lose altitude and spiral into the ground. I desperately wanted her to reconsider; I wanted the whole semester to be rewound so we could spend more than just this precious moment together. We stood up and I reached for her hand. Laurie instead hugged me and thanked me for coming by. Wishing me a wonderful life, she said "Goodbye" and walked toward the elevator. The elevator door opened. Laurie stepped into the elevator just as Suzie stepped out, neither knowing a thing about the other.

Suzie asked about my gloomy demeanor as we left the dorm. My only response was, for some crazy reason, my head was pounding, but so was my heart. I unlocked my bike from the rack and I walked it along as we slowly made our way to the O.K. Allen Cafeteria. Only a two-block walk away, it seemed to me we walked for hours. Once there, I found I had no interest in the food.

What had just happened? Would I have been any better off if Laurie left without this encounter? I don't think so. No, I don't want to think so. It could have been a major turning point in both our lives. Maybe more time around me would have convinced her that contacting me was not a good idea. But then, maybe not.

Thirty-four years or so have passed since that day. I sometimes wonder how Laurie's doing; hoping life has been gracious and kind to her. To this day, the memory I have of that morning is a tiny treasure I keep inside. How wonderful it is to feel she genuinely cared about me. Whenever I think of her now, I just close my eyes and Laurie's face appears, as well as those beautiful eyes...

The Fire

Wow.... What a blaze. I'll bet you could probably see it from Abercorn, if you were looking in the right direction on a clear day. I warned Susan, time and time again over the years, about having all those mini-lights hanging in the hedges year round. Even for minor holidays, the porch, the hedge, and the yard would be trimmed with lights and decorations, while strange mechanical props from Wal-Mart or Target went through their gyrations. It just wasn't safe, especially with twelve to fifteen extension cords plugged into one outdoor socket near the front door. But imagine, a husband being right about something. She continually tried to assured me Chinese decorative light manufacturers wouldn't sell those cute little lights if they were dangerous.

The clear mistake I made was assuming a large display of Christmas paraphernalia would be the holiday setup to short out and start a fire. It turned out the holiday destined to torch the house was Halloween, her downright runaway favorite. Yes, it was quite a scene. Dracula's fangs were dripping molten paint as plastic pumpkins exploded and the ghost and goblin recordings on the two CD players whirred to a stop.

It could have easily been one of several holidays, since Sue decorates for most of them. Well, it could not be the Groundhog's Day lighting, for I secretly Good-willed the box labeled 'Groundhog's Day Stuff' a few years back, unbeknown by Sue. In it was the large size pop-up groundhog, with or without sunglasses and a sign and a recorded message proclaiming a longer or shorter winter. This set of decorations included a string of cute little miner's lanterns to run along sides the front walk. Was I surprised when she flew down the attic stairway last January, declaring in horror, "I cannot find the 'Groundhog's Day Stuff' box in its place between the 'Greek Independence Day Stuff' box and the 'Guatemalan Labor Day Stuff' box." (She always ends the label with the word "Stuff.") I asked if she needed help, but she said she'd rather I would re-box MLK's bust into the appropriate container. Oh, and this time, she asked, "Please use two strips of tape to seal the box remembering to have the last strip circumnavigate the box with at least a 3 inch overlap of the tape's beginning." Back to the combustion...

Dale and Steve, a couple of neighbors, came running over, being concerned about my vast tool collection. I calmed their fears by pointing to the newly air conditioned, well lit, and impeccably clean workshop I just built two years earlier. Steve and his wife offered to store the boxes of home videos and photographs I managed to rescue as well as Susan's silly Nancy Drew book collection. Dale, "Mr.-Never-Throws-Anything-Away, " walks up with a 'still smoldering' section of hose telling me, "If you cut the burnt part off, we could put a new male swivel on it and it would be as good as new."

It was truly amazing to see our local firemen at work. The first fireman drove up within minutes of the fire and promptly parked across the street. When the fire truck showed up twenty minutes later, he was so embarrassed. He realized his Mega Cab hemi-powered, four-wheel drive pick-up was parked in front of the fire hydrant. What a pain it must have been for him to get up out of his lawn chair, put his beer down, and move his truck. I suppose I must be living in a vacuum, for I had never seen firemen with personalized lawn chairs. Do you think they'd mind if I help myself to one of their beers from the official "Northside Fire Department" beer coolers?

Suddenly, I heard a deafening, blood-curdling scream. As my ears rang, I realized Sue was standing in front of me, tears flying from her eyes. Now temporarily deaf, due to the high level of decibels of her scream, I could only read her lips. She was asking me, "What about MeNew?" At that moment, I'm sure she registered my expression of stupefaction as pure horror, but it was not the case. I WAS NOW FREE. MeNew was out of my life. As this realization flowed over me, the roof came down in a torrent of sparks and embers, meeting the floor for the first time with a thunderous crash.

Surely Misty MeNew was gone. Never again would I ever have to tolerate her twisting around my legs, tripping me as I walk around the house. Gone were the piles of her fur and dander in inaccessible places, clinging to the furniture, clogging the air filter, and fusing into the rug. At least once a week, I could be found blindly running into the wall, sightless and in pain, because of a cat hair between one of my eyes and its coordinating contact lens. Sure, I would still bear the scars and bite marks of our constant battles, but never again would a mere animal deprive me of my Easy Boy. I would soon be buying a new pair of waterproof slip-ons, ones never to be punctured by Me-

New's needle-like teeth, nor would she ever hide just one of them from me ever again. Dare I consider a life free of cold, squishy blobs of hairball between my toes as I walk across the bedroom carpet in the wee hours? LIFE will be GREAT. I AM TRULY FREE.

Thankfully my blubbering bride could not see my face, as I hugged her to my chest. She would truly miss MeNew. I had to think fast. At the right time, I would probably say, "Sue, maybe we shouldn't have another cat. We should not tarnish MeNew's memory by replacing her." Or how about, "Maybe we just aren't lucky with pets." I'd have to work on it.

Dale's wife, Liz, came over and took Sue to the ice chests to sit and console her. She was taking this really hard, so hard I felt I needed a plan of action. Yes, a quick trip to Wal-Mart for a couple dozen fish and an aquarium. Sure, a nice stand and one of those little treasure chests, always filling up with air and then pops its lid to showoff its plastic jewels and diamonds. She'll forget all about MeNew. Or how about a hamster? With my life-long interest and bachelor's degree in architecture, I could build a world-renowned hamster habitat. It would be the Eighth Wonder of the Rodent World. The tubing is relatively inexpensive and comes in a multitude of colors and materials. It would have a hamster hot tub, hamster escalators, 24/7 hamster buffet... nothing but the best. Wouldn't she love them? Of course she would. They also have fur; they eat and poop, and can be spayed or neutered. But dear reader, the important difference here is the $1/32^{nd}$ inch polystyrene thick tubing wall between the hamster infestation inside the habitat and... me. But I digress; there will be time to plan.

I stood there with a woeful crocodile face, having trouble keeping my happiness inside. Life is GOOD. Just then I felt a drizzle. No, the Northside boys hadn't even pulled the fire hoses off the truck yet, their pizza having just arrived. Ever notice you can count on rain if there's a fire? Isn't it funny how it always seems to happen? Just then I heard Sue yell, "MeNew." No longer crying, Sue was now pointing to the tree branches just above my head. She commanded, "John, don't just stand there, get her down."

Then I noticed the smell.

The Miracle Tree

All I heard of the call was, "Sure, Tina, I'll see what I can find." After hanging up, Cathy was back in the garage, creaking up the attic stairs. Before the phone conversation with Tina, Cathy had declared that she could not continue to clean the garage for a second longer. Now she was rummaging upstairs in the older Christmas boxes. I popped up the attic stairs halfway and asked, "What gives?"

"That was Tina on the phone. Her neighbor, Jodie, down the street in her subdivision needs help with Christmas. Her husband is on his third trip to Iraq and now her phone bill is larger than her rent and food bill combined. She and her two toddlers have nearly nothing to eat and of course Christmas isn't in the cards."

"And... so" I asked.

"Well, I have a stash of toys that I've had for years, you know, the ones I've been giving the kids in my class on their birthdays. Now that I'm about to retire, giving them to those two adorable kids will be doing us a favor in our effort to clean up the garage."

"Always Mrs. Claus, aren't you?"

"Andy, Tina's husband, is planning on cutting down a small bald cypress tree along their back fence so that the kids will have a tree. But they're having trouble finding ornaments." She closed up a box and after pushing it aside, she began to dig through another. "Jack, you know that the one thing that those kids will remember at their age is the magnificence of a beautifully decorated and well lit tree. Heaven knows we'll never use these old strings of lights and ornaments now that the boys are gone."

"But you've kept them all these years knowing that you'll never use them?"

"Jack, it was meant to be. What can I say?"

"Well, get everything together and I'll carry it all over to Tina's."

"No worry, they're on their way to get it now, probably be here in ten minutes."

Well, in about five minutes, we had everything boxed up and left it all on the front porch. Three hours later, we hear a car door slam shut and soon the door bell rang. At the door we found Tina and a quiet be-spectacled little lady with a big smile.

As I greeted them, Tina put up a hand to hush me as she continued to talk into her cell phone. "But... but...Momma, she... "She made a guttural sound deep in her throat as she slammed the phone into her thigh several times. "Momma, let me talk... Momma, I'm going to hang up... Momma, you know I love you, but you cannot give your one and only granddaughter a pony... But Momma, you can't...Momma, do you ever want to see Carly again?... You... But Momma... No, Momma that's not a threat, get her that pony and it's a promise." With that said, Tina flipped her cell phone closed. "Dammit if she gives her that pony she'd better buy Andy a snow shovel that he can use as a pooper scooper."

"Hey you all, this is Jodie. Jodie, this is Jack and his wonderful wife, Cathy, the Christmas Angel. She is here to enlighten all around her, empty the stores of Savannah of their bargains, and put up with Jack. Jack, do you ever not snicker when I'm around?"

Cathy entertained our visitors for at least an hour. Before they pulled away from the driveway, the back of Tina's convertible was loaded with boxes of ornaments, cheap discounted toys, and old boxes of cake mix (with names like 'Duncan Hines Double Chocolate Supreme Deluxe, now with Pecans.') As she closed the front door, Cathy had silent tears rolling down her cheeks.

"Jack, that poor family... and it's Christmas. It's all so sad. I hope that the little I gave them helps. I feel as though we should do more." She hugged me and as we stood there, her tears soaked through my shirt. Just then it dawned on me, I'd better look through Cathy's checkbook. I was sure she "accidently" dropped a check in one of the boxes.

The next morning, the house phone was ringing off the wall. Cathy was asleep, so I dashed madly to intercept the call. I didn't make it. The answering machine picked up, offering to take a message. The caller wasn't interested because the answering machine issued a loud dial tone after giving its initial apology for our absence. Immediately, Cathy's cell phone began to chime. Grabbing it, I read the display. It was Tina.

"Hello Jack, is the little woman in bed? No matter, this is so important I'll tell you. Last night after midnight, Andy was waked by a commotion in the backyard. Grabbing his shotgun, he went out back half naked and found a bunch of teens dragging Christmas trees across our yard. You know 'The United Shelter,' that fancy, up-scale church at the beginning of our subdivision? They sell Christmas trees at a stand in front, providing their rich parishioners with the most beautiful trees in Georgia. Well, when they closed the stand around ten last night, these neighborhood kids decided to grab some free trees."

"So, anyway, at seeing these kids and knowing that they were up to no good, Andy fired the gun into the air and shouted, "Nobody move." Well, move they did 'cause within seconds, Andy was standing alone in the middle of the backyard surrounded with Christmas trees."

By this time, shaking with laughter, I can barely hold the phone.

"Control yourself, Jack. I'm coming to the best part. Andy and the cops didn't find the kids, but brought the trees back to the tree stand. We all went back to sleep. Well, I just got a call from Jodie. Guess what she found in her yard this morning? Yes, a big beautiful Christmas tree. Isn't that wonderful? Andy has already gone over to set it up. So tell Cathy to come over to help us decorate the tree. And tell her we may need more ornaments. This tree is huge."

"But Tina, shouldn't that tree go back to the tree stand with the rest of the stolen trees?"

"Jack, you pagan. Jodie's two babies are as pleased as punch. Their daddy might be half way around the world, but they have a Christmas tree. Do you think you should go over to their house, shake off the ornaments, and drag it out of there? Is your heart that cold? And besides, don't you see that it was a gift from God? Who are we to intervene in a Christmas miracle?"

"Anyway, have Cathy call me." CLICK.

The Recipe

Susan was startled when the doorbell rang. After having gathered all the ingredients on the kitchen counter to make the Cereal Crunch, she was sure an interruption was not part of the recipe. She quickly glanced around the kitchen and living room for anything drastically out of place. Damn, she thought, how many times have I asked John to get his box of tools out from in front of the fireplace and into his tool shed? She grabbed his woodworking magazines from the couch and stacked them neatly under her Lady's Home Journals on the coffee table. She checked herself in the hall mirror and added a smile before she looked through one of the front door's side windows. Oh, crap, it's the neighborhood gossip, Judy from three doors down. She reapplied the smile, took a deep breath, and opened the door.

"Oh, Judy, come on in. Please excuse the mess. As you know, when we teachers take the summer off, we take the summer off. Why don't you come in into the kitchen for some coffee?"

Locking her thin frame into a forward leaning pose, Judy's quick eye scanned the room not missing a molecule. Her wrist came up to her chin as she flipped her hand forward and exclaimed, "Oh this little mess doesn't bother me any. The burden of house-cleaning perfection falls squarely on my job description, the stay-at-home mom."

Bitch, thought Susan. Judy's only child, Liz, had been off at college for the past three years. The only person she watches now during the day is Oprah.

As they settled in for coffee, as if to answer Susan's thoughts, Judy took a loud sip and continued, "Well, now that Liz is off at school, Bill and I have gotten used to our routines. He can be sure he will come home from work every night to a good home-cooked meal, a clean house, and an evening in his recliner with his satellite remote control. He watches T & A programs on Spike TV, sports on ESPN, and back-to-back episodes of *Law and Order* on the tube. The Easy-Z-Boy provides heat and roller-bar massage while I serve him gin and tonics till he falls asleep. What more can he ask for?"

Susan fought to control her laughter. Yes, and that's why he weighs the same as a small compact car and complains to John about not having marital relations since this new century started. She opened the white almond bark she picked up earlier at Kroger. It was important she not use white chocolate because it would not yield the right results. As Judy chatted, Susan melted six squares of the almond bark for 45 seconds in the microwave.

Judy, resting her elbows on the countertop and her chin on the palms of her hands, asked, "So, Susan, you're cooking at two in the afternoon? What's up?"

Susan next stirred the melting almond bark with a large plastic spoon, and then microwaved the mixture for another 45 seconds.

"You know John, always looking for new adventures. He's been bitten by the writing bug. He meets with a bunch of other writer-types every other Tuesday over at the Books-A-Million on the Southside."

"So he's bringing food to them tonight?"

Susan removed the bowl from the microwave and the stirred in two cups of Honey Graham cereal and a half can of mixed nuts.

"No, One of the members is throwing a party at her home for the group and everyone has to bring a dish or a snack. John wants to wow them, so he asked me to make cereal crunch. I don't mind and it's pretty easy to make. Besides, it gets him out of the house so I can watch my reality TV shows. He detests them."

Susan then poured the mixture on to a large piece of aluminum foil, spreading the confection evenly. In roughly thirty minutes, the mass will be cool and dry. She will then break it into small pieces and store it in a Ziploc bag.

"A writer's group? Do men really join writer's groups? Is he going to try writing a book like one of those Harlequin romance novels?"

Susan looked Judy squarely in the eye. "I visited just last month and I saw three other guys there. Granted, there were more women. Who knows, maybe he will write a novel or a woodworking how-to book. He's got so damn many how-to books; you'd think he could write one. You know how a nut doesn't fall far from the tree? If a nut falls in his home office, it's sure to hit a how-to book. John is just trying to find his writing niche."

"You'd better hope that's all he's trying to find."

"Judy, please."

"He was not bad-looking back when he had hair."

"Well as long as he's happy writing, I'll encourage him."

"Didn't he just get a degree at Armstrong? Wasn't it an education degree?"

"Yes, it's probably what started up his writing binge. He did have to write quite a few papers," said Susan.

"Judy, can't you wait for it to cool? I'll send you home with a bag full." Not soon enough, she added mentally.

"Sue, you know I can't pass up an almond. He was just looking up at me and I heard him yelling in his little almond voice, 'Help me. Help me. Please pick me up and eat me. You can do it.' Sue, I just wanted to save him, quiet him down."

"Well, Judy, you've walked down here. I'm sure you've got something juicy to tell me."

"Susan. Are you inferring that I would stoop to conveying embellished bits of unsubstantiated information? Believe me, I'm not one to gossip. But I did hear that down on the other end of the street, Elaine found out her husband, who is ten years younger than her…"

The Strong Scent of Pines

The yells of the Rebels rang through the trees as they came over the crest of the ridge. Michael rose from the prone position to sitting with his back to the flaky bark of the mighty pine. The excitement of anticipation roared through his body as his heart pounded in his ears. Twisting his upper body to the side of the tree, he lifted the rifle to his shoulder. His hearing was just clear enough to identify the voice of Sergeant O'Shay barking the command to open fire. He singled out a particularly large enemy silhouette rushing toward him, but the sweat pouring into his eyes and the uncontrollable shaking of his limbs made it impossible to draw a bead. Just then, the wind was punched out of him as he felt a burning fire in his lower left ribcage. His body's reaction to the blow threw his arms forward, causing him to launch his rifle from his chest. Trying to gain control, he rolled onto his stomach at the base of the pine. His brain was screaming. It just could not have happened to him, not so soon, not before his first shot. Though in pain, he managed to push himself up onto his hands and knees, searching for his rifle.

Around him there was a sense of much movement and screaming, as gunshots rang out. Suddenly he was knocked flat and stepped on by a rush of escaping figures. As that crowd moved away, another group followed in hot pursuit. An eerie silence then prevailed, broken only by rifle shots that seemed to be fading away. Opening up his eyes, he found that he lay across another soldier dressed in a uniform similar to his. Leaning to the left, he realized that the lifeless body was that of O'Shay. The sergeant was now missing a portion of his head and nearly his whole jaw. Michael began to crawl away from the corpse, but after only a few painful yards, he felt a cracking thud to the back of his skull as his forage cap flew away. Before he passed out, he felt that his pockets were being emptied, as his boots were removed.

The smell of the damp forest floor filled his nose as he came to. Michael began to cough as he realized that he had a mouth full of earth. Reeling in pain, he rolled on to his right side and managed to spit out the debris. Gulping huge amounts of air, he noticed that his hands were holding his wet blouse tightly to the fire in his ribs. The trees above began to darken as he again lost consciousness.

In his mind, Michael began to see glimpses of his dad's farm in Ohio. Wheat grew there for what seemed to be miles in all directions. One could almost get dizzy watching the wind whip the golden waves to and fro just before harvest time. Like an abandoned ship at sea, the old broken harvest wagon sat in the middle of the shallow pond near the orchard. With rolled up knickers and naked wet feet, he and Elizabeth sat in the bed of the wagon with their backs to the rotting seat. He was telling her how he would be off to war next month and later returning to marry her if she would have him. As she strung the clover blossom stems together from the rust pail, she went on and on about how going off to war seemed all so romantic and manly. Her dad felt that Michael should hurry off soon or miss the war. The South would surely be defeated by the end of the year.

She had been on the platform to see him off the morning he left. He hated to leave her, but he was eager to return a hero. While in training, he had received three long letters from her, scented with the imported French cologne that her Aunt Lucy had sent to her from Paris. He had managed to write a little bit to her every day, but had to wait till Saturday, mail day, to post each week's worth of letters.

His regiment, the Ohio Volunteer Infantry, trained and drilled for nine weeks under the tyrannical Sergeant O'Shay. The sergeant did finally take a liking to Michael, for he was astonished by the boy's marksmanship and his keen sense of hearing and sight. At the end of training, the Ohio regiment was sent to a large collecting camp where his group received its uniforms, gear, and weapons. After three more weeks of intense training and a camp visit by General Grant himself, Michael's regiment began to move south by road and rail. It was at this point that life became difficult for Michael. The ill-fitting uniform began to chaff him and the clatter of his equipment as he marched just about drove him crazy. Even the several short trips by rail were unbearable. Each day found him exhausted due to the heat and the swarming flies, while his nights were filled with the droning and bites of the waves of mosquitoes. But worst of all, he was unable to send or receive mail from Elizabeth.

The food was bountiful on the weekends and sparse on weekdays. To stabilize his diet, he became friends with the cooking staff, volunteering to help them whenever he could. Michael had always enjoyed the pleasant, quick rainstorms in Ohio, but here in the South; the rain came down in monsoon fashion and went on for days. For nearly a week he and his colleagues were drenched to the bone.

Rumor had it that this infantry battalion was chasing a Rebel army, that was always just a day or so ahead. Everyone in his company was ready to make contact with the Rebs, kill as many as they could, and chase the rest home.

Finally, Michael's regiment made it to the north central pine forests of Georgia. On the third evening of this bivouac, O'Shay called his men together to say that the battle with the Johnnie Rebs was imminent in the next day or two. For their part, O'Shay's group would be assigned to entrench themselves on the right flank of a ridge, and if the enemy challenged them, they were to hold the Rebs till the larger part of the Union army could take over. O'Shay lead the group in a prayer, then handed out a few bottles of whiskey. Out came a harmonica and the men began to dance and sing. Michael unbelted his campaign bag and pulled out paper and pen to write Elizabeth. He propped himself against a small pine just at the angle to have the campfire illuminate his pad. After explaining the excitement he felt for the upcoming action, he began to wander into the subject of their life after the war. Their beautiful spring marriage, his plans for the farm and the crops they'd raise, he even named their first three children, be they boy or girl. The partying lasted till midnight, then the men bedded down for the night. Some men could not sleep but the ones that did dreamed of the whipping they would give the Rebs come the following day.

Michael, not having participated in the drinking the night before, got up in the early light before the rest to get his gear in order and help with breakfast. Looking around, he found an old split oak that had been hit by some ancient bolt of lightning. Not being a pine in this pine forest, he was sure to be able to locate the oak later. Examining the tree, he found in its base a nice size hollow. Using a stick and his shaving mirror, he found it to be free of hornets, snakes, and spiders. Next, he laid a dry pile of pine straw down in the hollow's bottom. Next Michael carefully rolled Elizabeth's letters, with the locket that held Elizabeth's picture and a lock of her hair and his extra pair of shoes into his navy woolen bedroll. After securing the bundle with a strap, he carefully placed it in the hollow, covering it with dried oak leaves. He would be back later to retrieve it. As he walked away, he buttoned his right breast pocket. In this safest of places, he carried the rather long letter he had penned the night before with the last letter that he had received from Elizabeth. In that posting, she had actually written what she had never been able to say to him. This letter had closed with "I love you, Michael."

At roughly seven that morning, the regiment began to move easterly to a position seven miles away. As he marched, Johnnie, one of the cook's boys, ran up and shoved a couple of dried biscuits into Michael's cartridge pouch. As he ran back, the boy promised more when Michael returned. Michael knew he would be glad to have the biscuits if the action lasted into the evening.

At the ridge, O'Shay began to place his men strategically behind a natural earthen berm, placing zoning pegs between and ahead of them. These pegs were placed on a line about ten feet before the line of defenders. Each defender fired only between his two pegs, thus insuring that the men could not fire on one another and could deliver lethal fire into overlapping zones of the advancing enemy. Sergeant O'Shay positioned Michael behind a fairly large pine and told him that he wanted to see him hitting the Rebels as well as he had shot the targets back at the Ohio firing range. After assuring him that he would be near if Michael needed him, O'Shay was off to assign other positions. Looking from peg to peg, then to his two closest companions, Michael was glad to see old Dave, a kindly old gentleman known for his sharp shooting on his left, and Grady, the battalion's finest boxer and wrestler, to his left. He was comfortable in the thought that the Ohioans would win the fight today. He chuckled at the surprise he'd see on the faces of the Rebels if they made the mistake of crossing over the ridge. Everyone was sporting one of these new repeating rifles and had been able to get quite used to them. His battalion was such a force this day that many positions on this berm held two of his fellow soldiers.

The smell of the pines there was overpowering but pleasant. The cool briskness of the morning faded as bright thin blades of sunlight broke through the pine canopy above as choruses of tree frogs sporadically sang their rain songs. Michael realized that a long line of carpenter ants were making its way down his pine. He marveled how these creatures, carrying all forms of portable vegetation and insect parts, marched both to and from the tree using the same path. How strange, no human army could ever expect to work together in such a silent and orderly fashion, he thought.

Word came down the line that the enemy had been sighted and that it would be wise to dig yourself into the earth of your position, affording a better defense. Michael reasoned that it would be best to rest up for the coming battle, and besides, if the Rebels ever made it to this point, a hole in the ground would be of little value, for he would be chasing the Rebs back south.

Early in the afternoon, the attack came...

The memory of the fighting woke Michael. Lying on his back, he noticed, by the angle of the rays of sunlight, that the evening was close at hand. He felt a strange coldness washing over him. The pain he had remembered earlier was faintly present but was being replaced with a loss of energy and control. Remembering the contents of his right breast pocket, he began to fight the button open to see if the letters were still there. Once open, he was relieved to feel the papers between his swollen fingers. Michael tried to raise the bundle to his eyes, but his arm would not cooperate. He was only able to hold them tightly in his grip.

At the sound of crunching branches to his right, he squinted his eyes to see a silhouetted figure leaning above him. Michael realized the figure was of a female form, an angel he surmised. As she leaned closer to him, he recognized her straw hat and red hair. It was Elizabeth. He tried to lift his handful of papers to her. The girl stood and called out, "Hey, Emily, over here. I found another one. Quick, he's moving..." He smiled as the sweetest of feelings washed over him. He could no longer hear his angel. His grip eased as a slight Georgia breeze grabbed the delicate papers, carrying them away. As the light faded, he could still smell the strong scent of the pines.

ANN WHITWORTH UNEMORI

"Panda" Ann Whitworth Unemori was born in Sandusky, Ohio in 1959. She graduated from Earlham College with a BA in English Literature and Japanese Studies, and has visited Japan. She moved to the Savannah area in 1989, helping her then-husband with his business. He is still successfully running the Masato of Japan.

Ms. Unemori has been a member of the Savannah Writers Group since 2005. She has been writing off and on ever since high school, but admits most of those years have generally been a warm-up. Currently, she is working on both a short novel and an epic novel of urban fantasy. She enjoys both the limitless nature of writing, and the challenge of using the respectable boundaries for creating the best writing.

Ms. Unemori has three children.

Contact Ms. Unemori by email to mrsmishima@aol.com.

The Unseen Member Speaks

They never notice me, but I have been to every single one of the writers' workshops that meet by the coffee shop, here at Zillions O'Words. I shouldn't be that surprised, this is *my* bookshop even now. One of these days I think I will say something, just to see what happens. But not quite yet. Usually I like to sit back and listen to what the group has to say. They're all talented, even if some keep themselves firmly under the bushel, and I always look forward to what they've written. Sometimes I get so impatient that I peek over the reader's shoulder, not that anyone would notice me. But I don't like to do that because it is rude, and I still believe good manners are important, even in my present state.

Believe it or not, I enjoy my shop when it's busy, and that's not something you'd expect me to say. But unlike a house, a shop, especially a bookshop, is meant to be active; people are supposed to use it. What's the fun of keeping everything to yourself?

People don't notice me much, if at all, but that's okay, I still notice them. They notice Abelard of course, whenever he's up to one of his many little tricks; how he snickers when they look around and can't find him. I really must get after him some day, though it's probably impossible to make a cat mind, especially now. But don't tell me a cat can't laugh. I've heard his prim little purr as he sits on the bottom shelf while some luckless salesgirl is listening to some fussy customer lecture her about letting filthy animals in here. If I'm in a kind mood I might clean things up that night, but I am only saying I *might*.

As it is, I just wander about the stacks, behind the scenes, tidying up a bit, pointing out promising works. I do my real work after sunset, but I'm not afraid to whisper a hint or two into customers' ears, pointing out this romance or that western or that renowned reference guide. I do so value good writing. Abelard is less subtle, he just slinks in behind the books and will knock one at a person's feet. If they still don't get the hint, he does that figure-eight thing around their ankles until they look down. While they don't see him, they do see the book.

I've been here since the beginning, it was my father, Samuel Wordsworth Barber, who founded this store way back before the turn of the twentieth century. He always believed that "People deserve ac-

cess to the wit and wisdom of the ages." Those are his exact words. I
cut my teeth on books, and learned to read before I could walk, as is
only natural for the child of a great bookseller. I missed quite a lot of
school as I had to help out in the shop, a common occurrence in those
days, but I graduated anyway, with honors yet, because I could recite
any and all lessons and problems tossed at me. That was no small feat
way back then, especially for a girl, let me just say. If anyone makes
fun of "book-larnin" I'm not afraid to set that fool straight on the subject, so there.

Then as now, I've always liked helping out the children most of
all. Anyone discovering the thrill of reading, the joy of learning what's
really between those two covers deserves a bit of help. I remember my
own excitement when I discovered Little Elsie and all her adventures.
After that, it was *The Wonderful Wizard of Oz* and the other Oz books
that had the little ones running to our shop, and after that it was
Nancy Drew, and then Tom Swift, and then that book about that little
man who found a ring and had all those adventures, and after *him*...
well, I've lost count. These days it's that boy wizard, Henry? or is it
Harry? Potter they all come to read, and I can see why, it's a grand,
magical story of Good vs. Evil, and a boy learning to grow up and be
a man.

I'll confess right here that I will read the books myself after clos-
ing.

I don't hand out the books personally anymore, though I admit it
would be fun, but I've been known to draw a child's attention to
Treasure Island, or the Willy Wonka books, or maybe the newest book
out on dinosaurs, horses, or how to survive school. Sometimes, if I'm
not careful, a sharp-eyed child will catch a glimpse of me, or more
likely that naughty Abelard, and then of course I have to make us
both hide, while the mother remonstrates, "Now, now, Johnny, you
just *imagined* you saw that lady with the flying cat," while Johnny in-
sists, "I did too see it. That kitty flew right through that wall." Oh, it's
not easy tending the shop these days, I can tell you, and I hate it when
the children get punished just for telling the truth. Still, it's bad manners to let people see a person in my current state, and I am a stickler
for manners, just as I was and still am for good grammar.

Abelard thinks it is so funny when he creeps up behind some poor
soul with allergies. You'd think he couldn't affect people anymore, but

when he hunkers his little grey body down, and bristles up all his fur, then he can spread his dander just as much as he ever did. I can tell he does it on purpose because we've been together long enough for me to know him very well. Still, he's a good cat, and a friend on lonely nights, and his little trick can come in handy. Once, when a thief broke into the shop, Abelard snuck up behind him while I was trying to figure out how to use the phone. The man was just opening the cash register when Abelard, who was still hiding behind the thief, *bristled* for all he was worth, and if a cat can growl, Abelard was giving it all he had. The man looked around, rather nervous, and then– *Katchoo. Katchoo. Katchoo.*

"Help. Help. Police. We're being robbed." I yelled in my best ghostly voice, as the robber stumbled around and knocked over several shelves of books. Fortunately this set off the alarm system and our intruder was swiftly dealt with. All he could do was keep saying, "Where'd they go? There was a lady and a cat. Where'd they go so fast?" only to be told, "Where'd who go? Nobody's here at night."

Oh yes, I am a ghost, in case you haven't noticed, I'm telling you. I've been here since the beginning, and I am not going to let a little thing like death stop me from doing my job here with the books, especially when it's something I love. It's kind of fun, really, as now I can spend all the time I want reading at night, knowing my father can't really punish me for it.

In case you're wondering, he has "gone ahead" to his Eternal Rest, as we ghosts say; virtuous souls are allowed to do that if they've done their duties in life. But once in a while he does sneak back to make sure I'm doing a proper job.

Most of the time I wander the stacks, remembering to keep myself invisible, and keeping an eye on Abelard to make sure he does the same. I do wish the current owners would allow animals here; what fun is a bookshop without a cat or a dog to curl up invitingly? I've gotten pretty good at levitating books and little things, always being careful not to let people see. Once in a while I do like to cheat, just a little; if there's a lonely looking girl, and a nervous young man nearby I will push down a book of Shakespeare, or the poetry of Keats, or maybe just a good Agatha Christy mystery, near his or her feet. Of course one will go to help the other pick it up and, when sometimes I give it a nudge, one will nervously apologize as the other tries to explain, and that's all I need to see.

Sometimes, especially around Halloween, I do let the children see me for a few minutes. It's fun to scare them, just a little mind you; children still believe in us ghosts before their parents teach them otherwise. I don't really mind not being believed in, as children have so much to learn as it is, no sense letting them get distracted too much. Besides, it is good manners not to let everyone just gawk at you, and I do place an emphasis on politeness. I am not above giving some rude boy a shiver when I see him dog-earring a book.

There is also the fun of sneaking up behind some stuffy old professor who "doesn't believe in ghosts." and whispering "BOO," which I did do once or twice. But I must also confess to my favorite prank on that wild-eyed young man who came here about three years ago, determined to prove the store was haunted. He came here with special cameras and recorders, strange radio-like things, and boxes of special powder. He stayed here for three nights, staring into the dark, waiting and watching for his proof. Of course, Abelard and I stayed firmly out of sight the entire time. I suppose it was mean, but how could I resist? The one thing more fun than spooking some close-minded scoffer is popping the bubble of the poor soul ready to believe *anything*. And, as any respectable ghost can tell you, we do prefer our privacy.

But I don't do things like that very often, preferring just to glide behind the scenes, tidying a shelf or two, nudging a book or two out for the children's story hour. If I am lucky, some of my old customers come in, as they still do after all these years, many of them bringing along a favorite grandchild or two. A few have already crossed over, and we meet for tea every full moon or so. But I tend to stay in the shop as a rule, sometimes overhearing a conversation or two, or tending to Abelard, or trying to understand the computer; I *think* I've figured it out by now.

My favorite pastime, along with helping with the children, is sitting in with the writing group that meets every other week here. They've been coming here for quite some time now, ever since Zillions O'Words built this nice big bookstore; the group never could have fit into Father's old building. There's a roomy alcove next to the coffee area, very nice and quiet, perfect for groups like this. That's one reason I didn't mind the Zillions people buying the old Barber Bookshop; they always treat their customers well. When they moved all the books, my cat and I just went with them; we don't take up much room. Once they unpacked and set up things we just settled in and have been staying here ever since.

My, I do tend to wander from the point, don't I? Okay, now I'll tell you about our little group. There are about eight to ten regulars, and maybe a few who stop by on an irregular basis, who meet over coffee and muffins, who meet and discuss their writing, what they are working on, how to polish it up, how to get it published. They'll sit and talk about first-person versus third, the uses of commas, and the importance of a good cover letter. Some write how-to articles, some do poetry, many of them create fiction and essays drawn from their own experiences.

It's usually more women than men, but everyone is bonded by a love of writing. The *de facto* leader is a pleasant, sharp-witted lady with an excellent grasp of how to put words together and how to make them work. She's better than me, I must admit; no stray commas or split points-of-view on her watch, no sir. She's written several how-to articles for scientific journals so I know for a fact she is a master of what she's doing.

She has a nephew who's sort of the second-in-command, a big boisterous fellow who's always cracking jokes with and about the various budding authors. But he's a good soul at heart, having written several children's books; sometimes he brings his own kids along. They're in high school now, so they tend to go off with their friends. But, when I peep round the corner, just to keep an eye on them of course, as often as not they are sharing some favorite book with a companion or three.

There's so many fine people in the group, a few have had their writings published, most are still planning. I like the lady who's writing about her childhood in Jacksonville; it was only fifty years ago, but so much has changed since then. There's another, an artist, who is setting down what led her to begin a late-life career in painting; and her friend who has created a series of articles about her Boston Terrier for the local "Current Events" weekly. One of my favorites is the South American girl who is taking a great deal of time and effort to write a romance set in her home city, all the more remarkable as English is not her first language. She's the one Abelard likes, for he always sits at her feet, and pays attention when she reads. He's never that patient with me. But that's how I can tell she has potential; cats are very perceptive. Didn't all the greatest writers, Mark Twain, Ernest Hemingway, Emily Dickson, keep cats?

I know what the members write because I usually peek over their shoulders. Yes, it's impolite, but I'm hardly in a position to ask if I may borrow their manuscripts to read. On the other hand they often read them aloud, and I sit just as enraptured as the rest.

There's an Englishman who's writing a ghost story, and I always wonder if I should let him see me for a minute, hee hee. He always comes with his friend from Chicago, the one who is into adventure-action stories. Then there's that weird lady who always dresses in black and writes about the Indian girl with a pet manatee; she always gets strong black coffee. We've a few poets, how-to writers, but the most promising is a very attractive young woman who may be the break-away writer, the one capable of writing a real best seller, the kind that makes the *New York Times* list, with her *opus* of a young woman returning to Georgia. That would be a real feather in the cap for everyone.

But whether that happens or not, I don't think it matters to the writers at Zillions O'Words. Their real reason for meeting is a love of books and words and the wonderfully creative business of writing. Even after they all cross into the incorporeal state I think they'll still get together every week to talk and share manuscripts, accompanied by good ghostly coffee and muffins, of course. One of the best parts of being in my present state is that I can enjoy all the muffins I want and I won't gain an ounce.

Again, in case you're wondering, we ghosts use the aromas of earthly foods to create our own. Everyone knows how good fresh coffee and new-baked rolls smell.

But the exciting part right now is that my little group is going to publish a book, and every single member is going to write something for it. Each member has been fussing over their contribution, whether it's a story or a poem, or just an insightful look at one of life's endless foibles, and I can tell they all are giving their best. I guess that's what's finally motivated me.

I've been practicing at night on the computers in the office. The people in charge never really turn them off, just put them into hibernation, the perfect state for ghosts. I've always been a good typist, even if I prefer longhand, and I decided not long ago that it's time I learned how to use this newest variation of how to put words to paper. It's a bit tricky, but I think I've finally mastered all the various diddly and doodly buttons; being dead is no excuse for falling behind the times. The hard part was having to push down the keys.

So that's what this is, this story you nice people are now reading, my first attempt, at least in my current state, at getting into print. I wanted to introduce you all to a fine collection of stories and ideas from people I have grown to know and admire. Stop and enjoy them, dear reader, and if you feel the motivation, don't be afraid to take up pen and paper and try setting down a few words yourself.

If you don't, Abelard said he'll haunt you.

This Is For My Brother's Dog

[Notes for a rejected news article]
[Observations of Saddam in prison.]
[Notes from private interview with the sol-
dier in question.]

Look, I still don't talk about this much, it's too personal. I know the Captain still thinks I'm nuts. Any chance I got in the Army is over thanks to him. The Sarge, he supports me, most of the guys do. But he doesn't believe me either. Can't really blame him. Heck, I wouldn't believe it myself if it hadn't happened...

They used to rib me about it, but now they just leave me alone. Because it isn't funny, it never was. I'm probably still in trouble, but I don't care anymore.

Sure, there's a couple guys who believe me, but what's it matter now? Who cares what they think? *[soldier pauses]* My wife, yeah, she'd listen. My wife and my little boy, they're the only ones whose respect I want now.

[The author was unable to speak to either the
sergeant or to the captain in question.]

Okay, let me begin at the beginning. My name is *[edited for security reasons]*. We're based in Texas, but I grew up in *[edited]*, Michigan. Mom and Pete still back there, she runs the bakery, he just fishes. Cori and Jimmijohn are in Texas for now, and right now the most important things in my life. That's what I'm fighting for, my wife and my little boy. That's what Tasha must have known...

[Notes from fellow soldiers, that the subject
was reliable, a good buddy in the clench,
generally that he was honest.]

I'm getting there, don't worry. My dad...well, we don't talk about him anymore. But, see, just before he left us, Dad got me a puppy, a Lab/something mix from a neighbor. Just eight weeks old she was, and already sharp as a tack. Loyal? Ran up to me and began licking me to death at once, like we'd known each other all our lives. A puppy. A complete surprise that afternoon, I never would have expected it from Dad...just like I never expected him to leave two months later.

I still wonder why he got her. Was it to make up for what happened later? And yet even now I wouldn't have given her up for anything, not even to get my father back.

Oh, Mom said "no," of course. But she didn't say it very much, or with any meaning. Once she saw my dog and me laughing and rolling in the yard, it was too late. Mom later said she'd always approved of Tasha. That's what I named her, Tasha, after a family friend.

Raising a dog gets messy, I won't go into detail into all trouble that we got into–that I got into. I know you got a time limit. But I loved that dog like nobody's business, and in the tough times she was the only one who loved me. Yeah, I screwed myself up good, when I tried pot, when Mom married again, got into some real bad fights. Got sent away once, even Mom ready to write me off. That dog was maybe the only one who stood by me when I got nabbed for possession...oh, why dwell on it? *[he sighs]*

I want to say one thing. See, every kid says, "I'll take care of the puppy." But I kept that promise, especially after Dad left. I fed her, walked her, bathed her, cleaned up after her, and I did this every day. Every day, except when I was in juvenile hall, every day I took care of my dog.

Every. Goddamn. Day.

Please. I'm sorry. I'm been in the Army maybe too long. I shouldn't talk like that around a lady... *[break]* Well, only if you really don't mind. But I still want to watch what I say.

What matters is that Tasha stuck to me when no one else did. I know I'm going on; this is as short as I can make it and still stick to all the facts. I finally cleaned up my act because of my dog, though I also thank God for my mom, after all I put her through. I'd run with the fast girls, but not anymore; I was romping with Tasha when I met Corinne.

Tasha knew she was the one for me, even then. Rolled over and let her scratch her tummy, licked her ice cream. Cori said she married me because my dog made her laugh.

Okay, I joined the Army after 9/11, hell, who wouldn't have-sorry. I probably would have anyway, what with Jimmijohn on the way. We have a family history going back to the War Between the States. I remember Grandpa telling us about WWII, how proud he'd been to serve. That's a lot to live up to. Must have been the best thing I ever did, and I don't mean the job training. The military structured me, strengthened me, knocked the final [crap] out of me. And yet, would I have joined if I knew what would happen? [sigh, long pause]

Okay, here's what I mean. What matters is that, while I was in training, Tasha refused her food. She didn't play, didn't run, just sat in the driveway, waiting. Cori was staying with Mom and Pete at the time, Tasha let them comfort her, but nothing they did coaxed her into eating. She was pretty old by then. Did she know she was dying? Cori finally found her out by the drive, about a week before my son was born, my dog, still waiting for me...I never saw her alive again...

[pause, the speaker is broken up]

It...wasn't easy. Of course I got mad, but what could I do? You can't plead for leave because your dog needs you. My family meant well, trying to spare me the worst until it was too late, but try telling that to my Captain, the filthy, [several swear words censored at the speaker's request]. All I remember that day is breaking down and bawling like a child...if it hadn't been for the birth of my son about then I'd have had no reason to go on...But I have to go on, Tasha would have given her life for me, and I would do the same for my little boy.

Almost there. My training wasn't complete so I missed Afghanistan. But I'd seen Gulf War I on TV when I was young and stupid, so I figured I was ready for Iraq. Don't think my wife was happy about my shipping out. Yet she never questioned why I had to go; she never would have married a coward.

Okay, about the night in question. We really didn't know much at the time. What we, I mean we grunts, knew was this was a high-profile case, that this time our quarry was still there and we had to catch him. We probably knew who we were chasing, but didn't say so out loud, didn't want to spook the thing, just called him "Elvis." The Captain doubted it was really him after all this time. Nevertheless we headed to Tikrit, on the Tigris River.

It was about dusk. Most of us hit the ground running and fanned out. The Wolverines, that's the two main farmhouses, had proved empty, but there still remained the little hut among the orange trees. Even so, a few guys muttered that Saddam had flown the coop once again. Still, we pushed on.

The hut we found easily, under a date palm, We swarmed over it and over and around the surrounding orange trees. Outside lay a soiled prayer rug next to the date palm tree. There was the rotting fruit and chocolate, the clothing strewn across his bed, you've seen the pictures. But the Ace of Spades himself was nowhere to be seen. Several of the men began to doubt Saddam had been there at all, that we'd ever catch him. A few wandered back to the road, uncertain. By then, the Captain may have been thinking to call the whole thing off, another bust. It was then I thought I heard a dog, digging, whining, scratching...

"Keep looking. He's there. He has to be." Sarge never doubted it, never gave up, even when some of us drifted back to the Captain's Hummer. See, none of us were certain what to expect. Saddam was a monster. Saddam would have come out blazing, would have grown wings, and would have flown off laughing. We believed anything was possible with Saddam. A bunch of half-informed guys, some of us just kids, grubbing in the woods, who'd wanna depend on us? I wanted to agree with the Captain. Still, I heard a dog scratching...

Nothing was too small to overlook, we knew, but by then the darkness had deeply invaded, making the search difficult even with night-vision goggles. We knew what we were doing, what to look for, but everyone had been fooled so many times. Already talk began about pulling out, but Sarge wouldn't hear of it, insisting, "He's here. He's still here. I know it." But where? Not in the hut or lean-to, not among the oranges, not up in the date palm in the courtyard. Had he escaped to the Tigris? Would we leave empty-handed yet again?

That's when it happened. "Wuff. Wuff. RUFF." A bark I knew as well as I did my own name.

"WUFF. RUFF. Ruff-RUFF."

That's when I saw her. My dog Tasha, who'd died nearly two years before. I stepped outside the hut to discover my dog waiting for me. She was under the date palm, lying on a small white rug among little red flowers. You know how it is with someone you deeply love, love more than life itself? You know their face, their voice, no matter how disguised, whether on the moon or in this hell called Iraq. The face, the voice you'd know anywhere, the one you'd trust your life to...my dog had come back to me, to join me in the game I was playing...my beloved dog we'd buried in the yard, my dog Tasha.

"WUFF. WUFF." She stood up, waiting for me, tail wagging.

"What? What is it?" I asked automatically.

"Who the [bleep] are you talking to?"

"Tasha…"

"What the hell —"

"No, look. Under the tree." I'd turned to face the speaker. When I looked again I saw nothing but the white prayer rug.

The rug my dog had been sitting on.

I bent down to look at the dirty thing. "Sarge, this carpet, it doesn't look right." Other soldiers had been ransacking the house, now they were walking toward the tree.

"It's just an old carpet."

"No, look underneath, something about the ground…"

"What the —"

"Wait a minute, he could be on to something."

Beside the tree a shout, "There's a pipe sticking up. This could be it."

"Sweet Mother of God…"

Somebody yanked the rug aside, and then we saw the dirt and handles of a Styrofoam brick set flush with the ground.

"Remove it." Who pulled it out I don't know.

There it lay, at our feet. A hole in the ground, nothing more. Something was moving inside it. Something my dog had wanted me to see.

"Someone's in there."

"Not for long." God help me, I knew who it was, what he'd do.

"No. Wait." I said and grabbed the soldier's hand. "Hold it. He's coming out."

His hands, empty, open, his tangled grey hair, his defeated eyes. In a dusty voice he stated, "I am Saddam Hussein. I am the President of Iraq and I wish to negotiate."

This tired, disheveled man the entire Army sought. The Ace of Spades. The Butcher of Baghdad. The man my dog had found…

"President Bush sends his regards," said Sarge.

And from behind I heard, "Holy shit."

At Sarge's command, we swooped in, dragged Saddam out of his hole like the rat he was. Yeah, that's when the other thing happened, the one they left out of the papers. A bunch of us were securing him, standard procedure for prisoners. One guy found the pistol the coward never bothered to use. Someone had already cuffed his hands behind his back, when Saddam suddenly spat in my face.

I slugged him–hard. "And Tasha sends hers, bastard." Saddam glared but said nothing. Someone covered his head with a black hood. Like I said, we know what we're doing. We cleared out of there pretty fast after that. You know the rest.

There's one thing I haven't told anyone, not even the guys. I'm in trouble enough with the Captain. When someone asked me who Tasha was, I should have lied, said it was my girl or something. Right now they don't say it, but the Captain and others think I'm nuts. He also knows I made him look bad and swears he's going to ruin me. Sarge backs me up, but right now nobody can help me. I don't really care anymore.

I don't even know if I want to stay in the Army or not. The one thing I want to do is see is my wife and my little boy.

The one thing is what I saw on the ground, just before we caught Saddam. It was lost almost at once, so I can't prove it was there. But neither can anyone prove it wasn't there. I know what I saw, and I will stake my honor as a soldier on it: On the rug, I saw the paw prints of a large dog; in the dirt were scratches, as from claws, around the hole...

JIM WALLER

Jim Waller was born in Atlanta, and attended Fulton County Public Schools. At age nineteen, he joined the U.S. Air Force and served in the Pacific and in the continental U.S. While stationed in New Hampshire, he attended classes part-time at the state university at Durham.

Upon discharge from the Air Force, he enrolled at Georgia State University (GSU) in Atlanta and earned the BA in English and journalism. He later received the MEd and the EdS in education from GSU.

He is a former high school English teacher/education consultant/school principal/technical college English instructor. His education experience has taken him into numerous public school systems in all areas of the state. He is a seasoned traveler throughout continental America, compassionately observing the human condition along the way.

The author has dabbled in poetry and fiction since elementary school, and in 2002 embarked on writing for publication. He has composed poems, short stories, and novels, inspired largely by his career in education, and observation of life in his beloved South.

Waller currently resides at Tybee Island, Georgia, and can be contacted at jrwaller@bellsouth.net.

Crossroads

Flashlight and Paul were neighbors, about the same age, and sons of farm laborers. They could have been friends, but were bitter enemies. It wasn't that their enmity began with some terrible thing said or done, it was just the difference in the molecules of pigment in their skin. Paul's diminutive stature and his position at the bottom of the socioeconomic ladder made him an easy victim. Flashlight was a bottom feeder, too, in the pecuniary fishbowl of life. And, Lord knows, he could never ascend even to the *bottom* of the social structure. But to say that the white citizens of Bonds County, Georgia, did not take kindly to coloreds getting all uppity in the 1950s would be an understatement the size of Gulliver on stilts in Lilliput. Retribution for uppity could be severe. And it often was.

Flashlight was eighteen now, and for a number of years, the position of Negroes weighed heavily on his sensibilities and sense of self. It didn't seem right that he had to take to the street to let whites pass on the sidewalk in town, or take his hotdog and Coke at the back door of Rachel's Diner. With these observations and the passing of time, frustration and bitterness festered in his heart, his mind, and his soul. He discovered an outlet of sorts in frequently venting his feelings onto Paul.

Paul's only route to school and town was by way of Flashlight's home at the crossroads.

If there was any other route, Paul would surely take it. But he had to pass the house every day, six days a week. Flashlight's school day began later and ended earlier, and there he would be, sitting at the crossroads, waiting to inflict verbal or physical pain onto the hapless Paul.

But in the winter of 1958, a strange metamorphosis came over Flashlight. His aggression toward Paul vanished.

The change in Flashlight's attitude happened suddenly without warning. It was a cold February morning that he stood on the red-clay road waiting for Paul, riding cautiously up the hill on the bicycle that he used in his part-time delivery job at Liebman's Mercantile.

"Hold up, white boy. I want to talk to you."

Paul braked the bike to a halt and stood facing Flashlight. For sometime now, Flashlight had bullied him only verbally. Neverthe-less, he felt apprehensive. He did not want trouble.

"I want you to know I'm not going to bother you anymore."

"Well. That's nice to know," Paul replied sarcastically. "To what do I owe such benevolence?"

"Don't be a smart-ass, white boy. I might change my mind and wrap that bicycle around your red neck."

"OK, OK. What is it you want to talk about? It's too cold to stand out here jawing about nothing." A burst of cold air descended from the northwest. Paul tucked his jacket tighter around his neck.

"You ever heard of Martin Luther King Jr.?"

"Sure. Heard about him on the radio and the TV at school. Every-body's talking about him. Since him and that Rosa Parks woman over in Alabama started that bus boycott three years ago, he's been stirring up all kinds of mess. But that's not going to happen here, not in 1958. Maybe a hundred years from now. Anyway, we don't have busses–unless you count the school bus, and you don't even have that."

"That's right, smart-ass, but Dr. King says we ought to. He's pretty smart. Went to college when he was fifteen. He says all the whites and blacks oughta quit fighting and get along with each other."

"Is that a fact? I don't believe it'll happen here in Bonds County."

"Rev. King says it will. I've been reading a lot about his work yon-der in Alabama. And I watch him on the TV at school sometimes. By the way, I'm going to miss that TV when I graduate in the spring. You graduating, too, aren't you?"

"Yeah. It's about time. I'm going on nineteen," Paul answered, and noticed that the boy's enunciation had improved considerably since their first encounter eight years ago.

"Well anyway, Dr. King says everybody oughta have the right to sit anywhere they want to on a bus, and vote, and go to school, and sit down in a restaurant and have a glass of sweet tea and a hotdog."

"And you believe that?"

"I sure do, and that ain't all he says. He says black folks oughta have the same jobs as white people do. And I oughta be making fifty cents an hour like the white men at Mr. Bid's sawmill instead of just a quarter."

"You working at the sawmill?"

"Yeah, man."

"How long?"

"Long time. After school and on Saturdays. But that's not important. What really matters, Dr. King says you and me can be friends and go to school together."

"And you really believe that'll happen here in Bonds County? This Dr. King of yours sounds like he's got a loose screw." Paul felt good standing up to the bigger, more muscular boy.

"All right, white boy. You'll see. But I'm not going to bother you anymore anyway."

"Well I appreciate that, but I don't think you'll ever go to my school. Anyway, how can we be friends? I don't even know your name. And you won't call me by mine."

"OK...Paul. Grandma and Grandpa call me MG, but the fellows down at the Saturday night crap-shoot behind Rachel's Diner call me Flashlight, Flashlight Jackson."

"Well, then, Flashlight Jackson, why do they call you that? Anyway, what's a crap-shoot?"

"It's a game you play. There's these little gray cubes with black dots on them. They're called dice. You roll 'em and if the right number of dots show on top, you win."

"Win what?"

"Money, fool, Money."

"How much money?'

"Depends on how much you bet."

"How much do you bet?"

"Look, man, this is going to take all day. You so dumb. Why don't you come around to the back of the diner Saturday night when you get off work and I'll show you."

"Isn't that gambling, and against the Bible and the law?"

"Yeah, white boy, uh, Paul. But you won't get caught. Nobody cares. Nobody ever gets caught, And we ain't in no temple or nothing. Jesus won't care."

Intrigued by the prospects of quick money, Paul asked, "Are you sure?"

"Yeah I'm sure, man."

Pedaling along the road to school, Paul's mind replayed the conversation with Flashlight. The money he could win playing craps would help ensure his passage to college. This Flashlight Jackson may be on to something.

Flashlight Jackson did his best to be a good American, but his roots were firmly embedded in the soil of Africa.

In the Western Sudan–Mali perhaps, a country some say of remarkably beautiful women–a young princess neared womanhood, pampered, virginal, and happy. Of African-Portuguese descent, she was short and well proportioned. Braided bangs hung low on a square forehead. Wide eyes twinkled with the joy of abundant life. Full, inviting lips reposed in the space between a soft, wide nose and a chin congruent with the squareness of her forehead.

She was indeed a creature of loveliness on the day she was captured by a neighboring tribe. The conquering chief thought at first of making her his own slave, but determined more valuable the number of guns and kegs of rum and bolts of cloth she would bring in a trade with the white European slave merchants.

Dragged into the hold of a big ship, she lay chained together with other Negroes, male and female, adult and child; some puking, some urinating, some defecating where they lay. Before the weeks-long journey would end, many would go their graves in the great Atlantic Ocean. Those who survived, heaved and bobbed with the ship, and cursed the heat and the stench until the vessel finally docked in a strange place called Virginia.

Although possessed of defiance and determination, the fragile young princess survived only because from time to time, the ship's captain summoned her to his quarters to bathe and wash her only dress. And while her garment hung drying, she shared the captain's food–and his bed. At first she was terrified, but as the ship sailed slowly westward, she acquiesced to the forays and realized that they were her only means of survival. After the first few trips to the Dutchman's quarters, it wasn't so terribly bad. The bad part didn't last that long, and she didn't even have to pretend that she enjoyed it, and anything was better than the misery of the ship's hold.

The long, hot, humid days and nights wore on. And after an eternity of heaving and bobbing, and puking and cursing, and urinating and defecating, and dying, the surviving slaves found–at least momentarily–some measure of relief in reaching land once more.

They trod chained in single file from the ship, while a large, red-faced auctioneer catalogued for each slave a name followed by a brief description: "ideal field hand," "excellent mammy," "bawdy breeder for a young buck or a frisky master, *ha, ha.*"

The young princess, recently returned from a final go in the captain's quarters, trudged defiantly into the blinding, blistering sunlight. She glared at the white faces assessing the bound commodities like cows or mules or goats at a stock sale. After her name, appeared the words "tight little breeder," a description shortly to lose some of its validity; for as she dragged the chain bound to her left leg, she also bore the burden of the white captain's child growing in her womb. And in due time, following three days of excruciating labor, the baby tore painfully into this new world. The healthy girl-child, beautiful like her mother, would twelve years later marry Howard Jackson's Elijah, and thus begin a long line of descendents, some of whom would eventually find themselves in Bonds County, Georgia.

The first one came at the outbreak of the Civil War. Elroy Jackson, like most Southern white men—and many boys soon to become men before their time—volunteered to fight. His young bride, with a male to protect her and two females to serve her, was sent from Virginia to wait out the war at the home of an elderly aunt in Georgia.

The impatient young wife waited. And even though the battles were a long time coming this far south, they raged savagely and endlessly in the border states to the north. The relentless year after year waiting and the denial of her young body became more than she could bear. With her husband and other white males miles away fighting a never-ending war, she felt it a harmless diversion to count the days of the month and order her male slave to her bedroom from time to time.

The dreadful war dragged on, and when Elroy Jackson's young wife conceived a child, she cinched her protruding belly with torn bed sheets, successfully concealing her condition from the elderly aunt whose vision was as poor as her hearing. The baby was delivered in a slave cabin and remained there to be raised as a Negro child, a man-child. He matured and sired children of his own, and after four generations hence, a descendant known by some as Flashlight Jackson was born.

Flashlight Jackson's features were much like those of that slave girl who trudged full-bellied upon the American Continent so long ago. His wide eyes radiated quiet, congenial intelligence. The skin of his face was flawless. Of medium height, his broad shoulders easily supported his muscular arms and canopied his narrow hips. Bright in school, he was one of the few Negroes to graduate Bonds County Victory School.

From age fourteen, he worked after school, on Saturdays, and in summers at Mr. Bidwell Bonds's sawmill. In the beginning, he applied himself full-bodied to each assigned task. But as he matured with the passing years, he came to realize that he and other Negro hands labored at the hardest and most dangerous jobs. Those assigned to white workers required minimal effort and afforded occasional rest periods. Flashlight and his people never rested and were paid only a portion of the wages of whites.

The months, the years, the meager paydays passed, the inequities of the Bonds County work place weighing heavily on Flashlight's mind. He struggled with the conflicts and confusion vexing his soul. The inequities of the sawmill seemed unjust but somehow fair, because they were meted with such conviction and authority, as natural as springtime in March.

In school he read everything he could beg, borrow, or scrounge about black-white relations and engaged Headmaster Augustus Martin in long discussions. Slowly the Bonds County perception of Negroes materialized in bold, white letters on the chalkboard of his soul. They possessed a few characteristics of humans, but were fundamentally trained animals that, through the Christian patience and benevolence of the white man, had learned a crude imitation of civilized speech rising to a tongue roughly considered language, lacking the capacity for wanting, feeling, or tiring. That was merely the natural order of things, as natural as the white man's Bible-endowed dominion over all animals.

There had to be another way, and Flashlight set about finding it. He fell into absenting himself frequently from his job at the sawmill. In time, his absences increased. He spent hours reading all the books he could gather.

He read of a mysterious Negro who appeared from nowhere in

Detroit on the Fourth of July 1930. Professing to have come from the Holy City of Mecca, he called himself Prophet W. O. Farrad Muhammad. He taught his followers that they were not Negroes. They were "black men." Christianity, according to Farrad, was the white man's religion. The natural faith of the black man was Islam, and Allah the true God.

Unconvincing, but interesting, was the story of Elijah Poole, a young black man from across the state in Washington County, who migrated to Detroit to become Farrad's disciple. Rejecting Poole as a slave name, Farrad renamed him Elijah Muhammad.

The Black Muslim movement attracted a large following. One of his converts was Malcolm Little, son of a Georgia preacher, slashed to death in Lansing, Michigan when Malcolm was still a child. He grew up and adopted the name Malcolm X.

Flashlight found little interest in the movement, but embraced the Black Muslim call to emulate the white man's ways in business and industry and to aggressively seek education and good-paying jobs and political power and to abandon the practice of eating pork and possum and cornbread.

Flashlight Jackson once had a real name. But on days absent from his job at the sawmill, he read; and on Saturday nights in the darkness behind Rachel's Diner, he played craps with anyone–black or white–willing to lay their money down. A three-celled flashlight he carried in a hip pocket provided light. The gamblers began calling him "Flashlight," and the name spread. Eventually almost everyone forgot his real name.

Occasionally Mr. Bid met Flashlight by chance and demanded that he report to his job at the sawmill. "You coloreds gotta work, or next thing you know you'll be up to devilment, prob'ly trying to rob or kill some white man." At Mr. Bid's often repeated remark, Flashlight clenched his jaws and tolerated the abuse. He needed the job at the sawmill even if he didn't work a regular schedule. And besides, he had heard too many stories about the abundance of long ropes and tall trees in Bonds County.

When he grew tired of reading, or ran out of material, Flashlight returned to work at the sawmill. He enjoyed the physical labor and camaraderie with the other black men. But in time, he observed that they had hopelessly acquiesced to their way of life. He decided that he could not. His identity reflected through the white man's eyes branded him a virtually worthless human being, merely an object to be used and exploited like a sawmill draft horse. He longed to be accepted a man of dignity and worth.

He read, watched TV at school, and searched for understanding of the oppressive, static society of Bonds County, while geographically afar, transformation slowly germinated and grew. In May of 1954, the U.S. Supreme Court in the case of *Brown v. Board of Education* in Topeka, Kansas, erased the "Separate but Equal" doctrine of *Plessy v. Ferguson* enacted in 1890, a decision that validated racial segregation from that time forward. The *Brown* decision precipitated a series of court cases granting more freedoms than ever to blacks in America.

In 1955, Martin Luther King Jr. completed theology studies at Boston University. Soon thereafter, he found himself–somewhat reluctantly–leader of a well organized, non-violent protest movement that revolutionized the place of blacks in America by transmitting court decisions from paper to practice. Flashlight Jackson obsessively observed protest marches, boycotts, sit-ins and other civil rights activities. *The Atlanta Constitution* printed pictures of black men and women standing courageously in the face of snarling dogs and vicious humans. Television news programs broadcast appalling images of black men, women, and children rising defiantly after falling under the brutal and merciless blows of police clubs. With faces set in pain fear, and hope, a determined people plodded relentlessly on.

Flashlight witnessed these events and resolved to somehow join the struggle for equality, justice and freedom in this land of enough for everyone. His soul ached to walk head-high and proud; to greet white people openly and equally with a feeling of dignity and self-worth; to be free of the need to conceal his blackness. He dreamed of walking unafraid through the front door of Rachel's Diner and ordering a hotdog and Coke at a table. He felt no need to impose on white people, or take anything from them, or infringe upon them in any way. He simply wanted to be a man with all the qualities of other men; and the opportunity for him and his people to pursue education, wealth, and political power like other Americans. He longed to be free, not merely emancipated, but *free*. Really *free*.

High school graduation neared in the spring of 1958, and Flashlight sought the address of the man who, for him, had become the symbol of delivery and salvation. He composed a letter.

Dear Dr. King,

I read in the newspaper about your work and watch you on TV.

We need you awful bad here in Bonds County. Of course, I know you don't have time right now for us country folks because you got work to do in Birmingham and Little Rock and Atlanta. But I figure if I come to help, you can hurry up and finish what you're doing there and come on down here and help us.

Anyway, I'm big and strong and healthy, and I'm powerful hungry in my soul to be free. Dr. King, I want to be free. Sir, I just got to be free.

He carefully folded the letter and placed it in an envelope, methodically addressed it, and checked the return address. At the post office, he asked the white postmaster to weigh the letter. The postage must be correct. He watched closely to make sure it by-passed the trashcan for placement in the basket with other mail. He left the post office thinking about his letter mingling with all the white people's mail and visualized a day when everyone would blend and mingle freely.

The next day after school, he reported for work at the sawmill. He had to earn money for bus fare and be ready when Dr. King sent for him. The Great Man would summon, and he would be ready.

Paul decided to accept Flashlight's invitation to join the Saturday night crap games. He hoped to win money for college, but he soon learned that wins and losses balanced. Gambling for him was not worth the effort. He did, however, enjoy the excitement of the other players and their glee or despair with each turn of fate. He delighted especially in Flashlight's skill–and good fortune. He inevitably won with roll after roll of the dice. He played the game calmly, analytically, and impassively. The losers–mostly white men–cursed and anguished over the pitiable dollars earned at the sawmill or in the fields.

Paul came to admire Flashlight's quiet strength, determination, and unobtrusive intelligence. With each Saturday night behind the diner, their tentative friendship grew like a waxing gibbous moon, slowly but surely. And after the games, they rode home together, Paul on the store bike; Flashlight on the bicycle bought with winnings. Flashlight knew a lot about world events, science, and religion, and they talked. Paul enjoyed their conversations even more than the crap games.

Flashlight's luck held fast, and he carefully guarded the five hundred dollars saved in a Mason jar in the barn loft behind his house. He was ready for Dr. King's call.

And Rev. King did call.

The letter, postmarked from Atlanta, came addressed to *Mr. M.G. Jackson, Rural Free Delivery, Bonds County, Ga.* And even before Flashlight opened it, word spread through town that he had received mail from "them uppity rabble-rousers in Atlanta." Curiosity about its contents stirred through the county. Flashlight ignored the hostile looks from the white men, women and children he passed on Main Street and began preparations to accept the Great Man's invitation to join his Southern Christian Leadership Conference.

Word of his communication with black civil rights leaders spread like a California wildfire. Previously perceived as an acceptable, rather pleasant and courteous "nigra", he was now regarded as uppity, out to change everything.

The attitude of the white men behind the diner turned ugly. As long as Flashlight was considered relatively harmless, they found it reasonably palatable–with tolerable levels of bitter aftertaste–that he consistently won their money. Now he was uppity and a threat to their way of life. They would no longer allow him to take their money, even if it was won fair and square.

Led by Jack Savage, the gamblers learned of Flashlight's savings and devised a plan to recoup their losses. Pooling their resources, they challenged him to a winner-take-all showdown.

At first he hesitated. He had the funds to get to Atlanta, but on second thought, he really didn't know what to expect in a large, strange city. Maybe the extra money would come in handy. After days of ignominious dares and challenges, he relented and arrived at the familiar place behind the diner, tightly clutching the Mason jar containing five hundred dollars. In a hip pocket he carried a flashlight with three brand new batteries.

Flashlight, Paul, seven other white men, and two black men gathered for the duel. Prepared to begin the game, Jack Savage announced, "You two jaboonies can stay if you want to, but this match is between me and this moon-dog here." The two black men exchanged apprehensive looks, but curiosity and excitement overcame their fear, and they decided to stay for the action.

The competition began and became increasingly heated. For more than two hours, luck alternately smiled or frowned on first one and then the other gambler. But more often than not, fortune chose to graciously warm Flashlight's hand despite Jack Savage's best efforts. He continued to lose. The faces of the white men first registered concern, then fear and panic, and finally, anger. Flashlight had all the money except four ten-dollar bills.

Savage took the wadded bills from the pocket of his khaki work pants. "All right, you lucky bastard. You got all our money except these four notes. I'll roll you high dice for each of them."

Flashlight studied the faces of the men surrounding him, assessing the rage in their eyes. Their hate saturated him like the gathering dew. They were postured for more than a simple crap game. He felt a desperate urge to seize his friend and race their bicycles the dark road home. He would not leave here with the money. He knew that.

With fear strangling the sinews of his playing hand, Flashlight rolled the dice against the diner's concrete foundation. They clanked and rattled and rolled to a stop.

"Look at them damn boxcars." Savage exclaimed. You're either a cheating son of a bitch or the luckiest bastard alive. Gimme them dice." He could not beat a twelve, but he could match it and force another roll.

Savage scooped the dice from the ground and shuffled them over his shoulder. Flashlight silently prayed for a twelve. Maybe a return of some of the men's money would appease them. Savage viciously hurled the dice. Everyone jumped out of the way and the black-spotted, gray cubes rolled to a stop. "Damn. Look at that. A damn nine."

Flashlight picked up the money, retrieved the dice, shuffled them in his strangely cold right hand and rolled.

"Hot damn." Jack Savage exclaimed, and yelled an obscenity depicting an act no decent man would commit with his own mother. "A seven. I'm gonna beat your black chocolate-covered ass this time."

Flashlight drew a long, deep breath when the dice the white man threw rolled to a stop. The light-beam focused first on three black dots and then on six. Jack Savage whooped, almost grinned, and eagerly scooped up the money.

The game continued until well after midnight, money and luck moving back and forth. But despite Flashlight's efforts to lose, Jack Savage was down to his last two bills. He shuffled the dice and threw them. The white men moved closer, intently focusing on the roll. They loudly yelped their approval when they counted eight black dots.

Feeling confident now, Savage handed the dice to Flashlight. Through a sinister smirk, he snarled, "Let's go double or nothing this time. Roll 'em." He threw his last bill on the ground and Flashlight covered it.

Flashlight knelt on the damp ground and vigorously shuffled the dice for a long time. The white men hovered closer, listening to the sound like bamboo wind chimes in a hurricane. Flashlight continued to shuffle the dice. The circle grew tighter. He could feel the heat of the men's bodies pressing near and their anger and anxiety rising to an explosive pitch. *Please don't let me win,* Flashlight silently prayed. He clasped both hands around the dice and rattled them some more. Sweat beaded his brow and gathered in rivulets trickling down his face. He felt an urgent need to urinate.

"Three. Hot damn," Savage swore, and yelled again the familiar obscenity. "A trey. Where's the other'n?"

The die had skirted between their legs into the darkness behind them. They searched the ground, and when the light beam settled on the wayward die, the white men muttered in unison, "A damn six."

Flashlight picked up the forty dollars and rose to his feet. He turned off the light and warily eyed the men cloaked in darkness that could not conceal their rage.

Jack Savage lunged at Flashlight and collared him hard against the wall. "You white-eyed son of a bitch. You don't think we're gonna let you shuffle on out of here with our money, do you?" He pulled the dazed Negro from the wall and slammed him back again so violently that his knees buckled. Falling, he looked up to see Jack Savage standing over him with the steel encased flashlight drawn back to arms reach.

Paul bolted to the white man and frantically struggled to break the grip on his fallen friend. A hard blow from the flashlight sent Paul sprawling unconscious to the ground. The two black onlookers disappeared into the darkness. Negroes in Bonds County had been deprived of jobs, credit, and even life for lesser offences than assaulting whites.

Like wolves attacking a fallen prey, the men pounced on Flashlight, viciously pummeling and kicking him. He fought off the blows and managed to get to his feet. But at the moment of imminent victory, he failed to see the flashlight come crashing against the back of his head; neither did he feel the blows that followed.

When they simultaneously began to regain consciousness some time later, dew covered the two defeated men. The night was peaceful now and quiet, except for the sounds of frogs and crickets, and the frantic cry of a distant whippoorwill. They peered at each other in the glow of a blood-red moon rising barely above the horizon over the eastern landscape. Flashlight spoke first.

"Now that's a hell of a note. You laid there napping while I got my ass kicked."

"Oooh," Paul moaned. I wish I'd napped someplace else tonight."

Both men laughed weakly. Flashlight raised himself on one elbow. Unbearable pain forced him back onto the dry silhouette shielded from the dew by his outstretched body. "You OK?" He asked.

"Yeah, man. You're the one that looks rough. You look like you've been in a cock fight and you were the smallest one there."

"Hey, man, don't attack my manhood. You know what y'all say about us black men."

The two men laughed again. Paul eased himself up and leaned against the wall. Flashlight, much slower, joined him.

"They got my money, man. I don't know how I'm going to get to Atlanta now. Damn. Damn *all* white folks." For the moment, Flashlight had forgotten his friend's skin color. Then he remembered. "All but you, man. I didn't mean you." He raised a weak hand and patted Paul's shoulder.

"Well, we're not making anything better here. We may as well go home. We've got church tomorrow. You gonna be able to make it?"

"Yeah. You want to let's go together?" Flashlight asked. Both laughed at the absurdity of the question.

The turn of events in this night left little to laugh about–and even less to talk about. They pedaled home in silence, carefully avoiding clay-clods, potholes, and a slow-moving mother possum ambling leisurely across the road with an offspring clinging to her back.

Paul's high school graduation of eleven students passed unremarkably; the ceremony for Flashlight's class of three was even less notable; except that considering the station and circumstances of their lives, the completion of twelve years of school was of itself quite remarkable. They accepted their diplomas with pride and relief. Flashlight planned to work at the sawmill until he earned money for the trip to Atlanta. Paul would work at the store and save money for college.

In late June, on a Monday so hot and humid that eggs could boil in a hen's nest, Paul and Mr. Leibman stood outside the store in the shade of the covered sidewalk, watching heat waves dance skyward and disappear above Main Street. A rusted Dodge pickup braked to a dusty stop in front of them. Flashlight Jackson emerged.

"Good morning, sir. Hidy, Paul. I need some bolts for the sawmill. Mr. Bid said to put them on his account." Flashlight described his needs, and the merchant took the young man's arm and ushered him inside. Paul followed.

At the display bins, Mr. Liebman found the items requested. "These ought to do it," The merchant said and moved to the counter to record the transaction. The two young men exited the store. On the sidewalk, Paul asked, "How's it going at the sawmill?"

"Just fine," Flashlight answered. "I'm getting some of the easier jobs now. Guess my high school education is paying off." The two men laughed.

Flashlight drove away and Paul returned to the store. Mr. Liebman was still at the counter thumbing through account ledgers. He looked up and spoke when Paul entered the store. "That fellow just in here, isn't he the Jackson boy?"

"Yes, sir. Flashlight Jackson. That's all I know. Says his name is

MG, but I call him Flashlight."

Mr. Liebman slowly rubbed his chin. "Oh yes. Lives with his grandparents about two miles out of town at the crossroads. They're good people. Always pay their bill on time."

"Yes, sir. It's too bad about what happened to him."

"What was that?" Mr. Liebman took a seat in a straight-backed, cane-bottomed chair beside the cold pot-bellied heater in the center of the store. Paul pulled up another chair and sat facing him.

"He got beat-up and robbed. Lost all the money he saved to go to Atlanta to join Dr, King."

"I heard something about that letter. How much did the boy lose?"

"I think it was about five hundred dollars. He's working at the sawmill to earn money for the trip."

Mr. Liebman sucked a soft whistle. "That's a lot of money." He grew quiet and contemplative. He rubbed his chin for a long moment then spoke again. "You know, I've been thinking about rearranging the shelves and showcases. We would need another strong helper for that. Do you reckon the Jackson boy will help us?"

"Yes, sir. I reckon he will. He'd probably be happy to make some extra money. He's really eager to get to Atlanta."

"Ask him about it next time you see him. We'll do it on a Sunday. You can help, can't you?"

"Yes, sir. I'll have to miss church, but I'll be here."

The designated Sunday came, and the three men worked steadily throughout the morning. At noon over a lunch of Vienna sausages and saltines from the store shelves, they talked of the growing support for civil rights activities and Flashlight's desire to join the Movement in Atlanta.

They completed the work in late afternoon, and Mr. Liebman counted out 15 twenty-dollar bills and placed them in Flashlight's hand. "But, sir, that's too much," he protested.

"You want to go to Atlanta, don't you?"

"Yes, sir. I do. More than anything, I do. But three hundred dollars is a lot of money for one day's work."

Mr. Liebman smiled. "Well, let's just say this is my contribution to the Movement. Now, take it and go."

Flashlight hesitated and the two men stood looking deep into the others eyes. Mr. Liebman offered a handshake. White men in Bonds

County did not offer a hand to Negroes. After a long moment, Flashlight grasped Mr. Liebman's hand. "Good luck, young man," the merchant said. "God bless you and keep you safe."

Flashlight wasted no time. Early the next morning, ticket in hand, he anxiously waited for the bus to Atlanta. What if it had broken down, or had an accident, or maybe turned back because of a washed bridge? He smiled and took a deep breath when–forty-five minutes late–the bus finally hissed and squealed to a stop at the boarding point in front of the diner. Dust swirled about and lingered a long time on the still morning air.

At that moment, Bidwell Bonds parked his new, automatic shift Oldsmobile and walked toward the diner for breakfast. He stopped when he saw Flashlight with his brown paper bag of belongings. "Where in hell do you think you're going?" he demanded.

Flashlight placed the brown bag on the ground. Sweat began to bead his brow. He had not anticipated facing the most powerful man in northeast Bonds County today. Finally he spoke. "I'm... I'm leaving, Mr. Bid. Going to Atlanta.

"Oh hell no you ain't. Now get your jive-ass on out to the sawmill. I'll be out there to check on you soon's I finish my breakfast, and you damn well better be there."

Flashlight raised his body to full height and stiffened. "No, sir, Mr. Bid. I'm going to Atlanta." For a moment he stood resolute, his jaw set. He then picked up his bag and moved to board the bus. Mr. Bid stepped quickly between him and the doorway.

"Now you listen to me, boy. You belong here. In the old days, I would have owned your sorry ass, and I ain't letting you go nowhere. Now you get on out to the sawmill like I told you."

The two men stood toe to toe, their gaze locked in a determined glare. The world suddenly stood still and quiet, even the birds seemed to pause in mid-flight. After a moment, Flashlight's demeanor softened. His face relaxed. A subtle smile crossed his lips. He gently set the paper bag of belongings on the ground. "Mr. Bid," he said, wrapping his arms around the large man's waist, lifting him aside, "go to hell."

Flashlight picked up his bag and boarded the bus. The white driver, with an amused look on his face, closed the door and quickly geared the vehicle into motion. Taking a seat in the middle of the bus, the young man did not see Mr. Bid shaking his fist and coughing, in the exhaust fumes and dust left in the wake of the bus. Flashlight Jackson never looked back.

Don't Cry Matilda

Sam Ratteree stood in the yard looking out over the farm he had tended the greater part of his fourscore years. The surname on the title of the land had not changed since the 640 acres were granted to Colonel Angus Ratteree for his gallant service in the Revolutionary War. The land had been good to the generations of Ratterees, and they lived well, each line passing along additional wealth to the next. And now at the dawn of the 1950s, he was no longer physically able to cultivate the land, but he didn't need to. The land was now leased to a neighbor, producing income for property taxes, and a few dollars for household expenses.

He and Matilda had raised three fine boys on the generosity of the land, even though there was never enough manpower to cultivate the whole farm. Matilda envisioned a day when the boys would grow up, have children of their own, settle into nice homes built on the property, and turn every inch of earth green and prosperous. And every morning she would look across the landscape and know that Sammy was at work on that section there; over yonder, toward the northwest, Billy would be plowing his cotton; and down in the bottom land near the creek, Johnny would be hard at work harvesting his corn. She would have her children, her land–and always–the Good Lord. The world would be peaceful, righteous, and productive. It would be good, the way it was supposed to be.

The boys grew up on the land, loved it, nurtured it, and respected it, working alongside their father. But as they matured and moved away to college, they discovered an infinite world of opportunities and wonders unencumbered by fences and property lines, and they never returned to the farm. They had their owns families now, and were doing well. Sammy managed projects worldwide for International Contractors out of Augusta, Billy taught economics at the University of Georgia, and Johnny anchored the morning news at the fledgling WSB TV in Atlanta.

The families revisited the farm often, and these were good times with everyone again together. The young children scampered unfettered about the vast open land. The adults fished or walked the fields and spoke of olden times, and of the present. Sammy spoke of the beauty of Paris, and Berlin, and Rome. Billy shared economics information and great tips on investing and the stock market. Johnny spoke of the day when television would be broadcast in color, and every household would own at least one, maybe more.

Matilda's singular joy of late was setting a gracious table with all her family gathered safely beneath her wings. She could see them, feel their presence, and hear their joyful voices. But when conversation turned to those strange places beyond the farm, she would set her fork aside, set her chin sternly, turn away, and stare blankly into nothingness while Sam hung on every word, openly displaying his excitement. He had gone once with his father to Atlanta to buy a new Ford pickup, but that was his only venture beyond the county of his birth. He longed to go again, to accept his children's invitation to visit, or move in with one of them. He wanted to do that, but Matilda was dead set against it. Their home was the farm. That was where she wanted them–all of them–to be. That was where they belonged.

But the boys were gone now, and it saddened her to the core of her being. When each of the children left home, she wept. And when they did not return, she cried. As time wore on, in her private moments she wept. And as of late, tears welled full in her eyes openly and often. On these occasions, Sam would kneel before her, take her hands in his and try to soothe her.

It was a long time ago that Johnny–the last son to leave the farm–said his goodbyes. The weeping begun that day seemed never to make its departure. It hung around hiding among daily chores, a cold dark cloud waiting for a vulnerable moment to reappear. And with the passing of time, the tears attacked more frequently with growing vigor. Sam quietly looked on, living her pain, hoping that she would relent and go with him to live with Sammy. He had plenty of room for everyone, a large house–a mansion that he built himself. Then she would be happy, and the crying would go away.

He had thought last summer that she would do that. She agreed and for a while seemed to anticipate the move. The three boys came with rented U-Hauls and worked with excited energy. The trucks were soon loaded and ready to go. Matilda sat on the doorsteps watching the drivers board the trucks. Sam smiled and walked to her side. He leaned over to lift her erect and escort her to their car. But she jerked her arm away from his reach, and staring blankly into space, murmured quietly, "No."

Sam stood erect, the smile gone from his lips. "No?" He repeated, "No? You're not going?"

"My place is here, Sam. I thought I could leave. I want to. I want it for you and the children. I want to do it for you, Sam, but I just can't. Can you understand why I can't leave the farm, Sam?"

"Yes, Mama, I understand," Sam lied. But his understanding did not matter. Her father had run off to California with a neighboring farmer's wife, leaving Matilda, her mother, and three other young siblings to fend for themselves, in the hard times of post Civil War Georgia. In an effort to survive, the family scattered to and fro and eventually lost touch. Matilda's husband and children and a safe place of her own was important to her–and she was important to Sam. That was the way things were. He loved her now as much as the day Sammy was born, and he always would. That was the way things were. The trucks would be unloaded. That was last year, and there would be no more talk of leaving the farm.

Sam completed his visual survey of the land and turned to go back into the house. It had been a while since he last checked on Matilda. He looked up to see her sitting on the doorsteps, staring blankly at an apple tree about fifty yards down the driveway. It was April and the limbs labored under the burden of hundreds of pink and white blossoms. Sam walked to her and sat beside her. She never looked up, just kept staring blankly at the tree.

She continued staring at the tree for a long while, and then in a soft voice barely above a whisper, she said, "I'm just like that old tree there, Sam. Every year it blooms so pretty. Just like one big bouquet of glory. And then the blossoms die. Just fall off the tree and die. Oh, maybe an apple or two, sometimes maybe three or four come, but they die and fall off, too. Gone. They're just gone. *Poof!*" She waved a weak hand as if shooing a fly away from a freshly bake banana pudding. "Gone, Sam. Just gone." She waved a hand again. "Do you know where apples and blossoms go when they die, Sam?"

"No, Mama. I don't know where they go."

"I do, Sam. They go right down into the ground. They become part of God's earth. That's where I want to go. When I die, I want you to bury me with those dead apples and blossoms beneath that tree. That's what I want you to do, Sam. Now promise me."

"I promise, Mama. I promise."

Sam marked well her plan for final arrangements, thinking that if fate allowed him the unfortunate circumstance of surviving her, he would indeed undertake the painful task of granting her request. But in September when the leaves began to turn colors and fall to the ground, and the soft warm breezes from the southeast shifted to brisk, cool northwesterly winds, she died quietly in her sleep. The boys and their families came, the preacher spoke consoling words, and the choir sang comforting songs in the capacity-filled sanctuary of the Baptist church. Matilda would want no graveside service, so the mourners went on their way, leaving Samuel and the children alone with Matilda and the doers of the remaining duty. They followed the hearse to the farm and reverently laid Matilda in her freshly dug home, where she would eternally mingle among the fallen apples and blossoms and leaves.

The family spent the night in the farmhouse and in the morning prepared to leave. Samuel gathered his personal belongings and loaded them into his car lined up behind those of his children. He seated himself in the car and started the engine, then hesitated a moment in thought. Leaving the motor running, he stepped to the ground. The boys watched their father walk slowly and deliberately to the grave site. Standing at the foot of the mound of red clay, he began speaking to his beloved wife.

"I'm going now, Matilda. The boys want me to, and I'm going with them. I know you are happy where you are, and don't you worry about me. I'll be OK. I'll be back to see you and talk with you every chance I get. My time is about over, too. And when the time comes, I'll be back and lay beside you. Until then, you rest easy and enjoy your time here with the apples and apple blossoms." Sam turned and walked back toward his car. After a few steps he stopped, staring down at the ground as if trying to remember something important. He turned back to face the grave. He raised an outstretched hand, needing to reach beyond the grave and take her hand in his one last time, needing one last touch to remember. His eyes moistened and he spoke.

"And Matilda," he said softly. "Don't cry, Matilda."